VALIANT

Gentlemen of the Order - Book 3

ADELE CLEE

More titles by Adele Clee

To Save a Sinner
A Curse of the Heart
What Every Lord Wants
The Secret To Your Surrender
A Simple Case of Seduction

Lost Ladies of London
The Mysterious Miss Flint
The Deceptive Lady Darby
The Scandalous Lady Sandford
The Daring Miss Darcy

Avenging Lords
At Last the Rogue Returns
A Wicked Wager
Valentine's Vow
A Gentleman's Curse

Scandalous Sons
And the Widow Wore Scarlet
The Mark of a Rogue
When Scandal Came to Town
The Mystery of Mr Daventry

Gentlemen of the Order
Dauntless
Raven
Valiant
Dark Angel

This is a work of fiction. All names, characters, places and incidents are products of the author's imagination. All characters are fictitious and any resemblance to real persons, living or dead, is purely coincidental.

No part of this book may be copied or reproduced in any manner without the author's permission.

Cover by Dar Albert at Wicked Smart Designs

CHAPTER 1

Keel Hall
Little Chelsea, London

IT WAS one hell of a storm. Lightning lit the night sky in a blinding burst of white. The angry grumble of thunder followed seconds later while raindrops the size of small pebbles pelted the windowpanes in Evan Sloane's drawing room.

The raging tempest stirred his restless spirit. A man with the blood of a pirate flowing through his veins welcomed life's trials and tribulations. Was that not the reason his friends called him Valiant? Did he not live by the Sloane family motto? He who braves the storm emerges stronger.

Still, the sudden thud echoing through the hall came as an unwelcome intrusion. The persistent caller hammered the door knocker against the plate as if afraid a lightning bolt might strike him down dead.

What fool ventured outdoors in a thunderstorm? With Evan's mansion house situated amid the sprawling fields of Little Chelsea, perhaps the sound of clashing clouds had spooked some poor devil's horse.

Then another thought struck him—one infinitely more alarming.

Had his stalker, Miss Hart, braved the inclement weather to

demand an audience? The wallflower had prised herself from the ballroom wall to follow Evan about town. Whenever he glanced over his shoulder, be it in the circulating library, the theatre or Gunter's, Miss Hart was there spying.

Had she heard of his pirate heritage and found it all rather fascinating? He'd spotted her loitering in Hart Street, staring at the house belonging to the Order. Perhaps her ancestor once owned the land. Perhaps the fact Evan's pursuer shared a name with his place of business was one of those uncanny twists of fate.

Amid a thunderclap that shook the heavens, Evan could not determine the butler's mumbled comments. But it came as no surprise when the knock on the drawing room door brought the somewhat agitated servant.

"You look like a man with something to confess, Fitchett."

"Sir, I fear you'll think me a dreadful disappointment, or worse, dismiss me without a reference."

A man with an eye patch and a jagged scar cutting through his bushy white brow should fear nothing except for losing his sight.

"Dismiss you? Not unless you've disobeyed orders and Miss Hart is dripping water onto my marble floor."

Fitchett's shifty gaze confirmed Evan's suspicion.

Damnation!

The pest would stop at nothing to gain his attention. "Did I not give explicit instructions the woman must never cross my threshold?"

"But the lady might perish in such terrible—"

"How is that my concern? If she persists in wandering the countryside in the dead of night, she must suffer the consequences." Evan spoke loud enough for Miss Hart to hear. "I pray she brought a chaperone."

Evan entertained actresses and widows. Never unmarried chits skilled in harassment. Miss Hart was fortunate he lived in the wilds of Little Chelsea, away from the prying eyes of those in the *ton* who enjoyed casting aspersions. Still, perhaps he would play the dissolute rake when he put the woman in her place.

"The lady arrived with two attendants, sir." Fitchett lowered his voice. "Both of Scottish descent."

Miss Hart could have arrived with the vicar; she was still a reckless fool. Time spent conversing with potted ferns must have dulled the wallflower's brain.

"Her companions, they're soaked to the skin, sir. Might I be permitted to show them to the servants' quarters so they may take a hot meal and dry their clothes?"

Evan raised a reprimanding brow in reply.

"Sir, the lady begs for a moment of your time. Surely you don't expect me to throw her out into the storm."

"Fitchett, while I allow you a certain freedom of speech based on your unfortunate accident, do not overstep the mark."

Fitchett pursed his lips. He bowed, yet couldn't help but say, "No man wants a lady's death on his conscience, sir. I shall not sleep tonight for worrying."

Hellfire!

The butler knew how to find the chink in Evan's armour.

Evan breathed a weary sigh. Maybe Miss Hart's audacious manner had worked to his advantage. It was time to put an end to the woman's meddling. Time to get rid of her for good.

"Would it ease your anxiety if I let her warm her hands by the fire, offer her a sip of sherry?" He would give Miss Hart one of his famous concoctions—rum, whisky and a dash of sugar syrup.

Fitchett slapped his hand to his heart and bowed again. "Sir, I could rest my aching bones with nary a care in the world."

"Then show the lady in." Into Lucifer's lair.

Evan smiled to himself as he tugged his shirt from his breeches and shook his brown locks free from its queue. How would the wallflower fare when faced with a rakish rogue?

Fitchett's eyes widened upon witnessing the outrageous spectacle. "Shall I have Randall bring your coat and cravat, sir?"

"Hell, no! The lady arrived without invitation and can damn well suffer the consequences."

Having already expressed his opinion, Fitchett didn't dare press the matter further. While the butler walked gracefully into the hall, Evan pasted a wolfish grin. One look at his open shirt and the wallflower's confidence would wither and wilt.

Fitchett returned and announced the intruder.

Evan's heart thumped against his ribs as he waited ... and waited. Had Miss Hart caught a sudden case of nerves? He coughed impatiently into his fist.

"Just one moment," the lady called from the hall.

Arrogance turned to annoyance.

But then Miss Hart strode into the room, and Evan found himself face-to-face with his insipid nemesis. The lady's dark, intelligent gaze drifted over his open shirt as if it were perfectly natural to find a man in a state of dishabille.

"Forgive me, Mr Sloane. I've deposited my cloak and gloves on the floor in the hall for fear of dripping water onto your expensive Persian rug. I did not wish to burden your butler."

Wet tendrils of chestnut brown hair clung to Miss Hart's pale cheeks. Her tempting bow-shaped lips were a deathly shade of blue. The damp green dress hugged the gentle flare of her hips and—devil take it—the imp's stocking feet poked out from beneath the hem.

Evan inhaled sharply. "Where are your boots, Miss Hart?"

"In the hall, sir." She raised her dainty chin. "They're in a dreadful state."

How novel. Women usually took a drink and engaged in saucy banter before undressing.

"Lady Godiva rode naked through the streets of Coventry to make a point. I suppose I should be thankful your only concern is for the state of my rug."

The lady's mouth twitched in amusement. "Come now, Mr Sloane. You've seen your fair share of naked women. I doubt another would earn more than a fleeting glance. If my aim was to shock you, I would have drawn the pocket pistol from my thigh belt and fired at the chandelier."

Evan's chin almost hit the floor. Yet it wasn't the outrageous comment that seized his attention, but the flicker of admiration in his chest.

"What, and fire your only lead ball? That would be a foolish move, would it not, Miss Hart?"

Her teasing smile seemed to mock him. "A lady does not walk the streets at night armed with only one weapon. That would be foolish, would it not?"

"Dangerously so."

Evan observed Miss Hart's keen gaze and the relaxed set of her shoulders. Weren't wallflowers supposed to nibble their lips and refuse to make eye contact? They were dull and dim, yet Miss Hart's blithe spirit illuminated the room like a bright ray of sunshine. Was it a facade? Or did this devil of a creature enjoy posing as the shy, awkward type? Indeed, Evan was so preoccupied with his study, he had forgotten to dismiss Fitchett.

"That will be all, Fitchett. See if a maid might dry the lady's outdoor apparel. Have Turton prepare the carriage and show Miss Hart's servants to the—"

"Their names are Buchanan and Mrs McCready," Miss Hart interjected. "I'm sure you will come to admire their talents in the coming weeks."

The coming weeks?

The misfit made it sound as if she had arrived with her port-manteau, ready to take residence.

"I doubt I shall have cause to make their acquaintance."

Another mocking smile accompanied Miss Hart's knowing look. "Don't tell me you've lost your sense of adventure. A grandson of Livingston Sloane should have found my comment intriguing, not dismissed it out of hand."

Suspicion flared.

So, this did have something to do with his pirate heritage. And what could this busybody-come-wallflower-come-spinster— for she must be five-and-twenty—know about adventure?

"I do have one question."

"Only one, sir? As an enquiry agent for the Order, I expected more."

Cursed saints! Did she know his inside leg measurement too? "You said you removed your boots so as not to ruin my rug. How did you know it was Persian?"

"I called a week ago, but Fitchett said you were attending a wedding in Surrey. The wedding of your colleague Mr Cole. I asked if I might see the painting of Livingston Sloane, and he obliged."

The soft-hearted devil. Fitchett would feel more than the whip of Evan's tongue. Still, he admired Miss Hart's honesty despite the mildly arrogant delivery.

"And why would you travel from Silver Street to Little Chelsea just to glance at a painting of a scoundrel?" Was this the moment she revealed some distant kinship? Would she claim her parent was the bastard child of the buccaneer?

"I journeyed from Silver Street to Little Chelsea to see you, Mr Sloane, as you're intent on avoiding me." Miss Hart seemed unperturbed by the fact he remembered her address. She glanced at the portrait of Livingston Sloane hanging in a gilt frame near the fireplace. "But I believe the painting holds a vital clue and so couldn't leave without persuading your butler to let me examine the piece."

Evan narrowed his gaze. It occurred to him that Miss Hart suffered from a form of mental instability. Perhaps she was a fanatical eccentric whose imagination ran riot. Perhaps she had grown so bored with hiding behind potted ferns she thought to invent an exciting heritage.

"A vital clue to what, Miss Hart?" he foolishly said, for the woman needed no encouragement. By rights, Evan should summon his loose-tongued butler to escort her to the door. Yet this annoying pest had piqued his interest.

Hell.

Miss Hart paused. She rubbed her hands together and gazed at the amber flames dancing in the grate. "Might I take a moment to warm myself by the fire? And could I trouble you for a glass of sherry?"

How could he deny the needs of a woman caught in a raging thunderstorm? "Please make yourself comfortable, Miss Hart, and I shall pour you a drink." It wasn't often one played footman to a loon.

"Thank you." She moved to stand before the fire and raised her hands to the flames. "When one has important information to impart, one should have a firm grasp of one's faculties."

Had Evan been entertaining a paramour, he might have

6

suggested his faculties needed a firm grasp, too. The lewd thought was undoubtedly the reason his hand shook as he poured the fortified wine.

"The information must be important to bring you out in this weather." Evan crossed the room and handed Miss Hart a glass of sherry. Her fingers brushed his as she gripped the stem. They were long and elegant and would look splendid wrapped around his—

"I used the weather to my advantage, sir," she said in so confident a manner he decided she must be a bluestocking, not a wallflower. "You've failed to reply to my letters, and so I had no choice but to play the damsel in distress."

"So, this is a game of sorts, Miss Hart."

Her expression darkened. "On the contrary, this matter will alter the course of our lives, Mr Sloane. In coming here, I have placed us both in grave danger."

Yes, the woman was most definitely a loon.

Evan huffed in frustration. During his work as an enquiry agent, he'd met his share of vicious villains. Every new case brought the prospect of death. Miss Hart had misjudged him if she thought to intimidate him with baseless threats.

"Madam, do I look like a man who scares easily?"

Miss Hart's warm gaze drifted over Evan's mane of brown hair, down to the open neck of his shirt.

"You're a man who rescues innocent children from their abductors, Mr Sloane. A man who thwarts poisoning attempts, who proves paid companions do not steal rare blue diamonds." Her slow, teasing smile was that of a courtesan, not a damn bluestocking. "Nothing terrifies you. Yet I will lay odds my proposal will chill your blood."

Proposal?

Hellfire!

"Miss Hart, while I find your honesty and resolve refreshing, stop dancing around the maypole and come to the point."

"Very well." She swallowed her sherry swiftly and placed the glass on the mantel. "While I've imagined this moment for a while, I must confess to being somewhat nervous."

Evan's heart softened. Then he remembered this woman was

potentially deranged. "Your confidence has served you well so far, madam. Be blunt, and I shall afford you the same courtesy."

Hopefully, she wouldn't weep when he threw her out.

She nodded, turned away from him and hiked up her skirts. Good Lord! So much for being a timid wallflower. He could damn well see her ankles.

"Perhaps we should begin with this." She tugged a tightly rolled scroll from what he could only presume was the thigh belt she mentioned. "Forgive the indecent display, sir, but it was the only way to protect the document from the horrendous downpour."

"Indeed."

Evan watched this odd creature whose character he struggled to define, annoyed by the thrum of excitement in his chest. Curiosity danced like the devil, too, as he considered what might be scrawled on the parchment. Miss Hart certainly knew how to hold a man's interest.

She dropped her skirts and faced him fully. "Perhaps you should sit down. The news will come as a terrible shock."

Evan stared down his nose. "Madam, nothing could be more shocking than discovering the woman I thought was a wallflower is a teasing scamp."

He expected her to gasp upon hearing the cutting remark, but Miss Hart laughed. "You see. You're already agitated. No doubt you'll fly into a rage when you learn of our ancestors' devious deed." She handed him the rolled parchment secured with a black ribbon. "My father broke the wax seal many years ago, but had no need to stake a claim."

"Stake a claim?" Mild panic fluttered in Evan's throat. He couldn't tug the ends of the ribbon quick enough.

"Before you begin reading, sir, allow me to offer some advice. One should not label a person without knowledge of their character. I'm no more a wallflower than I am a mermaid."

For a heart-stopping moment, Evan thought he'd misheard.

"Did you say mermaid?" Shock held him rigid. "Have you spoken to D'Angelo or Ashwood?" Evan's colleagues at the Order sought every opportunity to torment him. "Did they encourage you to tease me about my fondness for sea nymphs?"

When a man lost his mother in childbirth, was it not natural to fantasise about being rescued by an immortal woman?

Miss Hart frowned. "No, I noticed your mermaid fountain and used the mythical creature merely as a comparison."

"Mythical?" he mocked. "Livingston Sloane claimed a mermaid rescued him when he was shipwrecked off the coast of Malta."

"That is a myth. My grandfather rescued Livingston Sloane near Malta, and though I never met him, I'm confident he did not have a tail or fins." She gestured to the parchment in Evan's hand. "The heroic deed is documented. It's the sole reason we're standing here this evening."

"Then give me a moment to examine the testimony, so I am not battling blindly in the dark."

"Of course."

Miss Hart faced the fire and continued warming her hands.

The document, written in Latin, dated 1756 and bearing an official Spanish stamp, raised an important question. "You read Latin, Miss Hart?" Perhaps she had struggled with the translation and there was nothing startling about the information.

"My father insisted on it, sir. When a family is owed a debt of this magnitude, there can be no room for error." She glanced over her shoulder and cast a mischievous grin. "Do not think to dupe me, Mr Sloane. My lawyer confirmed it is a legally binding inter-generational contract."

Inter-generational contract?

Was there such a thing?

The hairs on Evan's nape prickled. With some trepidation, he read the agreement made between Livingston Sloane and Lucian Hart. It appeared Mr Hart had rescued Evan's grandfather when the French attacked his ship during the Seven Years' War.

"Why mention the war when my grandfather was a marauding pirate?"

Miss Hart continued to stare at the amber flames. "Our grandfathers were privateers, not pirates. The British Admiralty commissioned the men to attack French vessels in the Mediterranean."

Evan snorted. "Perhaps your family embellished the tale to

9

spare you the shame." To make her ancestor seem like an honourable gent. "Livingston Sloane looted and pillaged and would never have served the Crown."

Miss Hart glanced at the painting of the young bearded man with a devilish twinkle in his eye. "If you believe that, why display his portrait?"

Oh, the lady was as sharp as a blade.

It would be easy to lie, but he suspected Miss Hart knew the answer.

"Because while my family disowned him, and I have been raised to despise the name, I often feel like a misfit myself." Many times during his youth, he had imagined running away, imagined living life on the high seas, free from society's suffocating restrictions.

Miss Hart gave a knowing hum. "When Livingston Sloane died, your father was raised by his grandmother, Lady Jane Sloane. My mother said the matron intended to eradicate the memory of her wayward son, and yet she kept his portrait."

Lady Jane Boscobel, daughter of the Earl of Henley, had married Daniel Sloane, Viscount Leaton's youngest son. They had married for love, by all accounts, though having married beneath her, the lady had kept her title. The couple were blessed with two sons, Cecil and Livingston, and Cecil had inherited the viscountcy when his uncle died without issue.

"Lady Sloane reverted to her maiden name when her husband died and the admiralty pronounced her son a pirate. Consequently, I always refer to her as Lady Boscobel. When one holds rank and position in society, one is easily influenced by opinion. Yet beneath the bravado was a mother who still loved her rebellious son."

Miss Hart appeared doubtful as she stared at the portrait of the young Lady Jane. "And you display both paintings because you want to understand the mother and son bond. You wonder if your mother—"

"That's enough, Miss Hart!" Evan never spoke about his mother and had no intention of discussing a personal matter with a relative stranger. Despite his annoyance, he softened his tone. "You have an uncanny ability to distract a man from his mission. Cease prying and permit me to finish reading this document."

"Then, for fear of distracting you further, let me summarise the legally binding agreement." Miss Hart squared her shoulders. "In short, you're contractually obliged to marry me, Mr Sloane."

CHAPTER 2

"Like hell I am."

"It's written quite clearly, sir." Vivienne's pulse pounded in her throat. She had expected to encounter some resistance. Mr Sloane was known for his devil-may-care attitude when it came to relationships with women. According to retiring-room gossip, the gentleman had vowed never to marry. "A direct descendant of Lucian Hart may demand to marry a direct descendant of Livingston Sloane. It is payment for the debt incurred by your grandfather when Lucian Hart saved his life."

Mr Sloane waved the precious document in the air. "You may quote from the contract, madam, but this won't withstand the scrutiny of the law courts."

Despite her earlier protestations, Vivienne suspected he was right. Still, she had no choice but to persuade him otherwise. Their lives depended upon finding the rogue who would stop at nothing to obtain their hidden legacy.

"Perhaps you should finish reading the document, sir." She kept calm, for he would rant and rave upon learning of the penalty for failing to abide by the agreement. "I shall sit patiently and wait."

Mr Sloane arched a brow by way of a challenge. "Nothing written by a deceased relative—who must have been sotted on rum at the time—could induce me to marry."

Vivienne sat on the gentleman's plush damask sofa, one far more comfortable than the threadbare couch in Silver Street. "And I would prefer to marry for love, sir. But I'm sure we can come to some arrangement once the deed is done."

"The deed?" The gentleman laughed. "Miss Hart, are you always so direct when discussing amorous liaisons?"

"Amorous liaisons?" It was Vivienne's turn to laugh, though heat flooded her cheeks at the thought of slipping between the sheets with such a virile gentleman. "You mistake my meaning. We need my lawyer to act as a witness to the deed of matrimony. I see no reason why you would want to claim your conjugal rights."

Mr Sloane fixed her with a heated stare. "Call me a pedant, Miss Hart, but I am not marrying a woman I cannot bed."

The low, throaty tone of his voice would make any woman drool. Thankfully, Vivienne was made of sterner stuff. "What possible difference does it make? Many people marry for convenience."

"Marriage is a damnable inconvenience." The gentleman stepped closer until she was practically eye level with his muscular thighs. He looked down from a towering height. "But let's suppose I'm considering your proposition. Though let me add, I most definitely am not."

"Yes," she said, feeling somewhat intimidated by his raw masculinity. His open-necked shirt didn't help, for she'd caught more than a teasing glimpse of bronzed skin and chest hair. "Let's presume a man of your prestigious lineage agrees to shackle himself to the granddaughter of a privateer."

Bravery flowed in her blood. It would serve her well to remember it. If Lucian Hart could command a ship of fifty rowdy men, surely she could control a rake who spent his days solving crimes.

"If I make the ultimate commitment, Miss Hart, it will be for life. No more wild parties until the early hours. No more late-night visits from unscrupulous women. To put it bluntly, madam, I would do everything in my power to fall in love with my wife."

Vivienne focused on keeping her mouth closed for fear of gawping.

Mr Sloane had inherited his wild, adventurous spirit from his grandfather. Yet he had acquired his sense of duty and loyalty from his father, Louis. It was said the man never recovered after losing his wife in childbed, never brought another woman into his home, not even a mistress.

"So you see how marrying me, Miss Hart, would work in opposition to your plan." The man stepped back. His intense gaze roamed over the loose tendrils of hair escaping her chignon. "And, as you're an advocate of honesty, you should know I'm rather rampant between the bedsheets. As such, I doubt I'd be mindful of your delicate sensibilities."

Oh, the arrogance of the man. His lewd remark was nothing more than a weak attempt to steer her off course.

Vivienne relaxed back against the bolster cushion and forced a confident smile. "And I suppose I should offer a similar warning." Though she could hardly profess to know anything about bed sport. "I possess the blood of an intrepid privateer and a ruthless Scottish laird. Cross me at your peril."

Rather than offer a sharp retort, Mr Sloane's green eyes glistened with intrigue. He made no reply and eventually lowered his gaze and continued reading the document. Vivienne began silently counting to five, knowing the volcano that was Mr Sloane's temper was sure to erupt.

Four.

Five.

"Mother of all saints!" His irate gaze shot in her direction. "Madam, it seems I have completely misjudged your character. You're not a wallflower. You're a pirate come to pillage and plunder."

"I am considered somewhat of a paradox, sir." Vivienne hunkered down and held her nerve. "That said, had my grandfather not risked his life to save Livingston Sloane, you would not exist. They drew the contract to honour the sacrifice made, to ensure an heir of Livingston Sloane couldn't break the oath."

He continued to mutter and curse beneath his breath.

"Should you fail to marry me, sir, I can make a claim against your estate. Your father may have built this house, but the land once belonged to Livingston Sloane."

"How the devil do you know that?"

"I have a copy of the original deed. The copy given to my grandfather."

"You seem to be extremely well-informed, Miss Hart." Mr Sloane threw the document onto the sofa. He strode to the rosewood drinks cabinet and yanked the stopper from a crystal decanter. "How is it I am scrambling around in the dark?"

She knew the answer to that, too.

Lucian Hart kept his prized possessions in a mahogany tea chest. The heirloom had passed to Vivienne's father and then to her. But while Lucian wished to ensure every family member knew of the debt, it was said Lady Boscobel destroyed her copy of the contract.

"Upon your grandfather's death, Lucian Hart wrote to Lady Boscobel to remind her of your family's obligation. In her reply, she wrote that Livingston Sloane was no longer her son. She denounced all claims. Refused to accept responsibility."

Mr Sloane stood sipping his brandy. "And there lies the hypocrisy." Bitterness tainted the velvet texture of his voice. "Lady Boscobel openly condemned her son but made sure my father inherited this land. I presumed she came to an arrangement with the Crown, for they usually confiscate the property of a pirate."

"Livingston Stone served the Crown, so there was no need to intervene."

"Yet there is no evidence to substantiate your claim," he said, reluctant to accept her version of the tale.

Oh, but there was.

Vivienne sat, hands clasped in her lap, while he downed his drink and refilled the glass. She took a moment to observe her surroundings. The burnt sienna walls, the gilt-framed paintings and sumptuous gold furnishings confirmed Mr Sloane lived in the height of luxury. Having watched him move confidently through the ballrooms of the *ton*, impeccably presented, he seemed far removed from his swashbuckling ancestor—more in keeping with Lady Boscobel's highbrow pretensions. Yet tonight, with his long hair flowing wild and free, and his shirt gaping at the neck, one might mistake him for a master of the high seas.

"I must admit to knowing nothing of your background, Miss Hart." Cradling the brandy glass in one hand, he came and sat on the sofa opposite. "How is it the granddaughter of a privateer receives invitations to the grandest balls?"

Despite the distance between them, his commanding presence made her stomach flip and her legs tremble like a blancmange. Perhaps marrying such a formidable man was a terrible idea.

"I'm the great-granddaughter of Laird McFarlane." The powerful laird's influence stretched the length and breadth of the land and lasted long after his passing. "Sir Otterly Hart is my paternal great-grandfather. My mother and the Countess of Hollinshead were great friends because of their Scottish heritage."

"Otterly Hart? The explorer?"

Pride warmed her chest. "Yes, he led an expedition to Antarctica, made many discoveries in the field of astronomy. Lucian Hart inherited the same love of the sea, the same need to conquer."

Mr Sloane swallowed a mouthful of brandy, his gaze falling to her empty hands. "Forgive me. While in a state of shock, I forgot to offer you another drink."

With her nerves hanging by a thread, and with so much information still to impart, she needed something to bolster her courage. "May I have what you're drinking, sir? I should take something stronger, strive to keep the cold from penetrating my bones."

"A wily whistle?" He swirled the amber liquid in the glass. "It's one of my famous concoctions. Rum, whisky and sugar syrup, finished with a dash of sherry. It's far too potent for a lady of delicate sensibilities."

"Might I be so bold as to take a sip of yours, Mr Sloane? I would hate to waste good liquor."

The fumes would scald her throat, but she would be this gentleman's wife before the week was out and had to foster a certain intimacy.

The flash of surprise and the sparkle of curiosity in the man's eyes said he was fascinated by her request. "If that's your desire."

He leaned forward and offered her the glass. "Be warned. Strong liquor is said to stimulate one's appetite for pleasure."

Their fingers touched as she accepted the vessel. It took effort to maintain a confident smile, to hide the delicious shiver shooting to her toes. Vivienne brought the glass slowly to her lips, aware his gaze remained fixed on her person.

"I advise but a small sip." The throaty tone of his voice conveyed caution and a touch of amusement.

"I suspect even a small sip will roast my insides." Having spent many summers in the Highlands of Scotland, she was used to taking a dram or two of whisky. Still, the aroma alone made her gasp. "The smell reminds me of hills and heather and babbling brooks, though I suspect my mouth will soon feel like the inside of a blacksmith's furnace."

Mr Sloane's laugh reached his vibrant green eyes. The sight stole her breath and warmed her insides before the sip of wily whistle scorched her throat.

"Good Lord!" Vivienne coughed and spluttered and panted to cool the burn. A wily whistle? He should name the drink *holy fire*.

Mr Sloane shot to his feet and closed the gap between them. "I did warn you." He took the glass from her hand lest she spill the contents. "It's lethal to the untrained palette."

"That's the devil's drink, sir," she said, though she laughed too when he could not conceal his mirth. "Perhaps when we're married, I might tempt you to mix me a whipkull. It's a far better way to serve rum, and they say it's the drink favoured in Valhalla."

As expected, his smile faded at the mere mention of marriage. But he could not avoid their destiny.

"Miss Hart, though you are entertaining company, and nowhere near the dullard I expected, I refuse to abide by this ridiculous pact. Should you wish to prosecute for breach of contract, know my lawyers will have the case thrown out within a matter of hours. As to the claim on my land that you—"

"This is not about legalities, Mr Sloane. This is a matter of honour."

Despite talk of his pirate heritage and his wild antics in the bedchamber, men respected Evan Sloane. They believed his work as an enquiry agent for the Order served as an acceptable pastime for a man with an adventurous spirit.

"You owe my grandfather your life," she continued in earnest. "The debt must be paid. We live in a society where a son is accountable for his father's mistakes. Your failure to abide by the agreement will bring more shame to your name than any association with Livingston Sloane ever could."

Mr Sloane's glare carried a hint of disdain. "Do you think I care about ballroom gossip? Livingston Sloane may have escaped punishment, but I took the beatings. School can be an unpleasant place when one's grandfather is a pirate, and so one develops thick skin."

"Your grandfather was a privateer, not a pirate," she reiterated. "He carried a letter of marque. Do you not seek an opportunity to clear his name?"

"Such an effort will only rouse unwanted attention. And I have nothing but the word of a busybody as proof."

Vivienne's watery laugh held no amusement. "What about your duty to protect the innocent? I suffer because of your grandfather's misfortune. If we do not marry, Mr Sloane, I doubt I shall live long enough to witness the first buds of spring."

Mr Sloane observed her intently through narrowed eyes. "Is this about money, Miss Hart? Your mother died a year ago, and you live alone in Silver Street, I hear."

"I do not live alone. I have Buchanan and Mrs McCready for company."

Their ancestors had served every Laird McFarlane for the last two hundred years, and they were assigned as her protectors. Though that did not deter the devil determined to rob her of her inheritance.

Mr Sloane rubbed his jaw in thoughtful contemplation. "I shall have my lawyers prepare a new contract. You will be handsomely rewarded for agreeing to destroy this document." He plucked the old contract from the sofa, rolled it tightly and attempted to hand it back to her.

Vivienne waved her hand in refusal. "I implore you, keep the contract. It is no longer safe in my possession."

With a huff of impatience, Mr Sloane pushed to his feet.

"Miss Hart, this document isn't worth a guinea. Accept my offer of financial compensation, take your servants and go home. If you're so intent on marrying, know there are few men in the *ton* willing to take a wife with such a vivid imagination."

Oh, she should have known he'd be an obstinate oaf.

Yet when he scanned her from head to toe with his intense green gaze, a glimmer of hope surfaced. Yes, she had a wild imagination, but judging by the look in Mr Sloane's eyes, he appeared mildly captivated. That didn't stop him from crossing the room and tugging the bell pull.

"I assume you hired a hackney to bring you here."

"Yes, the jarvey parked a hundred yards from the front gate." The miser had charged an exorbitant four shillings a mile— danger money for having to make the journey in a thunderstorm.

"My coachman will see you safely home. And I shall send a footman to settle your fare."

Pride should have made her refuse his offer of assistance, but a villain might easily bribe a hackney driver to take a detour while en route to town. The intruder who broke into her house would go to murderous lengths to steal their bounty.

"Mr Sloane, there is so much more I need to explain."

He needed to know he held the second vital clue to finding their inheritance, that she held the first. They could only obtain the third clue with proof of their marriage. She needed to explain there was treachery afoot, that someone stalked her from the shadows, had ransacked her lawyer's office, too.

"Do not try my patience, Miss Hart. I've heard more than enough—"

"But our lives are in danger if—"

"What? If we don't marry?" he mocked. "While I admire your original approach to improving your prospects, you do not want to marry me."

Before she could challenge his opinion, Fitchett entered the room and Mr Sloane fired a barrage of instructions. "The storm is passing. I want the carriage brought round immediately. Turton is to take Miss Hart and her ... her Scottish companions back to town."

"Yes, sir." Fitchett nodded and left the room.

Mr Sloane turned to her. "I shall arrange a meeting with my lawyers," he continued in a business-like fashion. "We will thrash the matter of the contract out there. And as I have no intention of bringing children into this world, the debt ends with us."

There were two types of actions—those motivated by love and those motivated by fear. Could he not see she was at her wits' end? No doubt this handsome and physically powerful man had never been pushed to the limits of his sanity. Yes, it was utter lunacy to marry a stranger because of a pact made seventy years ago. But she had to say something to make him comprehend the genuine threat to their lives.

"You don't understand, Mr Sloane. We both hold clues to the missing treasure."

But he was already ushering her towards the drawing room door. "I understand, madam. Desperate people say desperate things. But I shall see that you're compensated for your grandfather's sacrifice."

Vivienne shuffled back into the hall. "Sir, you fail to see the gravity of the situation." She clutched his forearm. "Why will you not let me explain?"

Hard muscle flexed beneath her fingers and the gentleman shivered visibly. He glanced at her hand for a few seconds, his brow furrowing in confusion. When their gazes locked, recognition flashed in his eyes. He must have felt it, too, the prickle of excitement, the spark of recognition.

"We cannot fight our destiny," she said, reluctantly pulling her hand away and breaking the connection. Vivienne reached down between the valley of her breasts and removed the tiny scroll. Oh, she was more than desperate. "If you won't listen to me, then take this. Keep it safe. Should I meet a grisly end, you must return it to Buchanan."

Mr Sloane seemed more interested in the swell of her breasts than her prized possession. When he failed to take the parchment, she grabbed his hand and thrust it into his palm.

"I am placing my trust in you, sir. This is the first clue to finding our legacy. You already possess the second clue."

The gentleman appeared more confused than ever. "Why would you trust a stranger with something so important, Miss

Hart?" Suspicion darkened his tone. "Why trust the man opposed to your plan?"

Vivienne inhaled deeply. He would think her a candidate for Bedlam if she spoke the truth, but needs must. "You're floundering, I can see. But you will marry me, Mr Sloane. During the coming days, the devil will seek to destroy us. Finding our legacy is the only way to save our lives."

The crunching of carriage wheels on the gravel sent her pulse soaring. She was out of time, and he refused to listen.

Fitchett appeared, carrying Vivienne's wet cloak and gloves. "Miss Hart's servants are in the carriage, sir, and I sent Dawson to pay the jarvey's fare." The butler glanced at Vivienne, his expression brimming with sympathy. "Your outdoor apparel, Miss Hart."

Vivienne took her cloak and gloves. Perhaps she should leave before Mr Sloane attempted to return the scroll and the contract. She would visit Keel Hall tomorrow, after he'd had time alone to process the information.

"And what of my boots?" she said, noting their absence. A maid must have wiped the muddy footprints from the marble floor and mopped the puddle.

"They were in such a terrible state, miss, I fear they're ruined. Mrs McCready tried her best to clean them, but the lining is soaked through. She has them in the carriage."

In the carriage? "And pray, how I am supposed to walk across the gravel in my stocking feet?"

Fitchett stared blankly. "With the master's permission, I shall carry you, miss."

"Carry me?" Based on Fitchett's stick-thin frame, he'd struggle to cover a few feet. And with him possessing only one good eye, she envisioned him tumbling down the front steps. "Never mind. I shall tread carefully."

Fitchett glanced at Mr Sloane. "Sir, Dawson broke a lantern yesterday. Slivers of glass covered the gravel. A cut to the toe often ends in amputation."

Mr Sloane arched a brow. "Have you been reading those morbid seafaring stories again, Fitchett?"

"Sir, there's many a truth found in fictional tales."

If they continued in this vein, Mr Sloane was likely to forget all about the small scroll in his hand. Everything depended upon him honouring the debt to Lucian Hart.

"Perhaps you'd allow me to summon a footman to carry the lady to the carriage, sir," Fitchett said. "Carter is just finishing his supper and can—"

"Oh, for the love of God!" Mr Sloane slipped the scroll into his boot. "I shall carry Miss Hart to the carriage."

Mother Mary! Panic rose to her throat, coupled with a shiver of delight. She was about to protest, but did she not need to foster a level of intimacy with the man she hoped to marry?

"I shall be fine, Mr Sloane," she said with a lack of conviction.

Evidently, the man wanted rid of her quickly. Without a word of warning, he scooped her up into his muscular arms and strode towards the door.

Vivienne wrapped her arms around his neck and clung on for dear life. The musky scent of his cologne teased her nostrils, as did the smoky aroma of whisky on his breath. She resisted the urge to lay her head on his broad shoulder, to take comfort in the warmth of his body. A woman need fear nothing with Mr Sloane as her protector.

"I know you think me a terrible pest," she said as he descended the mansion house steps as if she were as light as a child. "But I am very grateful for your assistance, sir."

"Madam, the sooner I deposit you in the carriage, the sooner I can relax and enjoy the evening."

Rain pelted their faces as they left the cover of the Grecian-inspired portico. "It must be rather lonely living in such a large house."

"I manage perfectly well." He threw her a dubious look. "I know your game, Miss Hart. While your approach to snagging a wealthy husband is original, your veiled attempts to sway my decision are less imaginative."

"Given time, I could find more inventive methods of persuasion." Her quick reply sounded rather salacious, far too out of character for a woman who hid behind marble pillars and watched him from afar.

Thankfully, Buchanan leant forward and opened the carriage door, saving her any embarrassment. The Scotsman tipped his grey felt cap to their host as a mark of respect.

"Just promise me one thing," she said when Mr Sloane plonked her inside the vehicle. "Promise you'll—"

"I'll not take you as my wife, Miss Hart." He slammed the door shut and instructed the coachman to move on.

Clawing desperation saw Vivienne yank down the window and thrust her head through the gap. The wind whipped her hair into her mouth. "Promise you'll read the clue on the scroll!" she cried amid the distant rumble of thunder.

But Mr Sloane ignored her plea and strode towards the house. Despite one last effort to gain his attention, he did not glance back.

CHAPTER 3

"THE GENTLEMAN IS A STUBBORN MULE." Mrs McCready scowled at the window, though the carriage was already at Keel Hall's main gate. The thin woman's mouth rarely curled into a smile. Years spent battling the harsh Highland weather had left her with ruddy cheeks and a permanent frown.

"Och, the lad needs time." As usual, Buchanan's summary carried the measure of the situation. "The lass will have said enough to gain his interest."

Vivienne prayed he was right. "Gentlemen like Mr Sloane are content to keep a mistress and have no need to take a bride. Hopefully, he'll consider what I've said and be intrigued enough to grant me a second audience when I call tomorrow."

"Well, he didna seem too happy when he dumped ye in the carriage," Mrs McCready grumbled. "Though the butler's plan worked well enough."

"Plan? What plan?"

"To have Mr Sloane sweep ye up into his arms."

Vivienne's stomach grew hot at the memory. Any woman would relish the prospect of being held in his strong embrace.

"Aye, the butler is desperate to see his master wed." Buchanan chuckled as he twirled the ends of his grey moustache. "Though his motives are entirely selfish."

"No doubt Fitchett longs for the day he can retire before

midnight." During her time spent lingering in the ladies' retiring room, Vivienne discovered Mr Sloane's penchant for entertaining guests until dawn.

"The butler fears being hit with another vase and losing the sight in his good eye," Buchanan added.

"Hit with a vase? Is that why Fitchett wears an eye patch?"

"Aye, a woman in a devil of a temper threw a vase at Mr Sloane. He ducked just as the butler walked into the room."

Mrs McCready gave a scornful snort. "Mr Fitchett said the master carries a heap of guilt and canna forgive himself. Though he canna be that sorry if he still hosts his wild parties."

Vivienne silently contemplated her dilemma.

When a man lived with the freedom to do as he pleased, to entertain unscrupulous women, to fill his life with excitement and pleasure, what incentive was there to settle into the tedious humdrum of family life? Not that she expected anything from Evan Sloane other than proof of their marriage. After the deed, and after Mr Sloane had used his skills as an enquiry agent to capture the villain out for their blood, Vivienne would travel north and live out her days in the Highlands.

"Well, let's hope he reconsiders before the miscreant who ransacked my house ventures to Little Chelsea." The intruder had smashed drawers, ripped feather pillows, slashed paintings, pulled up boards. But he did not find the old mahogany tea chest buried in the garden.

Buchanan shrugged. "Yer mother—God rest her soul—said Lady Sloane destroyed all evidence relating to the contract. The scoundrel will find nothing of interest in the mansion house."

Vivienne squirmed in the seat. Buchanan would rant and rave when he learnt she had left the priceless documents with Mr Sloane, but she kept no secrets from her mother's companions.

"Apparently, the matron abandoned the Sloane name and preferred to call herself Lady Boscobel." Vivienne paused. "And as for the scoundrel finding nothing in the house, I've given Mr Sloane the contract and the clue to our lost legacy."

Buchanan gasped. "Blessed saints!" His cheeks ballooned and his grey eyes bulged. "Tell me I've misheard, lass. Tell me the damp air hasn't dulled yer brain. Ah dinna ken what ye were thinking."

"The gentleman is probably dancing around the bonfire," Mrs McCready chimed, "singing his good fortune."

Having spent his life believing his grandfather was a heartless pirate who plundered the high seas, a life tainted by the association, trust did not come easily to Mr Sloane. Especially considering the terrible time he'd had at school.

"If I expect him to abide by the contract, I have to show him I believe he is honourable."

"But to give him yer only proof of his family's debt, lass."

Vivienne raised her chin. "I have faith in fate, in destiny, in the fact there is so much more to the gentleman than some would believe."

She couldn't explain why she trusted Mr Sloane. The certainty of it sat in the pit of her stomach, heavy as an anchor. The man had rescued a child abducted from the street and held prisoner in the slums of Whitechapel. That made him a hero in her eyes.

"And I need a reason to return to Keel Hall," she continued, clutching the overhead strap when they bounced through a rut in the road.

"There's no reason to return if he's destroyed the evidence," complained Mrs McCready, her expression unsurprisingly glum.

"You must trust me," Vivienne implored. "Mr Sloane knew nothing of his grandfather's work as a privateer, yet he kept Livingston Sloane's portrait." Had he kept it for the reason he'd stated? Did he really think of himself as a misfit? "Mr Sloane is a man who seeks the truth. I'm confident all will be well."

Buchanan's moustache twitched as he smiled. "There's logic to yer madness, lass. I'll give yer that. Happen yer mother would be mighty proud."

The mention of Vivienne's mother brought a rush of emotion to her throat. The stricken silence that followed carried the gravity of her loss. The last words her mother uttered as she clung to life in her sickbed was for Vivienne to find Evan Sloane. Evan Sloane would honour the contract and keep her safe. Evan Sloane would be her protector.

They all sat in thoughtful contemplation, shivering and staring as rain pelted the windowpanes, their minds conjuring their own morbid memories of the past.

They might have sat quietly until they reached Silver Street, had the sharp crack not pierced the night air and dragged them from their reverie. The coachman's keen cry followed. The commotion must have spooked the horses, for the carriage rocked violently as the terrified bays bolted forward.

"Damn the devil to Hades!" Buchanan rubbed mist off the window and pressed his nose to the glass. "What evil is this?"

Fear sent Vivienne's heart slamming into her ribs. Why did she sense the coachman's issue had nothing to do with the heart-stopping thunderclap? What if someone had followed them from town to Little Chelsea? Someone who wanted to ensure she never found the third clue.

Buchanan shot back from the window. "Quick. Crouch down, lass." In a state of panic, he tugged her cloak. "That was gunfire, nae a thunderbolt."

Mrs McCready yelped. "I knew we should have—"

Another shot rang out. The sound of splintering wood suggested the lead ball had hit a wheel spoke. Everything happened so quickly then. The carriage careened left, abandoning the muddy dirt track for the sprawling fields of Little Chelsea. It hurtled over the uneven ground at breakneck speed, throwing them off their seats.

"Cover yer heads!" Buchanan yelled.

"Saints and demons! Stop, you mad beasts!" The coachman's curses brought some comfort, for at least the poor man wasn't dead.

The carriage slowed and lost speed, but the rush of relief came all too soon. The vehicle bounced into a ditch, the violent impact snapping the axle and launching them into the air.

Mrs McCready and Buchanan banged heads as the carriage tilted and overturned. The windowpane exploded as it hit a rock on the ground, sending shards of glass flying into Mr Sloane's plush cab. Vivienne felt the trickle of blood at her temple before noticing the pain. But it was Buchanan's odd comment that brought bile to her throat, that left her trembling to the tips of her toes.

"Hush, lass, the plague doctor is on the trail. Where there's a plague doctor, death follows."

Legs crossed at the ankles, Evan sat in the wingback chair closest to the hearth, watching the amber flames flicker in the grate. A little over an hour had passed since Miss Hart thrust the tiny scroll into his palm and pleaded with him to read the script—the clue. The clue to what? Pirate treasure? A long lost legacy?

He snorted.

When it came to imaginative plans to snare a husband, Miss Hart deserved a medal of merit. Yet there were many flaws in her tale. If they needed to marry to discover the final clue, surely their lives wouldn't be in danger until after the event. And he'd known nothing of the contract before this evening. So how had the villain discovered the secret?

But what of this confounding contract?

Livingston Sloane must have known it would never stand up to the scrutiny of the law courts. Perhaps he had meant to appease his rescuer. A way to repay the debt without parting with hard-earned funds. And typical of a scoundrel like Livingston Sloane, he'd left his descendants to deal with the problem.

And yet Evan couldn't help but smile when he recalled Miss Hart's earnest explanation.

You're contractually obliged to marry me, Mr Sloane.

Had she expected him to nod and race to the archbishop for a licence? Surely while spying, she'd discovered he wasn't the sort to make a lifelong commitment. Nor was he willing to trade his sanity and freedom for a pot of pirate gold.

So why couldn't he shake the damn woman from his mind?

Why could he think of nothing but the scroll tucked inside his boot?

I'm placing my trust in you, sir.

Oh, Miss Hart knew how to stir emotion in a man's chest. She knew exactly what to say to rouse his interest.

A light rap on the door drew Evan from his reverie. "Enter."

Fitchett appeared. "Sir, I came to see if you required supper."

Evan arched a brow. "No, you came to see if I'd read the scroll. I'm sure Miss Hart's attendants explained the reason for her visit."

"They're convinced the lady is in danger, sir."

"Miss Hart is a danger to herself. A young unmarried woman should know better than to call at the house of a man who entertains courtesans. What is it you want me to do, Fitchett? Marry the chit?" Give up endless nights of pleasure for a woman who was most certainly deranged? Definitely not. "And before you ask again, I have no intention of solving her imagined mystery."

Fitchett inclined his head. "Forgive my insolence, sir. It's just one cannot help but believe there is some truth to the lady's claim. It's a ten-mile round trip, so I know we shouldn't expect Turton back yet, but I cannot shake the feeling something is dreadfully wrong."

Evan glanced at the mantel clock and felt a niggle of apprehension. "Have a stable hand saddle my horse, and fetch my hat and greatcoat. If Turton fails to return within the next half an hour, I shall ride into town."

Fitchett's shoulders sagged in relief. "A wise decision, sir."

"How long do you intend to make me pay, Fitchett?" Evan referred to the reason the poor man had lost the sight in his left eye. An accident for which Evan was entirely to blame.

"Pay, sir?"

"How many times will you play the guilt card to force my hand?" Evan would do anything to turn back time and save his butler from the savage temper of a madwoman—and Fitchett damn well knew it.

The butler bowed gracefully. "For as long as my impudence serves your best interests, sir. Consequently, in light of Miss Hart's warning, might I suggest carrying a loaded pistol if you plan on venturing to town."

"As an agent of the Order, I am always adequately equipped."

"Of course, sir."

Fitchett left the room to attend to his duties.

Well, if Evan was going to give Miss Hart's warning any credence, he may as well read the clue to finding their grandfathers' supposed legacy. Considering she saw fit to trust him, did he not owe the woman the respect of reading the note?

Reaching into his boot, he removed the small scroll. Energy pulsed in his fingers. His heart raced as he slowly unravelled the piece of parchment. When working for the Order, one learnt to use one's intuition, to listen to one's inner guide. These strange physical reactions might convince a man this was part of his maker's plan.

The clue amounted to nine cryptic words.

A temple for a pauper of Egypt's icy bones.

Evan read it numerous times. Egypt? Surely Miss Hart didn't expect him to journey thousands of miles in the hope of searching desert tombs. Still, the lady was right about one thing. Reading the clue had fired his curiosity. Excitement thrummed in his veins at the prospect of solving the mystery. Indeed, he found himself suddenly more than interested to hear Miss Hart's opinion, more than keen to discover what the hell had happened to his clue.

The chime of the mantel clock dulled his enthusiasm.

Turton should have returned by now. Had a fallen tree blocked the road? Had the torrential downpour left the muddy thoroughfare impassable? A chill ran down Evan's back. What if Miss Hart's suspicions were correct and a devious devil sought to stop them finding this supposed treasure?

Evan shot to his feet, though didn't wait to tug the bell pull. He strode into the hall and was about to shout for Fitchett when the man came hurrying forward, clutching Evan's hat and greatcoat.

"I fear there's no time to lose, sir." Fitchett helped Evan into his coat. "Something is amiss. I can feel it in my bones."

The sick feeling in Evan's gut said his butler was right.

CHAPTER 4

A MAN NEEDED a raven's keen sight when scouring the darkness. With so few houses situated along the muddy lane leading to town, and with the moon obscured by dense black storm clouds, there was no light to illuminate Evan's way.

The driving rain forced him to wipe his eyes every thirty seconds, to steer his horse around broken branches being whipped about by the brisk wind.

How was a man to focus when guilt sat like a stone in his throat?

Turton was more than capable of driving in harsh conditions. But had Evan not ejected Miss Hart so abruptly, he wouldn't be out combing the road through Little Chelsea.

"Turton!" Evan cried through the roaring gale while scanning the adjacent fields, silently bemoaning his fate.

Damnation!

Perhaps Miss Hart had discovered Turton's grandfather served on Livingston Sloane's ship. While Mrs McCready warmed a meat pie and made him a hot toddy for the journey home, Miss Hart was probably quizzing the coachman about his pirate ancestor. Meanwhile, Evan was soaked to the skin, cold to his bones and taking a mighty thrashing from his conscience.

Damn the woman.

She was intent on turning his ordered world upside down.

Salvation came in the form of an approaching rider. If the gentleman had travelled from town, he would have passed a carriage stuck in a quagmire, would have noticed something untoward on the road. Any information would prove useful at this point.

But as the horse drew closer, Evan knew it to be one of his Cleveland bays. Seated on the muscular beast, which had cost him the best part of a hundred and fifty guineas, was a woman riding bareback and astride.

"Sir! Stop!" Miss Hart waved frantically while clutching the reins with one hand. The wind whipped her loose hair about her face, sent her cloak billowing over the horse's back and croup. She looked every bit a wild Amazonian charging into battle.

The sudden stirring in Evan's loins proved more shocking than discovering the lady had bunched her skirts to her thighs and rode in her stocking feet.

"Where the hell are your boots?" he said as they brought their horses crashing to a halt in the road. His temper stemmed from his unwelcome arousal, not his mounting frustration. "Madam, I can almost see your thighs."

It seemed Miss Hart had the ability to turn a rake into a prude.

"Oh, Mr Sloane, thank goodness." Her breathless pants sent puffs of white mist into the air. "Hurry. Your coachman has been shot in the arm, and your carriage is overturned in a field."

"What the blazes!"

She gripped the bay with her slender thighs and turned the horse around. "Follow me, sir. I've left Buchanan tending your coachman's wound."

"Your servant allowed you to ride alone in the dark?"

"Buchanan knows I ride like the devil, and someone had to fetch help."

For a reason unbeknown he found that comment arousing, too. Hell's teeth. Miss Hart was a temptress in the guise of a blasted wallflower.

"Come, Mr Sloane. Come quickly."

Oh, he was one teasing comment away from spilling himself

in his breeches. In his current state, he feared following this conundrum of a woman lest he suffer an embarrassing accident.

"Remember, she means to marry you," he muttered to himself, which dampened his ardour considerably. "Lead the way, Miss Hart."

She barely gave him time to finish the sentence before bolting off into the blackness, but he easily caught up.

"Where did you learn to ride?" he called as their horses cantered side by side along the muddy track. She had complete command of the powerful animal, and he couldn't help but wonder if she would take the same masterful approach in bed.

"My father taught me when we lived in Derbyshire," she replied against the biting wind. "But I learnt to ride properly when visiting my mother's family in the Highlands."

"You've ridden bareback before?"

She laughed. "Many times. Highland terrain requires one to have better control of one's mount."

Perhaps she enjoyed feeling something solid between her legs.

Cursed saints! If he didn't calm his rampant thoughts, he'd be begging the chit to marry him just to satisfy his curiosity.

"Do Highlanders ride without footwear?"

"Not when the cold nips the toes. My only concern was to fetch help quickly, and I struggled to find my boots amid the chaos."

The comment drew his mind back to the more important matter of the wreckage and Turton's wound. "What happened to Turton? I doubt you were set upon by bandits, not on this road."

"Buchanan said a plague doctor fired the shots, though he had hit his head when he made the strange comment." Miss Hart's attention drifted to the fields on her left. "We're almost at the site of the accident. I'm sure Buchanan will give you an account of what happened."

Evan followed Miss Hart to the overturned carriage. Someone had released the team of bays from their harness and secured their reins to the rail around the driver's box seat. There was no sign of Turton or the lady's Scottish servants.

"Buchanan dragged your coachman behind the vehicle to tend to his injuries," Miss Hart said as if party to Evan's thoughts. "The poor man was thrown from his seat when the carriage tipped, and I fear he may have broken his ankle."

Evan dismounted. It occurred to him that without the luxury of stirrups to aid her descent, Miss Hart would need his assistance. Yet in true bluestocking-come-hellion fashion, the lady leant forward, gripped the horse by the withers and mane and slipped down to the ground.

"There," was all she said, brushing her hands and giving a satisfied grin.

Women usually used erotic means to gain his attention, yet Miss Hart's competent manner held him spellbound.

"Come, Mr Sloane." She tiptoed over the wet grass and beckoned him to follow. "You should assess Buchanan's work while I attend to Mrs McCready."

Evan hurried to the brawny Scot who was pouring whisky from a hip flask over the wound in Turton's upper arm. Turton lay on top of his greatcoat, a red plaid blanket draped over his legs. Blood soaked the shorn sleeve of his shirt. Thankfully, he was conscious.

"I hear someone shot my coachman."

The Scot pushed to his feet. He was almost as tall as Evan—half an inch shorter than six-foot-three—and his strong, muscular frame belied his age. Judging by the creases around his eyes and his grey beard, Evan guessed Buchanan had seen sixty summers.

"Aye, I managed to dig out the ball and stitch the wound. I think the injury to the ankle is just a wee sprain, but I've made a splint from the damaged wheel spoke and strapped it with material torn from Miss Hart's petticoat."

You'll come to admire their talents in the coming weeks.

The lady's earlier comment drifted through Evan's mind, as did a vision of her inadequate undergarments. "You're a resourceful man, Mr Buchanan." A quick inspection of the man's fine wool coat and quality riding boots suggested he was not a servant.

"Call me Buchanan. Only men of the cloth call me mister."

"Then I thank you, Buchanan, for taking good care of my coachman." Evan crouched beside Turton and examined his injuries. He doubted a surgeon could have done a better job. "Might you explain briefly what happened on the road?"

Turton grimaced in pain. "The bandit ... he must have followed us from Keel Hall, sir. He had ... had two loaded pistols. I can't rightly say what happened after the f-first shot."

"Don't trouble yourself now. We can discuss it tomorrow when you've rested." Evan stood and faced Buchanan. "Miss Hart mentioned a plague doctor. Though when the mind is consumed with fear, one is often mistaken."

"I saw the devil astride a black stallion fifty yards away. He wore a caped coat and a tricorn, hid his face with a white mask."

Was this a failed attempt at highway robbery, then? The person had an exceptional aim if they hit a moving target while on horseback. And the mask must have hindered his vision.

"Where is he now?"

"The lass fired a warning shot from her pocket pistol, and he disappeared into the night."

It seemed the lass was as brave as she was reckless.

"So the mask had an extended beak, like the ones once worn by physicians treating victims of the disease?" The ones worn to masquerade balls by weak men who enjoyed intimidating young women. Was it the shooter's intention to frighten Miss Hart? Was Turton's injury a case of the person firing blindly in the blackness?

"Aye, sir."

"And you determined that from such a distance in the dark?"

"When the devil fired, I glimpsed the mask as the charge ignited." Buchanan glanced at Miss Hart, who was kneeling on the wet grass, examining the Scottish woman's head. He shuffled closer to Evan and lowered his voice. "The intruder, the one who ransacked the lass' home." The man spoke as if Evan knew of the incident.

"Yes, what of it?"

"He left a mask at the scene, though I couldna tell the lass for fear she'd never sleep soundly again. I took it and hid it in my room."

"A plague mask?"

"Aye."

Then Miss Hart's fears had merit. Someone was willing to go to great lengths to terrify the woman. "And did the intruder steal anything?"

"The lass is canny enough nae to leave prized possessions where some devil might find them. And she owns nothing of value save for the documents passed down from her grandfather."

As Evan suspected, money was Miss Hart's motive for wanting to marry him and obtain the third clue. So why had she not readily accepted his offer of compensation? Maybe she believed their legacy was worth a king's ransom.

"Logic suggests the shooter had no intention of killing anyone, that his motive was to scare Miss Hart into abandoning her plan to have me honour the contract." A pang of doubt said Evan was wrong in his assumption, and so he took a few seconds to consider what he'd learnt so far. "Or, the devil wants to scare us into marrying and solving the mystery of the missing legacy so he might steal it from under our noses."

"Aye, I'm inclined to agree with yer second theory."

Yes, the second explanation sounded more plausible.

A host of questions bombarded Evan's mind. Indeed, he would need to interview Miss Hart and gather a list of suspects. Who knew about the contract? Who had the skill and cunning to commit a crime? The person had followed Miss Hart to Keel Hall, unperturbed by the storm, and waited patiently for her to leave. Would he have approached the carriage if Miss Hart hadn't shot at him in the dark?

No, the villain was orchestrating events to suit his purpose, biding his time. Plotting. Planning.

Evan's pulse soared at the prospect of working this case. He would have to meet with Lucius Daventry, the master of the Order, and explain the situation.

But then another thought struck him.

With the carriage overturned in the field, the villain knew someone would return to Keel Hall for help. Which meant while they were conversing over his coachman's injured body, the miscreant could be inside Evan's house, ripping the place apart.

Damnation!

He'd left the blasted contract on the sofa in the drawing room. And Fitchett would fight to the death to stop the thieving blackguard.

"We must return to the house at once." Evan spoke loud enough for Miss Hart to hear. He crouched beside Turton. "I'll lift you onto my horse and take you home. Are you able to manage the short journey?"

Turton winced in pain but nodded.

Buchanan swigged from his hip flask before bending down and pressing the lip of the vessel to Turton's mouth. "Down this, laddie, and we'll soon have ye tucked into yer bed."

Miss Hart approached. "Mrs McCready took a bump to the head but can ride with assistance. Buchanan will need to ride with her. We can lead the other two bays back to Keel Hall."

Buchanan muttered something in Gaelic under his breath.

"It's your head she hit, Buchanan," Miss Hart said as if used to their petty quarrels. "It's only right you take responsibility." The lady touched Evan's arm, leant closer and whispered, "Mrs McCready is a terrible patient, and likes to find something to complain about."

As if on cue, the woman with the dour face began lamenting her fate. "Och, we should have waited. Should have visited the hall at a reasonable hour like normal folk."

"Well, we cannot waste time here." Evan decided a woman with Miss Hart's fortitude could handle the truth. "The villain may be using the opportunity to ransack my house."

"Ransack your house?" Miss Hart's captivating brown eyes widened. "Blessed saints. Then we must hurry. Please tell me the clue is still in your boot. And what of the contract?"

Evan was annoyed at himself for not taking the threat seriously. "The clue is in my boot." He'd slipped it back inside his Hessian before shrugging into his greatcoat. "But I left the contract in plain sight."

While Miss Hart's pretty mouth fell open, Mrs McCready whined, "Did I nae say it was a mistake to trust him?"

Miss Hart closed her mouth and fixed her determined gaze upon his person. "It matters not. Mr Sloane has seen and read the contract. As an honourable man, he will do what is right."

Why did she seem so sure of his character? How was it a lady he had never spoken to until tonight had such faith in him? And why did he find the notion so damnably arousing?

"To anyone else the contract is worthless," she added.

Evan begged to disagree. "Unless we're looking for two villains who intend to pose as us. Either way, now is not the time to ponder the possibilities. My fears may be unfounded, which would render this a pointless conversation."

"Then let us make haste, sir. We can discuss our plan once we've assessed the situation at Keel Hall."

Miss Hart liked using words like *our* and *we*. Usually, any hint of possessiveness had Evan darting for the hills, and yet he couldn't help but feel he had an ally in this fascinating woman. That didn't mean he had any intention of marrying her. Hell no! He'd seen what losing a loved one had done to his father. The man had been but an empty vessel going through the motions. A sad remnant of his former self, waiting to die.

Still, as Evan watched the lady ride the Cleveland bay back to Keel Hall, with her shapely calves on show, he decided he liked Miss Hart. Indeed, there was something wild and spirited about her, something he admired, something he longed to tame.

Chaos erupted when Evan barged into his house carrying Turton. "Fitchett! We need help! Mrs Thorne!" Thank heavens he'd only had to walk a short way, for the man was heavier than expected.

Fitchett appeared, almost tripping over his polished shoes as he hurried through the dimly lit hall. He summoned two footmen to carry Turton to the servants' quarters, then rang for the housekeeper to attend to Miss Hart's companions.

"Send a groom to Chelsea." Evan paused to catch his breath. "To the physician who lives opposite the Botanic Gardens on Paradise Row. Tell him we need assistance now, tonight." He turned his attention to his housekeeper. "And Mrs Thorne, have the maids prepare rooms for our guests."

"Yes, sir," the flustered servants said in unison.

Mrs Thorne, a woman of middling years who had served his

father and liked to fuss and dote, sent a maid to heat some water and then escorted Buchanan and Mrs McCready upstairs.

Miss Hart had hurried into the drawing room within seconds of entering the house, desperate to see if the devil in the hideous mask had stolen her precious contract.

Evan entered the room and found her gawping at the fire roaring in the grate. The room was so hot it was hard to breathe. His gaze drifted over her windswept hair, down to her wet cloak and bare feet.

Bare feet!

What the devil had she done with her muddy stockings? She must have removed them and stuffed them in a concealed pocket for fear of soiling his expensive Persian rug. Most women of his acquaintance would dart for cover, ashamed to have a gentleman see them in such a sorry state. Miss Hart didn't give a damn. He liked that. He liked that a great deal.

"I see you've found your contract." He breathed a relieved sigh upon noting the rolled scroll in her hand. "We have a lot to discuss if I'm to accept your case, Miss Hart. Though after such a dreadful ordeal, you need rest. Mrs Thorne will find a suitable room and arrange to have your clothes cleaned. I'm sure we can find new stockings somewhere."

"Sir, I fear we have more important concerns than my stockings." Miss Hart pointed to the empty space left of the marble fireplace. "The blackguard took advantage of the carriage accident to steal the painting of Livingston Sloane."

"What!"

Shock stole the breath from Evan's lungs. He covered his mouth with his hand and stared at the dusty mark on the wall. Guilt surfaced for the umpteenth time. The masked rider appeared more cunning than his usual foe. Yet he couldn't have predicted Evan's coachman would take Miss Hart home, or that he would mount his stallion and ride out into the night. The quick-thinking devil took advantage of every opportunity, and that made him unpredictable. Dangerous.

He stepped forward but was suddenly distracted by the fire's amber flames. A toxic smell wafted from the grate, hitting the back of his throat, attacking his nostrils, forcing him to cough.

Chunks of wood and broken board lay scattered amongst the glowing coals.

Merciful Lord!

Evan shot back. He gripped Miss Hart's arm and pulled her away from the flames. "Cover your mouth, Miss Hart. Do not breathe in the fumes. The devil did not steal the painting of Livingston Sloane. He snapped it into pieces and used it as firewood. Quick. Help me open the windows."

Miss Hart did not stop to question him, nor did she vocalise the crippling panic flashing in her eyes. She threw the scroll onto the sofa, darted to the far end of the room, dragged the heavy brocade curtains aside and raised the sash. Oh, there was nothing timid about this woman. Indeed, after tonight's debacle, she deserved the moniker Valiant.

Wind rushed into the room, howling in protest.

"This window is already open." Miss Hart's comment came as no surprise. The intruder had to have found a way in without alerting Fitchett.

Evan joined her at the window so they might talk while inhaling fresh air.

"You were right, Miss Hart," it pained him to say. "Right to voice your concerns, right in your belief that someone has learnt of our ancestors' pact and wants to ensure we never find the supposed treasure. Forgive me for not taking the matter seriously."

The lady blinked in surprise. "There is nothing to forgive. You acted as any man would when confronted by a stranger demanding marriage."

A gust of wind whipped wet locks of hair from her heart-shaped face. It was then Evan noticed blood at the hairline near her temple.

"You're injured." His heart raced, though he resisted the urge to cradle her head and examine the wound.

Miss Hart pressed her fingers to the area and winced. "It's nothing, just a scratch from a shard of glass." She glanced at the spot of blood on her finger and wiped it on her cloak.

"May I take a look?"

Her eyes widened. "If you think it necessary, but I assure you, all is well."

"Still, if we're to work together, you need to be in optimum health."

"Work together?" A weak smile played at the corners of her mouth, yet he sensed excitement rushing through her like a fast-flowing river. "You would work with a woman?"

He refused to work with anyone but his colleagues at the Order. And yet a small part of him wished to make amends for his earlier mistreatment.

"I'm a logical man, Miss Hart. Our combined efforts will bring rapid results."

"Does that mean you're going to marry me, Mr Sloane?"

Evan couldn't help but laugh. "I've made my views on marriage clear, though perhaps we might find another way to gain the third clue." A mountain of questions formed in his mind, but they would begin their investigation in the morning. "We can discuss the matter tomorrow. For now, I wish to check your cut and hear your thoughts on the villain's reason for destroying the painting."

Miss Hart nodded. She bent her head. "See, it is just a scratch."

A coil of desire swirled in his stomach as he clasped her head in his hands and narrowed his gaze. A different sensation filled his chest, one infinitely more worrying—an overwhelming need to play protector.

Hell! He must have inhaled the toxic fumes.

Evan tried to focus on the task.

"Ow!" she cried when he touched the small gash.

"It should heal perfectly well on its own, but you must wash it thoroughly before you retire tonight. I'll have Mrs Thorne bring you some ointment." He released the tempting minx and stepped back. "Now, tell me why you think the painting of my ancestor has been reduced to a pile of ash."

He sensed an inner conflict. "I must confess, I'm unable to lie to you, Mr Sloane. Please know I dislike condemning those who cannot offer a defence."

"Madam, honesty is a quality I admire. Speak freely."

Miss Hart exhaled before saying, "I do not believe Lady Sloane, or Lady Boscobel if you prefer, cared for her son. I believe she cared about money and title, and so kept the painting because she knew it held a clue to finding the hidden legacy."

Evan attempted to remain impartial while he considered her point. "And that is the reason you persuaded Fitchett to let you study the painting?"

"Indeed."

"Did you draw any conclusions?" Natural suspicions surfaced. Would she have bothered coming back if she had gained the information she needed? Would she have found another way to obtain the third important clue?

The lady's teeth chattered as she thought about his question. It occurred to him that her clothes were soaked, her feet cold, and she would likely catch a chill if she did not strip off the wet garments and warm her icy limbs.

"The first point to note is that the portrait was painted in 1756, and yet Livingston Sloane is depicted as a much younger man."

"Vanity is a trait enjoyed by the masses. He wished to be immortalised as a handsome charmer, not a weather-beaten buccaneer."

She wrapped her arms across her chest and shivered. "I think the date might be a clue to the meaning behind the painting."

"And I think you need out of those clothes, Miss Hart, before you catch your death." Evan strode to the bell pull and rang for his butler. He needed time alone to think and had to interrogate Fitchett while the man could still recall the night's events. "Fitchett will escort you to your room. We can discuss the case in the morning."

A pretty blush stained her cheeks. "I cannot stay the night, Mr Sloane."

Evan arched a brow. "As you're determined to marry me, Miss Hart, I don't see the problem." Indeed, he should be the one worried, worried the woman would force his hand. And yet for some unfathomable reason he trusted this less than timid wall-flower. "Besides, it is unsafe for you to remain in Silver Street at present."

"Oh, but I must return home, sir. There are—"

"A woman who rides astride can surely have no issue sleeping without nightclothes," he said, anticipating her complaint. Indeed, he had no problem imagining the alluring scene. "Get some sleep, Miss Hart. We have work to do tomorrow and must make an early start."

Fitchett's timely appearance left the lady no option but to take her scroll and bid Evan good night.

"Return to the drawing room once you've seen Miss Hart to her chamber, Fitchett."

"Yes, sir."

As soon as the lady crossed the threshold, Evan released the tempest of oaths he'd kept at bay. It was easy to remain impartial when solving a stranger's case, easy to maintain a facade for Miss Hart's sake. But the masked devil's personal attack had Evan seething. He stared at the space on the wall and let the unholy rage overwhelm him.

Once the anger dissipated, he would be left with the steely determination to catch the blackguard, regardless of the cost. Even if he had to shackle himself to a wallflower, Evan would have his revenge.

CHAPTER 5

"TO WHOM DOES THIS GARMENT BELONG?" Vivienne asked as the maid helped her into a pretty white petticoat with frills at the hem.

Having spent weeks following Mr Sloane about town, scouring ballrooms and listening out for the latest gossip, she was confident the gentleman did not have a mistress. Nor did he have a sister or aunt. Mr Sloane was alone in the world, except for a distant cousin who had inherited the Leaton viscountcy.

"I don't rightly know, miss."

Vivienne caught Theresa's flush of embarrassment in the looking glass. "Ah, I see. One of Mr Sloane's guests misplaced the item." That explained why there was a spare petticoat and stays, but no shift or gown. She plucked the clean white stockings from the bed. "These are expensive, new."

Theresa swallowed deeply. "B-bought as a gift, miss."

"A gift for whom?" It was unfair to pressure the maid into revealing her master's secrets. Besides, Vivienne suddenly found the idea of wearing clothes belonging to Mr Sloane's lover rather distasteful. "Never mind. Are you certain my undergarments are ruined?"

Theresa nodded. "I've never seen so much mud on a petticoat, miss, and it's ripped. Bessie has been boiling and poking it in the laundry copper for the last three hours. And your stockings are fit for nothing but the bonfire. Your dress is almost dry, but it smells none too pleasant."

That's what came from traipsing about in a field during a thunderstorm. "Thank Bessie for her trouble, but I've changed my mind and do not wish to wear another woman's underclothes. Help me out of this petticoat, Theresa."

"But the master said you were to wear the new stockings."

"And have Mr Sloane thinking about his paramour during breakfast?" That was hardly conducive to her plan. "Speak to Fitchett or Mrs Thorne and explain the situation."

Like the rest of the household, Theresa preferred plain speaking. Her lips curled into a knowing smile, and she set about undressing Vivienne before hurrying from the room to fetch the housekeeper.

Mrs Thorne entered the bedchamber five minutes later. "Good morning, miss." Her wrinkled face exuded a wealth of warmth and kindness. "Theresa explained there's an issue with your undergarments."

"Yes, perhaps you might provide a solution to the dilemma." Vivienne explained her problem. "I cannot wear my clothes and refuse to wear a courtesan's discarded raiment."

"Hmm." Mrs Thorne pursed her lips. She studied Vivienne's figure as if mentally taking her measurements. "The master will dismiss us all if you join him for breakfast wearing maid's attire, and we've nothing else suitable. Might I send a footman to town to fetch clean clothes?"

Vivienne was already late. Mr Sloane had summoned her to the dining room half an hour ago. The man might be a libertine, but he behaved with the utmost professionalism when working on a case.

"There's no time. The return journey takes an hour."

The housekeeper gave a reassuring smile. "Mr Fitchett might have a few suggestions." She crossed the room and removed a blanket from the armoire and handed it to Vivienne. "I shall be back shortly."

Once again, Vivienne was left in the shift she had insisted on wearing to bed. She sat in the chair near the fire and waited. Mrs Thorne returned with Theresa, their arms laden with garments.

"We've a few choices here, though I'm not sure you will approve of Mr Fitchett's suggestion." Mrs Thorne placed the assortment of articles on the bed. "But he said you're a lady willing to embrace a challenge."

Vivienne took it as a compliment. She hurried to the bed and began sifting through the clothes. The thought of wearing the ridiculous garments warmed her insides and lifted her spirits, particularly when she anticipated Mr Sloane's stunned reaction.

"Fitchett is right. Few women have the courage to wear these gaudy garments."

Indeed, poor Mr Sloane was in for another mighty shock.

Vivienne burst into the dining room. "Do not take the trouble to stand, sir. I wouldn't want you to suffer from indigestion."

"You're late, Miss Hart." Mr Sloane did not look up from his newspaper, though it was evident he wasn't reading anything of interest. "If we're to work together on this case, know I shall not tolerate tardiness."

He looked devilishly handsome with his hair tied in a queue and his cravat fastened in a fashionable knot—like the perfect present one longed to unwrap.

"Of course." She smiled at the footman who pulled out her chair, though the distraction did little to calm the flutter in her chest. "I had a terrible time finding suitable clothes."

The gentleman raised his gaze above the top of his newspaper. Any pretensions of appearing indifferent to her plight vanished. "What in blazes are you wearing?"

"This?" Vivienne stroked her hand down the embroidered pink waistcoat. "Yes, it's a little garish. I heard it belonged to a libertine who attended one of your house parties."

Mr Sloane threw the paper onto the table. The chair legs scraped the boards as he shot to his feet. "Madam, you're wearing the clothes of a degenerate. And I do not care to be reminded of why I still possess Monsieur Lamont's wardrobe."

Mrs Thorne had told the tale with great delight. While highly intoxicated, and despite his small stature, the Frenchman had stripped off his clothes, bathed then piddled in Mr Sloane's mermaid fountain.

"You're somewhat of a conundrum, sir. You entertain debauched members of society, yet are shocked when they behave disgracefully. Mrs Thorne said you chased the naked Frenchman halfway to town."

With a curt nod, Mr Sloane dismissed both footmen.

"Had I caught him in the act, I would have drowned the blighter." He scanned her blue tailcoat and silver breeches. "If you think I am going to town with you dressed like a dandy, think again."

Vivienne bit back a grin. "Then, I shall wait for you to change."

Mr Sloane arched a brow. "Miss Hart, do not try my patience. Wear the popinjay's clothes, if you must, but you will change the moment we reach Silver Street. Is that understood?"

Firstly, Vivienne was not in the habit of being treated like a child. Secondly, Mr Sloane did not make decisions on her behalf.

"You're not my husband yet, Mr Sloane. And before you make the ultimate commitment, know you cannot browbeat me into submission."

Mr Sloane dropped into his seat. "As we have already established, marriage to me is out of the question."

"Perhaps." Vivienne smiled. She hadn't had such fun in years, though their situation was far from amusing. "Are you happy for me to serve myself, or will you ring for a footman?"

Mr Sloane gestured to the toast rack. "Do as you please, madam. I shall save my demands for the bedchamber, not the breakfast table."

Vivienne swallowed to hide her nerves, but couldn't let the comment pass without challenge. "Talk of the bedchamber must mean you've changed your mind about marriage."

"While I might be opposed to marriage, Miss Hart, I find I'm not opposed to bedding you."

Good heavens!

The sly devil! Illicit talk was an attempt to unnerve her, to force her to mind her tongue. Perhaps Mr Sloane was unaware the women in the Highlands spoke more freely than their English counterparts.

"You surprise me, sir." Vivienne reached across to take toast from the rack. "Not that I know much on the subject, but I was told men who focus on pleasing their partner make the best lovers. Those who make demands are often found to be boring in the bedchamber."

Mr Sloane almost choked on his coffee.

"Might you pass the strawberry jam when you've recovered?"

"I can assure you, Miss Hart," he began but paused to cough into his fist, "women find me anything but a bore in bed." He pushed the jam pot across the table as though moving his chess piece into an attack position.

The urge to tease him took command of her senses. "Well, they would hardly make the complaint directly. Perhaps you lack your grandfather's adventurous spirit." Before he replied, she said, "And as an agent of the Order, I thought you would approve of my costume. After all, do we not want to throw the masked devil off the scent?"

Mr Sloane seemed more concerned about the slight to his prowess than the need to focus on the case. "Trust me, there is nothing tiresome about the way I make love."

"Make love? The words suggest a meaningful alliance, a deep connection."

"Oh, I can do deep, Miss Hart."

Heat crept up Vivienne's neck and warmed her cheeks. Still, she was the granddaughter of the hero who had saved his drowning relative. She had to say something to make it sound as if she were not floundering out of her depth.

"And yet from you, it all sounds superficial. Besides, when it comes to daring, sir, I am the one who braved the storm. The one willing to risk everything to find our legacy. The one dressed in ridiculous clothes because our mission is too important to worry about appearances."

Mr Sloane's intense gaze drifted from her lips to her breasts, squashed into the foppish waistcoat. "Superficial? Are you not the one demanding to marry a stranger? Perhaps this boring-in-the-bedchamber routine is a means to have me seduce you, Miss Hart."

"Ha! Are handsome men always so self-assured?"

"You think me handsome?"

"Undoubtedly." Why lie? "Handsome and misguided. You're the one who has been seduced, sir. Your head is spinning. You do not know what to make of me. You're intrigued by my unconventional character, excited by the prospect of solving this case. The question is, how far will you go to seek answers?"

Mr Sloane's slow smile pinned her to the seat. The simple movement of the man's mouth caused a sudden pulsing at the apex of her thighs. How was he able to caress every inch of her body with nothing more than a sweeping gaze?

"You're right, of course." His buttery-smooth voice melted over her. "I am finding it difficult to determine your character. You possess the wicked mouth of a hellion, yet blush like a wallflower."

When one's life hung in the balance, one had to adapt. "There is nothing wicked about the truth. Perhaps you're used to hearing falsehoods, having ladies pander to your whims. We haven't time for misunderstandings."

"Then let's have nothing but honesty between us."

Vivienne nodded. "Agreed. Is there something you wish to say?"

"Indeed." He moistened his lips. The mere sight of his tongue made her stomach flip. "You're a riddle, Miss Hart. You possess a man's courage and a woman's vulnerability. Logical comments follow illogical statements. Your mouth moves in a way I find annoying and alluring. I have nothing to prove, and yet I need to prove something to you. Why is that?"

From Mr Sloane's mouth, the truth was like opium. It brought a wave of euphoria, a rush of confidence. She could become addicted to his compliments and flattery. Never had a man found her mouth alluring. Later, when her mind dulled, she would be plagued by the fact he found her annoying, and another dose of the truth would be the only remedy to banish the doubts.

"Perhaps you've never met a woman willing to hold you to

account. If you wish to prove your skill in the bedchamber, know the only man I will bed is my husband."

Mischief danced in his verdant eyes. "You may have a change of heart." Arrogance dripped from every word. "We can discuss marriage and seduction during dinner this evening. But for now, we have a busy day ahead of us. Write a note to your lawyer and arrange for us to meet with him today. Buchanan will ride into town and deliver the missive."

Being preoccupied with her lack of clothes this morning, she had not visited Buchanan or Mrs McCready. That said, Mrs McCready would have come to Vivienne's bedchamber if she were well.

"You've spoken to Buchanan?"

"Yes, he's taken a few stable hands to the site of the accident. He left a little after dawn and assured me he would have my carriage returned soon. He's a competent fellow." Mr Sloane poured coffee into her cup. "I presume you like the beverage."

"Yes."

"Good."

"And what of Mrs McCready?"

"She's suffering from a terrible migraine and is still abed. The doctor said to expect as much, and she should rest for a few days."

While Mrs McCready enjoyed playing the poorly patient, Vivienne wondered if she had another motive for keeping to her bed. The woman's nerves had been in tatters since learning an intruder had rummaged through her belongings. No doubt she felt safe sleeping beneath Mr Sloane's roof. Or was she using her injury as an excuse for Vivienne to remain at Keel Hall?

"While waiting for you to dress, I sketched this." Mr Sloane removed a folded piece of paper from the inside pocket of his coat and handed it to her. "I haven't mastered Hogarth's realistic portraiture, but I've tried to record every memorable detail."

Vivienne scanned the sketch of Livingston Sloane's portrait. The devilish gent sat by a window overlooking lush fields in the height of summer. To the right of the window hung a painting of a galleon at full sail. In his hand, Livingston held a compass.

She glanced up and smiled. "It's a fair attempt, sir."

"Only fair?"

"More than fair considering it's from memory."

"I tried to capture everything pertinent." He leant closer, close enough for her to catch a whiff of his cologne. The sensual smell of cedarwood and frankincense spoke of a man confident in after-dark pursuits. "But there's nothing of interest except for the compass in his hand."

Vivienne felt certain he had missed something. She closed her eyes and summoned the image of the painting. "Hmm. I recall there being a small table with a book resting on top." She opened her eyes to find Mr Sloane staring at her mouth.

He blinked and shook his head. "I once took a magnifying glass to the book but found it impossible to decipher a single word. As such, I don't see how it's relevant."

"Perhaps it's not." When Fitchett kindly let her study the painting, she had squinted at the book until her eyes hurt. "The needle on the compass pointed north, if I remember rightly."

"Yes. It pointed to the window. It must mean something because my grandfather held the instrument upside down."

Vivienne had made the same observation. A seafaring man relied on his compass the way he relied on the wind. "I agree. Livingston Sloane respected the instrument and would not have allowed the artist to make such a foolish mistake."

Mr Sloane relaxed back in the seat. His keen gaze drifted over her simple chignon and the complicated knot in her cravat, tied by his reluctant valet.

"As we've agreed to speak honestly, Miss Hart," he said, his eyes brighter than she had ever seen them before, "let me say I'm quite impressed by your logical deductions."

Vivienne's heart lurched at the compliment. "I'm glad you can take me seriously when dressed in foppish attire."

"Oh, I'll soon have you out of those clothes." The gentleman caught himself and added, "You can change the moment we arrive in Silver Street. While my colleagues are all forward-thinking men, I would prefer they understood the gravity of our situation. Dressed like that, D'Angelo will think you're an actress persuaded to play a prank."

"We're to visit the office of the Order?" A wave of trepidation washed over her at the thought of meeting the intimidating men.

"I must explain that I cannot take a case while working on this one."

Would his friends at the Order sway his decisions? Would she find herself pushed to the periphery, ousted from her role so his colleagues could assist? Had she placed her trust in a man who would discard her at the first opportunity?

"And as we get closer to discovering the identity of the plague doctor, we might need their support," he added. "Like Buchanan, they're highly resourceful."

Well, at least he intended to include her. But his colleagues were bound to frown upon the stipulations in the contract. She wondered what they would advise when marriage was the only way to gain the third clue.

Vivienne pushed to her feet, and Mr Sloane stood, too.

"Then let us not waste time," she said. "I presume you have another carriage and coachman."

"I do." Mr Sloane glanced at the toast on her plate and the full cup of coffee. "Do you not want to finish your breakfast?"

"No. We have a busy schedule." Once they'd visited Silver Street and she had shown him the documents in her possession, they would make the next necessary call before advancing on the men of the Order. "And we do not need an appointment to visit Mr Golding."

"Mr Golding?"

"The lawyer at Golding, Wicks & Sons."

Lucian Hart had hired Mr Golding to oversee all legal matters, though his elderly son now dealt with issues concerning the contract. Before Mr Sloane posed his next question, Vivienne knew the lawyer would be on the gentleman's list of suspects.

"So, Mr Golding knows about the clues and the treasure?" Mr Sloane asked, his smooth voice slathered in suspicion.

Vivienne explained her family's long-standing relationship with the firm. "Mr Golding knows of the legacy and the clauses we must satisfy to obtain our inheritance. That makes him a suspect. Greed consumes the best of men, does it not?"

"Indeed. But Mr Golding must be in his dotage."

"He'll soon turn seventy. His nephew, Mr Wicks, dealt with most clients but has been relegated to the role of clerk. And yes, before you say anything, we must add Mr Wicks to the list of potential villains, too."

"You've given the matter considerable thought," he said with admiration. "Have you added anyone else to your list?"

Vivienne had thought of nothing else since the night the intruder ransacked her home. "Two people. My father's friend, Mr Ramsey. He was rather attentive to my mother during her final months and has developed a sudden interest in my welfare."

Mr Ramsey often arrived at her home without invitation. He'd asked personal questions about her financial affairs—merely out of concern, of course. Buchanan didn't like the man and made his feelings known.

"And the fourth person?" Mr Sloane asked, listening intently.

Vivienne cleared her throat before broaching the delicate subject. "The fourth person is Charles Sloane, the current Viscount Leaton." Before he voiced his objection, she added, "I believe Lady Boscobel's eldest son would have known about the contract she destroyed. She must have forewarned him. Therefore, it stands to reason your relative is aware of what we might gain should we marry. And based on the fact your family believe Livingston Sloane is guilty of piracy, the lord might feel he has a right to claim what should be legally his."

Looking somewhat impressed, Mr Sloane said, "Miss Hart, should you ever tire of playing a wallflower, perhaps you might like to work as an enquiry agent."

"Are you mocking me, sir?"

"Mocking you? Madam, you have me on the edge of my seat, hanging on your every word. Indeed, I am beginning to wonder why you need me."

It was easy to offer a few insightful comments. Not so easy to tackle a cunning villain alone. But perhaps the gentleman needed reminding why she'd sought him out.

"I need you to marry me, sir, so we might obtain the last clue. I need your power and influence so we might catch the villain, so

I might sleep easily at night, so I might travel the roads without being shot at by a lunatic in a plague mask."

"And you need money."

"Doesn't everyone?"

He smiled. "If they awarded titles for persistence, Miss Hart, you would be a duchess."

"I would make a terrible duchess, sir. I'm wild and unruly and say inappropriate things." London life was not for her. It had taken a tremendous effort to loiter in the background, watching his every move. No, she was more at home roaming the Highlands. "But rest assured, once we've pledged our troth, you need never see me again."

Mr Sloane straightened. "Is that a promise?" His amused grin belied the regretful look in his eyes. "If so, let us make haste so I can be rid of you for good."

"You might miss me when I'm gone," she teased.

"I doubt I shall miss the antics of a wildcat."

So why did he sound unsure?

CHAPTER 6

"I CANNOT DIG if you persist in standing so close, Miss Hart."
And the fact her shapely thighs filled Monsieur Lamont's silk
breeches played havoc with Evan's concentration.

There were many things a man might do with a woman while
alone at the bottom of a secluded garden—scrambling about in
the dirt wasn't one of them. Evan contemplated pulling the lady
behind the apple tree and kissing the last breath from her lungs.
That would stop all ridiculous talk of marriage. He contemplated
kissing her just to see her confidence falter, and to sate the
damnable craving that hardened his cock whenever she opened
her delectable mouth.

"I am trying to prevent you from getting wet." Miss Hart
kept her cloak raised above their heads to shelter them from the
chill wind and drizzling rain. "Heaven forbid you take ill and I'm
left to face the blackguard alone."

"Yes, heaven forbid I no longer prove useful." Evan plunged
the shovel into the damp earth. The sudden thud as he hit something hollow brought instant relief. "It's unwise to keep a
wooden tea caddy buried in the ground. It's likely to rot."

"It's not in the ground but hidden inside a brass-mounted
trunk. Your task isn't over yet, I'm afraid. You must dig a much
larger hole. Should I call Buchanan?"

If she thought he'd surrender his shovel to a man twice his age, she was sorely mistaken.

Evan dropped the tool and stripped to his shirtsleeves. "Take my coat and wait inside. There's no point us both getting wet."

Miss Hart hesitated. "I'll not leave you," she said, ignorant to the fact the words struck a chord deep in his chest. She lowered her cloak and draped the damp garment around her shoulders before grabbing his coat. "And my need to remain here has nothing to do with distrust."

"You don't fear I might steal what's hidden in the trunk?" Evan gripped the shovel and continued digging, aware of the lady's gaze lingering on his biceps.

"I trust you to do what is right, Mr Sloane. Everything about our situation is difficult. I'll not leave you to deal with any part of it alone."

Hellfire!

Never had he encountered a more accomplished temptress. Miss Hart made sincerity as arousing as sin. One carefully constructed sentence had the power to reach deep down into his soul and stir hidden feelings. The old trunk wasn't the only thing buried. When a man had no memory of his mother, he filled the gaping hole of loneliness with any rubble he could find.

Evan continued working in silence. The beguiling woman behind him consumed his thoughts, not the need to uncover the chest.

"That should suffice," she said as he exposed the solid lid. "You should be able to slip the key into the lock and flick the catch."

Evan thrust the shovel into the dirt, leaving it upright. He brushed his hands and took the small iron key from Miss Hart's cold fingers. His only thought was sucking life into the slender digits, not crouching and sweeping away the soil.

The tarnished hinges creaked as he lifted the lid. "How long has the chest been buried here?"

"Two years. After my father's death, Lady Hollinshead persuaded my mother to move from Derbyshire to London. That's when my mother told me about the contract."

Evan removed the box wrapped in a coarse linen grain sack.

"Did she know I was Livingston Sloane's only direct descendant?"

"Mother knew your name, but didn't urge me to find you until hours from meeting her maker." Miss Hart gestured to the house. "We should go inside where it's warm and dry. Rosemary has lit the fire in the drawing room." She threw him a mischievous grin. "I shall let you look through the documents if you promise not to steal them."

He smiled. "Why would I steal them when you trust me with everything you hold dear?"

Evan followed Miss Hart back to the house. The young maid took their outdoor garments, then brought the tea tray and a plate of Bath cakes to the drawing room. Once nestled into the worn wingback chairs, and having banished the cold from their bones, Miss Hart removed the mahogany chinoiserie tea caddy from the sack and held it on her lap. She unlocked the caddy with a tasselled key before glancing up at him.

"First, let us put to rest any doubts concerning Livingston Sloane's chosen profession." The lady removed a folded letter, tatty around the edges and with slight foxing. "This is a letter of marque held by Lucian Hart, granting him permission to attack enemy vessels in the Mediterranean."

Evan took the letter, peeled back the folds and read it quickly.

"And this is a letter giving Livingston Sloane the same rights."

Evan gripped the parchment. The sudden surge of emotion in his chest took him by surprise. He felt a close kinship to his deceased relative, the one he was supposed to despise. Hell, he'd taken enough beatings at school for defending the scoundrel—until he found the strength to fight back.

"How have you come by this?" He absorbed the information on the page. Mild anger tainted Evan's tone, anger aimed at Lady Boscobel, not Miss Hart. "Tell me my family knew nothing of its existence."

"I don't know why your grandfather's document is in this box. I don't know why your great-grandmother disowned her son when he had legitimate cause to attack foreign ships."

Like the wind rattling the sash, Evan's anger gained momentum. Indeed, he would visit the pompous oaf who had inherited the Leaton viscountcy, the distant cousin who must know something of the tales spun by Lady Boscobel, and then throttle the truth from his lying lips.

"I can only presume your grandfather gave Lucian Hart the letter before he died," Miss Hart added. "Both letters bear Lord Anson's signature, who was the First Lord of the Admiralty. Whatever they were doing in the Mediterranean, it was of some naval importance."

Various questions bombarded Evan's mind.

Did Lady Boscobel believe her son had carried out acts of piracy? Based on the vile things she'd said about Livingston Sloane, she couldn't have known the truth. So why had she kept the painting? Why had she refused to use the name Sloane?

"And this is a copy of the letter instructing Mr Golding's father to ensure the contract is legally binding. It's signed by Lucian Hart and Livingston Sloane."

Evan gave an amused snort. Miss Hart's persistence in wishing to marry him distracted from thoughts of his family's antagonism. "Regardless of what Mr Golding says when we meet him today, the contract cannot be enforced."

"Perhaps not," she agreed, much to his surprise.

So why did he feel a pang of disappointment?

"But you will see something of interest listed amongst the articles given to Mr Golding's father."

Intrigued beyond measure, Evan took the letter and studied the contents. It seemed Mr Golding had taken receipt of various items of correspondence. One in particular leapt off the page.

Letter for the archbishop. Approval for a special licence.

"Were it not for the yellow stains and faded ink, I might be inclined to think you wrote this, Miss Hart. It seems our ancestors went to great lengths to remove any obstacles to a potential marriage."

Miss Hart looked quite pleased with herself as she sat in Lamont's flamboyant clothes, clutching her precious box. "Are you not curious to know why?"

"Curious to the point of madness." Particularly when the person who approved the licence must have influence with the archbishop. "Every passing hour brings a new riveting revelation." Indeed, Miss Hart had swept into his life and knocked him off his feet.

"Oh, we've only just begun, Mr Sloane. Wait until the masked devil discovers we've visited Mr Golding together." The lady's expression darkened, and she shivered visibly. "He is watching our every move and has been for weeks."

"Then we need to gain ground if we hope to catch him." He gathered the papers and handed them back to Miss Hart. "We will take the tea caddy with us. Change into something more appropriate and pack a valise. I've already asked Buchanan to gather clothes for Mrs McCready." And to bring the plague mask left by the intruder.

"Pack?"

"You cannot remain here. You and your servants will remove to Keel Hall." It was the only way he could guarantee her safety. "No doubt we will have a lot to discuss, and I cannot make the trip to town whenever I need to ask a question."

After a silent deliberation, she said, "You're right. Few people venture to the wilds of Little Chelsea, and considering the fact we shall soon be married, your suggestion makes perfect sense." She locked the letters away, clutched the casket to her chest and stood. "What shall I do with Monsieur Lamont's clothes?"

Evan stood, too. "Leave them here, or throw them on the bonfire. I doubt the poor will want them."

Before she left the room to slip out of Lamont's fancy breeches, he couldn't resist one last look at her tempting thighs. Miss Hart had a body made for sin. Lust throbbed in his loins as he considered every delectable curve. Ironically, she had everything he'd imagined wanting in a wife—strength, courage, a voracious appetite for adventure, a total disregard for propriety. One thing was certain. Miss Hart posed a greater threat to his sanity than the masked fiend.

●

For the second time this morning, Vivienne found herself alone in a carriage with Mr Sloane. His commanding presence filled the small space, as did the alluring smell of his cologne. The urge to press her nose to his neck and inhale the exotic scent left her shuffling in the seat. But it was the undercurrent of tension in the air, the strange spark of electricity, that held her in its grip and made it hard to breathe.

The ride to West Smithfield wasn't particularly bumpy, yet her stomach flipped like a skilled acrobat. Staring out of the window served as a distraction but did little to settle her racing pulse. She felt the heat of Mr Sloane's penetrating stare despite having her nose pressed to the glass.

It all became too much.

"I'm surprised you let Buchanan ride atop the box." She forced herself to look at him, and her insides fluttered all over again. "I thought you'd insist on a chaperone. What if I did something disreputable and tried to force you to marry me?"

The gentleman moistened his lips. "We're in a closed carriage, Miss Hart. Should we wish to partake in anything illicit, there is no one here to bear witness."

Vivienne sucked in a sharp breath to halt the rising blush. "As most men insist on marrying a virgin, it would be unwise to do anything scandalous in a carriage with you, sir." And certainly not with Buchanan in earshot.

"I'm not most men, Miss Hart."

No. He was vastly superior on many levels.

"While I'm confident you're chaste," he said in a sensual drawl, "I would prefer my wife had experience in the bedchamber."

The devil enjoyed teasing her, but she was used to bantering with Highlanders. "Bedding a virgin who happens to be your wife might prove highly satisfying."

"Fondling innocents is not my forte."

"You surprise me. Surely a man who values honesty would prefer to feel the true touch of a woman's lips. A passionate kiss must be better than one feigned for pleasure."

Mr Sloane laughed. "You want to marry me to gain our ancestors' treasure. What is there to feel from your lips but desperation and greed?"

The comment stung. The sudden constriction of her throat

came as a shock. Water welled in her eyes. Heavens, she couldn't let the gentleman see her sobbing into her handkerchief, but he'd noticed something was amiss.

"I apologise if I've upset you." He'd softened his tone. "We agreed to speak honestly, Miss Hart. If there is another reason you wish to marry me, then simply say so."

How could she speak? What could she say? Though blunt in delivery, his words rang with truth—not the whole truth. Yes, she needed to marry him to stop the murderous blackguard, to gain financial security. But she wanted to kiss him, had admired him for weeks. She wanted to feel locked in his strong embrace.

"You want the truth, sir?"

"I deserve the truth, madam."

Vivienne stayed her tears and raised her chin. "My reasons for wanting to abide by the contract stem from desperation, not greed. But I like you, Mr Sloane." Her skin tingled just being in his presence. "I'm drawn to the elements of your character that fit so perfectly with mine."

His searing stare fixed her to the seat.

She would give anything to know his thoughts.

"While our kin shared a love for the sea," she said, "we share a love for adventure. We both long to escape the humdrum of daily life, long to feel the wind whipping our hair. As a woman, my situation is more complicated. I must strive to provide for myself. Marriage to any man brings a loss of liberty."

"Not if you married me," he said, though seemed surprised he'd made the comment. "I believe we should appreciate people for who they are, not try to forge them into someone of our own making."

Mr Sloane was one of those rare men who shared her views.

"Which leads me back to my earlier point. You have many fine qualities to recommend you, sir. But most important of all, you accept my unconventional character."

A smile tugged at his mouth. "I'm far from accepting. I insisted you change out of Monsieur Lamont's ridiculous clothes."

"Only out of concern for me."

His heated gaze journeyed over her blue pelisse, lingered in shocking places. "And because a lady in breeches appeals to my rakish nature. I cannot concentrate on the case when eye-level with your shapely thighs, madam."

Vivienne's heart pounded under his visceral invasion. Mr Sloane had a way of making a woman feel like a wicked temptress. Thoughts of kissing him entered her head, as did the notion of him stroking his large hands over the thighs he so admired.

"However, I must confess to being somewhat curious." His rich voice raised her pulse another notch.

"Curious? About what?"

"Whether your lips taste of innocence. Whether you would struggle under the weight of experience. Or would the wild woman who rides bareback in the darkness take command of the reins?"

She might struggle at first, but Mr Sloane would tempt a saint to sin.

"There's only one way to know, sir."

Mr Sloane rubbed his sculpted jaw as he scanned her body. "Are you saying you want me to haul you onto my lap, Miss Hart, and plunder your mouth in true pirate fashion?"

Oh, he made debauchery sound so inviting. Yet she wasn't about to surrender just yet. "No, Mr Sloane, I'm saying you will have to wait until our wedding night to find out."

CHAPTER 7

ACCORDING TO MISS HART, the offices of Golding, Wicks & Sons occupied an entire townhouse in Long Lane, West Smithfield. Evan had been so captivated by his conversation with the lady seated opposite, he'd not considered the invariable problems they would encounter upon reaching their destination.

Being the third day in September, the first day of the infamous Bartholomew Fair, Evan's carriage came to an abrupt halt at the bottom of Holborn Hill and didn't budge.

"What's causing the delay?" Miss Hart gazed out of the window at the hordes of people heading towards Smithfield.

"It's the Bartholomew Fair. Every cloth merchant in the country has descended on the capital to set up stalls and sell their wares. I'm afraid we may have to walk the short distance to Long Lane."

"Walk through this rowdy rabble?" Miss Hart clutched her chest. "Then let's make haste before every cutpurse from the rookeries hones in on their prey."

Bartholomew Fair was a playground for the debauched and provided a host of opportunities for every crook from Southwark to Shoreditch. "If we're to walk, you must hold on to me, Miss Hart. Promise not to let go."

"I've heard terrible tales about the fair. I shall cling to you like a leech. Indeed, you will have to prise me from your arm once we reach Mr Golding's office."

Even when nervous, Miss Hart proved amusing company. And to think he'd presumed she would be tedious, a dullard, a bore. As with most men, the fault lay with him for not looking beyond the beauties vying for attention, for not appreciating those wallflowers who sat with their hands clasped in their laps, wilting from boredom.

Evan opened the carriage door and vaulted to the ground. He told Buchanan to follow discreetly behind until they reached the lawyer's office, instructed his coachman to turn right onto Shoe Lane and wait there.

"Take my arm, Miss Hart." Evan clasped her elbow and assisted her descent.

The lady didn't need to be told twice. As soon as her feet hit the pavement, she hugged his arm as if they were lovers who couldn't bear to be parted.

They bustled through the excited crowd, amid the din of hawkers flogging their wares and the raucous laughter of those huddled around a puppetry booth. Although Evan noted a few shady characters lingering in doorways, they arrived in Long Lane without incident.

"Mr Golding's office is opposite the Old Red Crow," Miss Hart said.

Like the coffee-houses and alehouses along the row, the tavern proved popular with cloth merchants and those seeking boisterous entertainment. It was only a matter of time before a fight broke out amongst the drunken revellers.

"I assume Buchanan accompanies you when you visit your lawyer?" Evan experienced unease at the thought of Miss Hart wandering these streets alone. Not that it was any concern of his, but still.

"He does, yes, though Lady Hollinshead was kind enough to lend me the use of her carriage the last time I visited."

Yes, he recalled seeing Miss Hart in the company of the countess. Surely a lady of great social standing would have found a suitor for the daughter of her closest friend. Lady Hollinshead knew enough eligible gentlemen to fill Miss Hart's dance card. Yet Evan had never seen his wallflower grace a ball-room floor.

"Does Lady Hollinshead know why you came to visit Mr Golding?" he said, directing her across the busy thoroughfare. As an agent of the Order, the smallest things roused his suspicions.

"Of course not. While she has been more than kind since my mother died, I trust no one but you with the sensitive information."

The swirling heat in his chest seemed to occur whenever Miss Hart vocalised her faith in him. While women fawned over his handsome features, praised his prowess in the bedchamber, none had commented on his character.

"Perhaps your mother confided in her closest friend."

"Not when the mere mention of hidden treasure would cause untold problems. You've seen the lengths people go to in the name of greed. Besides, Lady Hollinshead would have mentioned it. She noticed my preoccupation with you." Miss Hart brought him to an abrupt halt in front of a neglected townhouse and gazed at the facade. "This is the place."

Evan was curious to know how she had explained her interest in him. "Did you tell Lady Hollinshead you wished to marry me?"

Miss Hart looked up at him and raised a shapely brow. "I told her I'd heard you were a wild, adventurous sort. She agreed and said you were unsuitable company for an innocent. She will expire from apoplexy when she learns of our impending marriage."

"Had I a mind to encourage your fantasies, I might agree." But oh, how he admired her tenacity. "Now, let us harass Mr Golding until he gives us what we want."

Namely, the last clue without Evan sacrificing his bache-lorhood.

"You could strap the lawyer to the rack, crank the handle and stretch him a foot and still he will not give you the answers you seek."

"I can be extremely persuasive, Miss Hart."

"Then prepare yourself for a great disappointment." She pushed open the black paint-chipped door and slipped inside. "He insists on abiding by a set of written rules."

Evan followed her into the stark hall with its faded blue wallpaper and cracked floor tiles. "Are you sure this is the right place?" Based on the shabby surroundings, he could not imagine anyone hiring the lawyer to present a case. "Do they have many clients?"

"I have no notion." She mounted the narrow staircase without gripping the dirty handrail. "Perhaps things were different seventy years ago. Perhaps our ancestors chose Mr Golding's father for a reason unbeknown."

In retrospect, slovenly men were easier to manipulate. They lacked determination, were not as rigid when it came to rules. Hopefully, Mr Golding conducted business in the same slipshod way he treated his premises.

"We shall knock on Mr Wicks' office," Miss Hart whispered when Evan joined her on the first-floor landing. She moved to the door at the end of the corridor. "Mr Golding deals with clients, whereas his nephew fulfils the role of clerk."

Evan suspected the younger man resented his lowly position in the firm. "Might you permit me to speak on our behalf?"

Miss Hart smiled. "By all means, take the lead."

He inclined his head to her before knocking on the door three times.

The scraping of chair legs on the boards preceded the scuffle of footsteps and the incessant mumblings of a man who had nothing better to do than talk to himself. Mr Wicks yanked open the door and hit them with his brandy breath.

Excellent. The fool was half-cut at midday and probably didn't give a damn about rules and regulations. Evan would have the third clue in his possession before the mantel clock chimed the hour.

"Ah, Mr Wicks." Evan removed a calling card from his coat pocket and gave it to the bewildered gentleman sporting red eyes and a pitiful neckcloth. "I'm Evan Sloane, and you know Miss Hart. We wish to speak to Mr Golding as a matter of urgency."

The clerk gripped the card between trembling fingers and blinked numerous times in an effort to concentrate on the small script. "He's with a c-client at present."

"Then inform him we're here," Evan snapped. "Tell him we'll

wait." It grated that this imbecile held a position when there were many good men out of work, struggling to feed their families.

"Shloane. Shloane." Mr Wicks swayed as he glanced up at Evan. "Is this about the c-contract?"

"Inform Mr Golding we're here," Evan reiterated. He would not deal with a drunken lackey. "Else I shall knock his damn door myself."

From his room halfway down the hall, Mr Golding must have heard the commotion. A man with wisps of white hair combed over his pate poked his head around the jamb. He took one look at Miss Hart, gasped and retreated inside. Suddenly the door to Mr Golding's office swung open, and he ushered a woman dressed in widows' weeds out onto the landing.

"There must be something you can do," the young woman implored.

Mr Golding clutched the brass handle of his walking stick and stared over the round spectacles perched on his nose. "As I said, you've no grounds to contest the will as you were not legally wed. A bigamist has duped you, madam."

"But how am I supposed to feed my child?"

Evan couldn't bear to watch the exchange. Slipping his hand into his coat pocket and retrieving three sovereigns, he strode forward and thrust the coins into the widow's hand. "I'm afraid it's all I have with me, but you're welcome to it."

Astonished, the woman raised her black veil and gazed at the gold coins. "Thank you, sir."

With mild embarrassment, Mr Golding said, "Come back tomorrow, Mrs Davies, and I shall see what I can do."

"Thank you, Mr Golding," she said and hurried on her way before the man changed his mind.

The lawyer waited until Mrs Davies was out of earshot before turning to his sotted nephew. "Get back into that office and don't come out for the rest of the day." He glared at Mr Wicks until the man shuffled back into his den and closed the door. "Forgive my nephew. He's not been the same since his mother died."

It was strange how a simple comment altered one's perception. Suddenly, a drunken lout became a fellow tortured by unbearable pain. It was a lesson on how not to make assumptions without knowing the facts.

"Now, if you would both care to follow me." Mr Golding gestured to his office.

Miss Hart appeared at Evan's side and touched his arm. "What a kind gesture, Mr Sloane."

"I have a weakness for mothers down on their luck."

"Indeed."

Evan found he rather liked the glint of admiration in Miss Hart's brown eyes. It cleansed his soul in a way nothing else could. Equally, the act of giving had a way of lifting a man's spirits.

They followed Mr Golding into the cluttered office. Evan waited for Miss Hart to sit and then dropped into the seat next to her.

"We're here to discuss the matter of the contract made between Lucian Hart and Livingston Sloane," Evan said. "Miss Hart tells me our ancestors hired your firm to deal with all legal proceedings in relation to the matter."

"That's correct." Mr Golding hobbled to the old veneer side table. He retrieved a key from his waistcoat pocket and opened a secret compartment concealed by the faded marquetry. "As you're here with Miss Hart, I must assume you're a direct descendant of Livingston Sloane."

"He was my grandfather, though I confess to knowing nothing of the contract until Miss Hart made me aware of its existence."

"I feared no one would come forward to relieve me of my burden." Placing a steadying hand on the table, Mr Golding removed a leather notebook and doddered back to sit behind his oak desk. "I'm not sure your ancestors expected it either."

Evan was about to tell the lawyer that he had no intention of honouring the contract. No court in the land would force a man to marry based on a privateer's oath. But he was keen to learn more before dashing Miss Hart's hopes.

"Now, let us begin." Mr Golding opened the black book and

flicked to the relevant page. "The first thing to consider is that you can both prove you're related to my clients."

"You want proof of our lineage?" Evan scoffed.

Again, Miss Hart touched his arm to bring an element of calm to the situation. "What sort of proof is required?"

Mr Golding consulted his notebook and then glanced at them over his spectacles. "Do you have the men's letters of marque issued by the admiralty?"

"We do," she replied. "We have both letters, but they're locked away in a bank vault."

The lie fell easily from Miss Hart's lips. Like Evan, she wasn't sure she could trust the lawyer and so proceeded with caution. It was a wise move, a wise move indeed.

"Ah." Mr Golding examined the other notes written on the page. "Then you must both present the clues to the legacy left by your ancestors."

Clues to the legacy? How in the devil's name could he do that? The painting of Livingston Sloane was nought but a pile of ash in the grate.

"Present the clues?" the lady challenged. "Lucian Hart would not demand I reveal his secret correspondence."

"Excellent. It says here that should you give the lawyer the clues, you shall forfeit any claim to the legacy." Mr Golding ran his bony finger down the page. "Ah, I don't need to see the clues. But I must ask you both a series of questions, and you must provide the answers."

The process was more complicated than Evan had anticipated. Livingston Sloane's instructions were precise and left no room for negotiation. Did that mean the treasure amounted to a vast sum?

"So, the first question is to Miss Hart." Mr Golding glanced up from his notebook. "A pauper or prince, a knight or knave, who will you save?"

Evan glanced at Miss Hart, who beamed with confidence. "Why, I would save a pauper," she said, quoting from the nine cryptic words written on the tiny parchment.

"Yes. Good."

Evan's pulse pounded in his throat when the elderly

gentleman fixed him with a beady stare. "Now a question for you, Mr Sloane."

Hell. Evan knew nothing about his ancestor's clue, and could only assume it had something to do with the painting of Livingston Sloane.

"North, south, east or west, which direction suits me best?"

Good lord, it was like a line from a children's rhyme. Evan couldn't help but think their ancestors were mocking them from the grave. Still, with quiet confidence, he said, "The answer is north."

"Excellent. Now back to you, Miss Hart. If you could travel anywhere in the world, my dear, where would you go?"

"While I have a fondness for the Highlands, sir, I believe I am supposed to say Egypt."

Mr Golding consulted his notebook. "Egypt, yes. The land of the pharaohs." He glanced at Evan. "Is there anything, sir, that might distract a man from a beautiful view?"

It took Evan a second to realise that was his question. Clearly, Mr Golding referred to the lush fields depicted in the painting. He thought for a moment.

Miss Hart turned to him. "You know the answer, Mr Sloane."

"I do, Miss Hart." All thanks to her. Had Fitchett not granted her permission to examine the painting, had she not suggested he had missed something from his sketch this morning, he would be clueless. "I believe the answer is a book. A book might distract a man from a beautiful view." Yet when he looked at Miss Hart, nothing could drag his gaze away from her brilliant smile.

Mr Golding hummed with pleasure. "This is the point where I'm to ask for the author's name."

Miss Hart turned pale. "His name?"

Evan's heart sank to the pit of his stomach. "The writing was illegible. I couldn't read the name of the book or its author."

"Good. Good." Mr Golding fiddled with his spectacles before reading from the notebook. "Then I can tell you it's a poem by Thomas Gray."

Thomas Gray?

Was that supposed to mean something? Was it another clue?

"Well, I'm pleased to say you both passed the test." Mr Golding pushed to his feet, though Lord knows what he intended to do next. He reached for his walking stick and tottered to the veneer table. "No doubt you want to marry posthaste."

"As to that," Evan began, but Miss Hart tapped his arm and mouthed for him to wait.

"I presume you have the letter we're to take to the archbishop," she said.

Mr Golding bent over the table and inserted a key into a lock hidden at the back. The whirring of cogs preceded the opening of yet another secret drawer. "There are a few letters here for you, yes. I must say it's been a mighty strain on my heart, keeping them here all this time. But my father made me swear to abide by the oath, and I'm not the sort of man to break a promise."

Guilt flared, for Evan cared nothing about a pact made seventy years ago. Not when he was the one forced to make the ultimate sacrifice.

"I doubt our relatives expected two strangers to marry. And for what? So they might share a chest of pirate gold."

Mr Golding retrieved the letters from the velvet-lined drawer and hobbled back to his seat. "Who can say what motivated the men to invent the complicated scheme. Though I remember my father saying Livingston Sloane despised his family and hoped one of his ancestors might inherit his moral character."

"Moral character?" Evan scoffed but caught himself. Livingston Sloane was not the dastardly pirate he'd been told to loathe. The man had been permitted to hunt foreign vessels in the Mediterranean. Alas, many in society thought the term privateer was a polite name for pirate.

"Both your ancestors detested society's hypocrisy. Livingston Sloane told my father that an honest man was worth more to the world than the richest prince."

Pride filled Evan's chest. He agreed with the statement wholeheartedly, and yet he was the only Sloane who did not value money and position above all else. But an honest man would not marry a stranger in the hope of finding treasure.

"I don't believe our ancestors want us to marry," he said. "I believe it is another test to determine our strength of character. To test the depth of our greed."

Mr Golding pursed his lips and thought for a moment. "You must do what you feel is right, Mr Sloane, even if your choice proves unpopular. Unless I'm mistaken, that is the point your grandfather wished to make."

"But what are we to do about our *pressing* problem?" Miss Hart sounded alarmed.

"Rest assured, I shall discover the identity of the devil who seeks to steal our grandfathers' legacy." Evan fought the urge to grab the lady's hand and tell her she had nothing to fear. But he could not protect her night and day. She would return to Silver Street, and he would be five miles away in Little Chelsea.

"Having consulted the notes, I am obliged to offer you a choice." Mr Golding pushed the clutter of papers aside and placed two sealed letters on the desk. "This is the letter you must choose if you fail to abide by the terms of the contract." He pointed to the one with a sketch of a swallow perched on a dagger.

Something about the symbol often used by his ancestor roused a crippling sense of dread. Was Miss Hart the delicate creature teetering on the edge of disaster, the one left to fight the blackguard alone?

"Should you choose this option, you will both receive the sum of a thousand pounds and may leave this office without further obligation. Of course, Miss Hart may wish to make a claim for compensation—recompense for the unpaid debt."

"A thousand pounds?" Miss Hart repeated as if tempted to accept.

"Are you saying if we take the money, the debt to Lucian Hart will be considered unpaid?" Evan attempted to confirm.

Mr Golding's pale lips thinned. "Yes, Mr Sloane. I shall record that Livingston Sloane's descendant failed in his obligation to honour the vow."

Hell's teeth.

The words were like a sharp blade stabbing Evan's conscience.

"However, should Miss Hart decide she cannot abide by the pact, then the letters remain sealed until two other descendants come forward to claim the right. Though it will be my nephew who deals with all future matters."

As Evan had no intention of marrying or siring an heir, the contract would be void, the legacy lost. He found the thought unsettling.

Mr Golding directed their attention to the other letter, the one with a sketch of a heart wearing a princely crown. "Should you agree to marry and honour the contract, you will receive this letter along with permission for the archbishop to grant you a special licence. Though I must warn you. To satisfy the conditions stipulated by your ancestors, you must prove you hold some affection for each other. I have the right to deny your request, to stop proceedings."

Miss Hart gasped. "Proof? What proof would you need?"

A faint blush crept across Mr Golding's cheeks. He consulted the notebook twice to be sure. "You must seal the pact with a kiss, Miss Hart."

CHAPTER 8

"A k-kiss?" Vivienne stuttered. "You want me to kiss Mr Sloane while you bear witness?" Her pulse thumped hard in her throat. Not that she hadn't imagined kissing the gentleman—she had considered it twice during breakfast—but not while Mr Golding assessed their performance.

"I cannot believe Lucian Hart intended his relative to make a spectacle of herself in a lawyer's office." Mr Sloane gestured to the tatty black notebook on the desk. "Might I see the entry? Might I see where it states a sign of affection is necessary?"

Mr Golding folded the corner of the page, then closed the notebook and handed it to Mr Sloane. "Marriage is a serious affair. Sacrifices must be made when two people come together. This is a test of your mettle, so to speak."

"My mettle?" Vivienne snorted. "Kissing a man I hardly know in front of a witness seems a cruel way to test one's nerve."

The wrinkles on Mr Golding's forehead deepened. "But intimacy in marriage is key. Your ancestors married for love. It's the sole reason Livingston Sloane left London. He refused to abide by his mother's wishes and marry someone she deemed suitable."

"But we're not in love, and yet they expect us to marry."

Mr Golding scratched his head. "Yes, there seems to be a certain hypocrisy here, but we must satisfy the conditions in order to proceed."

Mr Sloane glanced up from the notebook. "How do you know that's why Livingston Sloane left London when it's the first I've heard on the subject?"

"That's what my father told me." Mr Golding gave a half shrug. "There must be a relative who can support the claim."

Vivienne craned her neck to look at the notebook, but her attention drifted to Mr Sloane's muscular thighs and the strong hands clasping the pages. Lord, the man exuded masculinity on every level. Yet those long, capable fingers had cradled her head with remarkable tenderness. There was so much she didn't know about this man, and yet she would take his name and swear an oath she had no intention of keeping.

"Is Mr Golding correct?" The nervous tremble in her voice was impossible to disguise. "Are we required to prove we share an affection?" There was a definite attraction between them, no more than that.

Mr Sloane met her gaze. One look from those mesmerising green eyes sent a shiver shooting to her toes. "Mr Golding must decide if greed is our motive for marrying. He can only proceed if he believes there is an undeniable connection between us, one that may grow into something lasting."

Heavens! He sounded remarkably calm, all things considered.

Mr Sloane stood and placed the notebook on Mr Golding's cluttered desk. "Excuse us for a moment. I would like to speak to Miss Hart privately."

"Of course. Take as long as you need. I've no clients today."

Mr Sloane cupped Vivienne's elbow as she stood. "We shall slip out onto the landing and return shortly."

Vivienne let him guide her from the room. She waited for him to close Mr Golding's door before saying, "This is ridiculous. I cannot possibly expect you to agree. The money doesn't matter. It is easy to live modestly in the Highlands. But if you would consider me your client, and seek to discover the identity of the masked devil, I shall be forever grateful."

She would pack a valise and leave for Scotland today if she thought the blackguard wouldn't follow. Without knowing the intruder's true intentions, it was impossible to make plans.

Still clutching her elbow, Mr Sloane drew her closer. "There's one problem, Miss Hart. I'm uncomfortable with failure. I cannot have it known I broke my grandfather's oath."

"Oh. I see." Vivienne frowned as he'd not cared a whit before. "Why the change of heart?"

"When reading the words written in that old book, I could almost hear my grandfather's voice. It is impossible for me to walk away now. Trust me, my sudden loyalty to a man I've never met shocks me to my core."

"What are you saying?"

He chuckled to himself. "I cannot believe these words are about to fall from my lips, but I think we should take the letter with the crowned heart. I think we should see this matter through to the end."

Could he not speak plainly? Could he not make a declaration?

"You think we should marry?"

He laughed again. "Yes. Surely you hoped I would agree. What did you intend to do once we'd found the treasure and caught the man who shot Turton?"

Vivienne heard his question, but could barely form a rational thought. When making arrangements to visit his home, she had planned for every eventuality. Yet she had not expected to feel an instant attraction when he spoke, not expected to admire the man's honesty or experience the fluttering inside whenever he paid her the slightest attention.

She'd thought they would marry and work on solving the clues, nothing more. Now she would have to kiss the gentleman. Surely he would feel something of her mild obsession when their mouths met.

"Once we'd dealt with our problem and found our legacy, I planned to leave London and return to the Highlands. Buchanan and Mrs McCready long to go home, and there is nothing to keep me here."

"The Highlands? So far?" He pondered the information for longer than necessary. "If you marry me, Miss Hart, you will never bear legitimate children, never be free to marry a Scot who shares your love for wild adventures."

A wave of sadness washed over her. She had not considered

what she would lose if she married Evan Sloane. Ever since her mother had frightened her half to death with mumbled tales of threats and imminent danger, Vivienne had thought about nothing but the contract, nothing except for forming an alliance with the valiant agent of the Order.

"I'm too reckless to make any man a suitable wife." She worked hard at being a wallflower. Holding her tongue and curbing her passions was the only way she could mingle in polite society.

"No one can predict what the future holds, Miss Hart."

"Nothing is guaranteed," she agreed. "My mother said it's called the present for a reason, and so the gift of today is all we have."

A sad sigh left his lips. "Mothers are infinitely wise, are they not?"

In the grave silence that followed, she could feel his pain. He must have spent his life wondering what his mother might look like, dreaming about the wealth of love she would have in her heart, feeling the crippling ache of her absence.

"Come, Mr Sloane. If we're to marry, we must prove to Mr Golding that we might suit." The longer she stood staring into his tortured eyes, the more she knew she had to pour every ounce of admiration she had for him into that one kiss.

The corners of his mouth curled in amusement. "Though I know you enjoy riding roughshod over me, Miss Hart, I wonder if I might take the lead when demonstrating our affection."

"Of course." At this present moment, she would do anything to distract his mind from painful memories of the past. "You should know I have only been kissed once, and that was on the cheek."

"You speak of a father's affection?"

Vivienne couldn't help but laugh. "No, of William Campbell's. I was sixteen, and it felt like being slapped with a wet fish."

Mr Sloane's laugh brightened his eyes. "Then I pray the second time proves more pleasurable."

The last word rolled smoothly off his tongue. She'd heard tell of his skill with his mouth and hands, but suspected Mr Golding was not looking for the mechanical movements of a seducer.

"On second thoughts," she said, "let me kiss you first. I will look terribly inexperienced. Then when you do whatever it is you do to make women fall at your feet, it will look more convincing."

"Agreed." He gestured to Mr Golding's door. "Shall we?"

"Certainly." She gave a confident nod, though her knees trembled.

When they entered the room, Mr Golding looked up from the notebook. "Have you arrived at a decision? If you need more time, you may come back tomorrow."

"No, we have decided to abide by the contract and wish to marry." Mr Sloane spoke as if he'd never had a doubt. "We will follow your instructions."

"Excellent." Mr Golding grinned. "That is excellent news."

"You seem most pleased, sir," Vivienne said, noting his merry countenance.

"I admit to feeling some relief, Miss Hart. One cannot help but think the intruder who ransacked my office was looking for a clue to locating your legacy. In all honesty, I long to be free of the burden."

Mr Sloane's gaze shot in Vivienne's direction before settling on the lawyer. "Someone broke into your office?"

"Yes. Almost two weeks ago now."

"I'd been to visit Mr Golding." She'd come to persuade him to let her have a peek at the final clue. "It was the day Lady Hollinshead loaned me her carriage. The incident occurred late that night."

"Did the devil steal anything?"

"Not that I'm aware." Mr Golding gestured to the pile of papers on the desk. "Though I'm still checking the files."

"Be sure to inform me if you find something amiss." Mr Sloane removed a card from his coat pocket and placed it on the desk. "You may contact me at the Order's office in Hart Street."

"There's nothing worth stealing here, Mr Sloane, except for your ancestors' letters." The lawyer turned his attention to Vivienne. "Hart Street. What a coincidence."

"Hart is a relatively common name, sir, but I prefer to believe in fate, not coincidence."

Mr Golding nodded and then consulted his notes. "Well, I suppose we should proceed with the erm, the erm ..."

"Kiss," Mr Sloane finished.

The tension in the air was palpable. That said, Mr Golding seemed the most perturbed. "Let's get the matter over with so we may progress to the next part. Erm, try to pretend I'm not here. Pretend this is your wedding day. Yes, yes, a chaste kiss with some measure of feeling will suffice."

Vivienne faced Mr Sloane. "There isn't much room. Shall we stand behind the chairs?"

Mr Sloane seemed to find something amusing. "We have all the room we need." He reached for her hand and pulled her close. "Relax. A kiss is nothing more than a physical expression of admiration."

"Yes." Lord! Her stomach twisted into knots.

"Begin when you're ready," Mr Golding instructed.

"Well, Miss Hart, it's time to satisfy my burning curiosity." Mr Sloane's sensual voice had her heart thundering in her chest. "Time for you to convince me why we should marry."

Vivienne mustered every ounce of courage she possessed. How could she make the kiss memorable when he had locked lips with a host of skilled women? While Mr Sloane had experienced more than his share of carnal pleasure, had anyone ever kissed him like they cared? A man who had never known a mother's love deserved to feel genuine tenderness.

Vivienne looked up into the emerald pools that made her knees weak. Without family, with no one to love him, he must feel dreadfully lonely.

She tugged off her glove, reached up and cupped his cheek. "Thank you," she whispered, stroking her thumb gently back and forth.

He closed his eyes briefly. "For what?"

"For understanding I'm not like other women."

"You're unlike any woman I've ever met."

Vivienne smiled. "I shall take that as a compliment."

"It was meant as such."

Heat swirled in her stomach. "Lower your head, Mr Sloane, else I shall be forced to tug on your expertly knotted cravat."

"I rather like the idea of you ruffling my clothes, Miss Hart."

Brazenly, she tugged his starched neckcloth. "Then be prepared to be crumpled," she teased, though her confidence abandoned her the second he bent his head.

His warm mouth met hers, the mere brush of his lips turning her insides molten. She felt instantly connected, desperately drawn to him in ways she couldn't explain—drawn to taste the man whose honey-smooth voice made her damp between the thighs.

His magnetic pull was so strong she wound her arms around his neck, melting into him, moving her mouth in the slow, melding motion that proved highly addictive. Somehow he coaxed her lips apart. Kissed her open-mouthed. Somehow he fired an urgency deep in her core. Stole the breath from her lungs.

Vivienne pulled away, panting, desperate for more. "Is that ... that enough to satisfy Mr Golding?"

Hunger burned in Mr Sloane's hypnotic green eyes. "Perhaps we might be more persuasive."

Mr Sloane did not bother consulting the lawyer mumbling in the background. Instead, he coiled his arm around her waist like the devil's tail, a means of drawing an innocent maiden into his inner sanctum, tempting her to sin, sin, sin again. His lips captured hers in a scorching embrace, searing her with his mark, branding her, ruining her for mortal men. Not that she could ever imagine kissing someone else like this—with raw, unbridled lust.

The first strokes of his tongue set her body ablaze. But he withdrew the pleasure, left her mouth empty, so empty she ached for the return of the wicked organ. Longed for it. Craved it. Yet he continued kissing her, continued rolling his hips against hers in a primal dance that left her sex feeling just as empty, just as deprived. And then he slipped his tongue deep into her mouth, so deep she couldn't help but moan, moan as he drove her wild with every erotic plunge, moan as he fondled every wet corner.

Lord have mercy!

The need to hike her skirts to her waist, to have him wedged between her thighs, proved maddening. It didn't help that beneath his burning passion she sensed the chill of loneliness. A loneliness she felt compelled to ease.

Mr Golding cleared his throat. "Yes, that should suffice."

But Mr Sloane did not release her from this carnal claiming.

The lawyer banged on the desk. "I'm perfectly satisfied, sir." He raised his voice. "Mr Sloane! I can find no objection to your marriage!"

Like a bucket of ice-cold water, the last word doused passion's flames. Mr Sloane dragged his lips from hers, yet his heated gaze held her captive. A slow smile tugged at his mouth. Oh, he appeared more than pleased with himself.

"Did you hear me?" Mr Golding croaked. "I said I am perfectly satisfied, sir."

"That makes two of us, Golding." Mr Sloane withdrew his arm from Vivienne's waist, though she feared she would struggle to stand unaided. "It's clear we have no issue conveying our affection."

Mr Golding dabbed his brow with his handkerchief. "No. No issue at all."

Vivienne's cheeks burned. Merciful Lord! Like a serpent tempting her to sin, desire slithered through her veins, coiled heavy and low in her loins. The need to grab Mr Sloane's cravat again and devour his wicked mouth left her breathless. Oh, she was out of her depth with this gentleman. So out of her depth, she would likely drown.

"Thank heavens you agreed to marry." Mr Golding seemed rather embarrassed. "Now, I suggest we hasten to the next part."

How could she proceed when lust held her in a tight grip? "I presume we're allowed to open the letter bearing the heart emblem?" The huskiness in her voice spoke of barely suppressed desire. Drat. She was related to a great explorer, surely she was equipped to navigate uncharted territory.

Mr Golding consulted his notes. "Yes, now you may break the seal and read the message." The lawyer gestured for her to proceed.

"Please, you open it, Mr Sloane." With trembling fingers, she would struggle to break the seal. "I believe I have had enough excitement for one day."

Mr Sloane's arrogant smirk did little to calm her racing pulse, for he looked every bit the confident seducer. He took the letter, tore the parchment around the seal to keep the wax stamp intact, then he peeled back the folds.

The slight arch of his brow spoke of confusion. "Here we have another clue, or riddle, though I have no notion what it means." He studied the words on the page before reciting, "*What the eyes do not see, the heart cannot follow.*"

While Vivienne repeated the sentence silently, Mr Golding took to mumbling it aloud.

"Perhaps it speaks of what I have just witnessed," the lawyer mused. "A physical attraction is the first step to any affair of the heart. If one notes the potential before them, love will blossom."

Mr Sloane snorted his dismissal. "I'm inclined to think it has something to do with the painting of Livingston Sloane. When I examined the book on the table, it was impossible to determine the author's name, yet you were instructed to give us that information."

Vivienne agreed. "Yes, the clue is the book. We couldn't follow it before because we were scrambling around in the dark. Now we have clarity we must look closely at the poems of Thomas Gray."

Mr Sloane cast her a sidelong glance and nodded in agreement. "Let us move to the matter of our wedding." He motioned to the parchment in his hand. "As this is potentially a clue to finding our legacy, I trust I can keep it."

"Yes, as you've agreed to abide by the contract, you may keep it." Mr Golding handed Mr Sloane a final letter. "You're to present this at Doctors' Commons. It's addressed to the archbishop, though his proctor will probably deal with the matter. There should be no trouble securing a special licence."

Vivienne's stomach roiled. She knew she had to marry Evan Sloane, but it suddenly seemed so real, so unnerving. Would he seek to solve the case quickly so they might go their separate ways? Would he expect more heated kisses?

"And once you've witnessed the ceremony," she said, "what then?"

"Then I am instructed to present you with your wedding gifts."

The slam of the front door followed the sudden thud of footsteps on the stairs. Mr Golding's eyes widened, and his bottom lip trembled. "Pay it no mind. It is just my nephew going about his errands."

If it was just his nephew, why did his complexion turn ashen? Why did the green vein in his temple bulge? Why did he jump up from his chair like a sprightly lad and dart to the door?

"Are you sure it's your nephew?" Mr Sloane suspected something was dreadfully amiss, too.

Mr Golding opened the door a fraction and peered out into the hall. He muttered to himself and hurried back to his desk. "In the coming days, you'll not know who to trust. I fear someone knows of your legacy and wishes to rob you of your inheritance."

The swift change in the lawyer's countenance proved alarming.

"Take this note." Mr Golding dipped his nib into the inkwell. He wrote a few hasty lines, sprinkled pounce from a pot over the wet ink, and shook off the excess. "Should I meet my end before I'm able to see this task through, you're to give this to Mr Howarth." He mouthed the man's name.

"Mr Howarth?" Vivienne had never heard of the gentleman.

"Hush. Yes, he's an optician and an instrument maker." Mr Golding lit the candle in the brass stick on the desk. He melted red wax over the folds and stamped his seal. "You'll find him on the corner of Newman Street and Oxford Street. He will only see you if the seal is intact. And place any information relating to the wedding ceremony in my hand, not my nephew's."

Then, before they could question the lawyer's reasoning, he thrust the note into Vivienne's hand and ushered them out of the door.

CHAPTER 9

EVAN LEFT Mr Golding's office feeling perplexed. Despite his refusal to marry, he had accepted Miss Hart's proposal, had agreed to abide by the ridiculous contract. Even more ridiculous were the questions and rhymes written in the tatty black note-book. Beyond the grave, their grandfathers must be laughing at their expense.

But more bewildering than the fact Evan would soon be married, was his reaction to kissing Miss Hart. Oh, he had kissed plenty of women. Never had he felt such an intense ache, such a desperation to cover a woman's body and thrust deep. Never had innocence been so damnably appealing. Indeed, he was still dazed by the experience, still compelled by the incessant thrum of lust.

"Are you in shock, sir?" Miss Hart said as they navigated the boisterous crowd gathered in Long Lane. "You've not said a word since Mr Golding shoved us out onto the landing."

No, he was too busy tamping down the flames of desire, too preoccupied by Mr Golding's odd reaction. "If we're to marry, Miss Hart, you must call me Evan."

"Then having shared a heated kiss, you should call me Vivienne."

Vivienne. Vivienne Hart.

He felt as if he'd known the name since the dawn of time.

Was that why the collective sound of vowels and consonants stirred such longing in his chest?

"But you didn't answer my question," she added. "I did warn you. Marriage to me is the only way to claim our legacy. Now is not the time to discuss our expectations, but I have one stipulation if we're to wed."

Curiosity burned. "Have no fear, I shall not demand my conjugal rights." His comment lacked conviction for he could think of nothing but bedding Vivienne Hart. "And you will have your own bedchamber at Keel Hall if that is your concern."

Miss Hart gripped his arm as they jostled past the insistent pastry seller, around the drunken oaf sprawled in the gutter, and across the busy thoroughfare. "I presumed those were a given. No, all I ask is you do not entertain your paramour while married to me."

Evan almost choked. "Madam, we shall be married until one of us is six feet under. Surely you're not asking I remain celibate for the rest of my God-given days."

"Of course not. I simply ask that you do not conduct affairs while we are living together as man and wife."

"Miss Hart, I may hold wild parties and partake in amorous liaisons, but I am not a cold-hearted libertine. I would not disrespect our union by having another woman in the house." Nor would he seek entertainment elsewhere.

He felt the heat of her searching gaze.

"Yes, I almost forgot your pledge. You vowed to do everything possible to fall in love with your wife."

The comment caught him off guard. More so, because he had made the oath knowing he would never marry. But he would be this lady's husband in a matter of weeks, less if the archbishop granted them a licence. Would their marriage be a means to an end or a grand love affair?

"That does not apply to me, of course," she added, missing the point entirely. "Ours is an arrangement made partly for profit."

It most certainly applied to her. The question was, would he keep the oath? And even if he made every effort to nurture romantic feelings, what's to say she—

"Miss Hart?" A gentleman aged sixty with wiry white hair and sagging jowls stumbled into their path. He seemed embarrassed to be seen amid the horde of rowdy revellers. "Miss H-Hart, it is you. How w-wonderful to see you out at the fair," he lied. The gentleman glanced nervously at Evan, waiting for the lady to make the introduction.

Miss Hart gripped Evan's arm a little tighter. "Mr Ramsey, you're looking well. Are you here to purchase silk or to enjoy the sideshows?"

"I thought to take advantage of the break in the weather, my dear, stretch the old legs." Again, he cast a surreptitious glance at Evan.

"Allow me to introduce Mr Sloane." She hesitated, clearly not knowing how to explain their connection. "Mr Sloane, this is Mr Ramsey, a family friend."

So this was the man Miss Hart had listed as a suspect. Judging by the size of his paunch and the fact walking left him breathless, he was definitely not the masked rider. Perhaps he had an accomplice. Either way, Evan wanted to ensure Mr Ramsey knew the nature of his relationship with Miss Hart.

Evan inclined his head. "What Miss Hart failed to add is that I am her betrothed."

"B-betrothed?" Mr Ramsey's eyes widened in shock, coupled with a faint flicker of horror. "Betrothed? But this is the first I've heard. You must have made the decision rather suddenly." He forced a smile. "Betrothed, by Gad! Well, I suppose I must congratulate you both on your upcoming nuptials. I trust Mr Buchanan has given him the once over." His watery laugh trickled to nothing.

Miss Hart glanced up at Evan with beaming admiration, purely for Mr Ramsey's benefit, of course. "Buchanan is not my keeper, sir, but he is more than thrilled with my choice. As am I. There is no finer gentleman in all of London."

An awkward silence ensued.

Not that Evan cared. He was busy trying to determine why his heart skipped a beat upon hearing Miss Hart's praise. Why he wanted to believe the comment reflected her true feelings.

"Is there something of particular interest to you in Long

Lane, Mr Ramsey?" Evan kept all hint of suspicion from his voice. Strange to meet a man on Miss Hart's list of suspects a hundred yards from Mr Golding's office, and within minutes of them leaving the lawyer, too.

"I'm to meet a friend at the tavern and then we're to watch a bare-knuckle prizefight at some point this afternoon."

Ramsey's rapid blinking said that was another lie.

"If it's entertainment you seek, those working the puppetry booth have turned a tragedy such as a plague into a comedic farce." Evan watched Mr Ramsey's facial expression with hawk-like intensity. "They've dressed the puppets in black cloaks and beaked masks."

Mr Ramsey swallowed deeply. "As I say, I'm to meet a friend, and he's determined to drink himself silly and shout at the brawlers." With a sudden urgency, he doffed his hat to Miss Hart. "Well, I best be off. I shall call to take tea with you on Friday, my dear. Better not keep Jeremiah waiting."

Evan watched the gentleman scuttle away through the crowd.

"You distrust him, don't you?" Miss Hart laid her palm gently on Evan's chest to gain his attention. The tenderness of her touch made his heart swell. It occurred to him that the more they grew accustomed to the idea of marriage, the more intimate their gestures became.

"He's meeting someone in the tavern, but not for the reason he explained."

"Perhaps we should walk to the tavern and see who enters."

"It's better to gather evidence before confronting the man. I'll ask D'Angelo to investigate Mr Ramsey's background." With the streets brimming with pickpockets, Evan refrained from pulling out his watch and inspecting the time. "Besides, we're due in Hart Street. We meet on Wednesdays for Daventry's briefing."

Miss Hart inhaled sharply. "Will you tell them we're to marry?"

"Of course. They're my friends and my colleagues." And he trusted the men implicitly. "We will need their help as the case progresses."

Villains behaved recklessly when cornered. The wild shot

fired by the masked rider had served as a distraction. But instinct said, at some point soon, they would find themselves staring down the barrel of a pistol.

"Forgive me. I must have something wrong with my ears." D'Angelo shuffled to the edge of his seat in the drawing room. The man had spent the last thirty seconds gawping. "Did you mention the word *marriage*?"

Evan gripped the back of Miss Hart's chair as he stood behind, scanning the men's shocked faces. "Miss Hart and I are to marry as soon as possible." He almost heard the clamour of questions forming in their minds. "And no, we were not found in a compromising clinch, nor am I deep in debt or under the influence of opium."

"But you're not in love," Daventry stated, for he did not mince words.

"No, we are not in love, sir," Miss Hart replied. "And if we knew of another way to solve our problem, we would not take such drastic action."

All four men stared.

"So let me understand the situation." Cole rubbed his bearded jaw and narrowed his gaze. "You say your grandfathers made a contract whereby Miss Hart can force you to marry her."

"Not force," she said, mildly affronted. "Mr Sloane has a choice."

"It doesn't sound as if you've given him a choice," Noah Ashwood added.

Miss Hart shook her head. "Lord Hawkridge," she began, deferring to Ashwood's title, unaware he despised the fact he had inherited a baronetcy. "Like Mr Sloane, I had no intention of marrying anyone. Rest assured, once we have satisfied the conditions of the contract and claimed our lost legacy, I shall leave London and never bother Mr Sloane again."

"But he will be obliged to care for you financially," Cole said, his expression as dark as Satan's sanctum. "Knowing Sloane, he will be forever obliged to act as your protector.

Evidently, he has the most to lose in this improper arrangement."

Rarely did Evan's colleagues annoy him, yet he couldn't help but jump to Miss Hart's defence. "It is not her fault my grandfather made the pact. She's been terrified by a masked intruder, shot at by the same devil who forced my carriage off the road. And while she is a capable woman, she cannot solve these problems alone."

Again, the room plunged into silence.

Evan caught D'Angelo's grin. "What is so amusing?"

"Nothing. I thought I detected a hint of admiration in your voice."

Evan flashed his friend an irate glare. The devil loved nothing more than to tease him. But then D'Angelo had witnessed the murder of his parents when he was just a boy, and so used amusement to mask his permanent pain.

"I admire any woman who thinks logically during trying situations." Though Evan rarely encountered one amid the widows and courtesans of the *ton*.

"And so you must marry to obtain a clue to a legacy. A legacy that might amount to nothing more than worthless trinkets." Daventry snorted. "Why bother? It's not as if you need the money. Take the thousand pounds offered by this Golding fellow and be done with it."

Daventry often made provoking statements to uncover the truth.

"You're missing the point. There is another factor to consider."

"You speak of this masked devil. Surely there's a way to stop him without making a lifelong commitment to a woman you hardly know."

Miss Hart flinched at Daventry's blunt reply, heightening Evan's frustration.

"I speak of the fact my grandfather was a privateer, not a pirate. The fact I've been lied to my whole life." He had been made to feel like an outcast, a misfit. Perhaps that's why he admired Miss Hart. He'd been made to feel inadequate, too, hence his valiant attempts to save the innocent, to approach everything he did with skill and finesse. "I intend to ensure people know the truth."

D'Angelo leant forward in his seat, his hands braced on his broad thighs. "And what of you, Miss Hart? Despite his heritage, there are women in the *ton* who would cut off an ear to marry Sloane. Most find it impossible to resist him. What if you make a dreadful mistake and accidentally fall in love with your husband? What if the decision to marry brings a lifetime of regret?"

Miss Hart cleared her throat. "You're right, Mr D'Angelo, your colleague has a way of stirring excitement in one's chest. I expect the more time I spend in his company, the more I will grow to like him."

Evan gripped the top rail of her chair as a rush of euphoria swept through him. Why did it matter what this particular woman thought? Why did he care for her good opinion?

"You're remarkably honest, madam," D'Angelo countered.

"Falsehoods are for fools, sir."

Pride filled Evan's chest. Few women would withstand the scrutiny of these men. Indeed, he touched her shoulder in a gesture of reassurance. "Honesty is an excellent foundation for marriage. Would you not agree?"

A smile tugged on Ashwood's lips. "So it would seem."

"And as for regret, Mr D'Angelo," Miss Hart said. "Those who count their losses live in a constant state of disappointment. I'm more inclined to count my blessings, and shall be forever grateful to Mr Sloane."

A darkness passed over D'Angelo's features. Miss Hart's words struck a chord. He had spent his life reflecting on his losses, using every form of pleasure to numb the pain.

Daventry spoke, breaking the silence. "Well, as you're intent on marrying, and we cannot persuade you otherwise, there must be a way we can help you find this masked fiend."

At the prospect of assisting in a dangerous venture, D'Angelo dragged himself from his melancholic mood. "Now we have overcome our initial shock, explain all that has happened so far."

With considerable input from Miss Hart, Evan gave a detailed account of recent events.

"You had to kiss the lady in front of the lawyer?" Cole's frown deepened. "Did you research his background before agreeing to his farcical demands?"

"Golding is acting on behalf of our grandfathers," Evan reassured. "Of that, there is no doubt."

D'Angelo grinned. "So you had no issue convincing him of your mutual affection?"

Evan firmed his jaw. "No. No issue."

"I think my lack of experience helped," Miss Hart said, "coupled with Mr Sloane's skill in that department. Mr Golding seemed more than pleased."

Evan inwardly groaned. D'Angelo would make jests about this until the end of his days. "And so now we need to marry and have Mr Golding bear witness."

"What happens then?" Ashwood asked.

"I assume our wedding gifts will provide the clues to finding our legacy. In the meantime, we intend to investigate all suspects. Namely, Mr Wicks, Mr Ramsey, Charles Sloane and Lady Hollinshead."

Evan knew the last name on the list would prove unpopular with Miss Hart, but he did not expect her to gasp and jump up from the chair in open challenge.

"Why have you added the countess to the list?"

"Because it's likely she knew about the contract, and you used her carriage to visit Mr Golding on the day the intruder broke into the lawyer's office. She persuaded your mother to move to town. She's visited Silver Street and knows when no one is home."

Miss Hart shook her head. "What motive would she have for wishing to steal our legacy? Surely you don't believe she rode through the fields of Little Chelsea wearing a plague mask?"

"Why not? Perhaps you're not the only woman to don breeches or ride astride."

"I might have been killed in the carriage accident." She touched Evan's chest lightly as she made her plea—an action that captured the notice of Evan's colleagues. "The countess swore an oath to protect me. As my mother lay groaning in her sickbed, the countess gripped her hand and promised to give me the life I deserve. Every ball gown I've worn since belongs to her. She has been nothing but generous and kind."

Evan might have offered an opposing opinion, but the comment about the ball gowns tugged at his heart. He scanned Miss Hart's plain blue pelisse, worn for warmth not style, observed the simple poke bonnet fixed with new lilac ribbon and a sprig of lavender. When he considered the state of her furnishings at home, it was evident the lady hoped their legacy amounted to a king's ransom. While Evan had inherited a vast sum from his father, who had inherited his wealth from Lady Boscobel, Miss Hart had been less fortunate.

Daventry coughed to gain their attention. "Miss Hart, good people commit terrible crimes when pushed to the brink."

Evan touched her upper arm, for he saw the war between logic and loyalty raging in her dark eyes. "Ask yourself why you haven't told the countess about the contract. You have a host of exceptional qualities, so why did she not round up eligible men to fill your dance card? Why did she leave you alone in the ballroom with those deemed unpopular?"

Tears brimmed as she looked into Evan's eyes, but she dashed them away. "You know how reckless I can be. I kept to the shadows because I did not wish to embarrass the countess. But you're right, she did not encourage me to do anything other than watch the merriment from my chair."

"Then like the rest of society, she is blind to what truly matters."

What currently mattered to him was making Vivienne Hart smile. He wanted to hear her laugh so hard her ribs ached, to see tears of joy. He wanted to draw a deep moan from her lips as she found her release. He wanted to buy her the finest silk gown, drape rubies around her throat, have every man see what he'd seen when she stood before him in a damp dress and muddy stockings.

Vivienne!

The urge to kiss away her feelings of inadequacy burned. This woman had pushed through his blockade to cause untold havoc with his conscience.

"Should I consider everyone a villain?" she asked, her voice thick with emotion. "Who can I trust?"

He squeezed her arm gently. "You can trust me, Vivienne."

She gasped upon hearing her given name fall from his lips. Wait until she heard him pant her name as he thrust into her willing body. The kiss had awakened her hidden passions, stirred a craving she would need to satisfy. And a woman need not feel ashamed about making love to her husband.

"You can trust all those who work for the Order," Daventry added. "Cole will find out what he can about Mr Ramsey. D'Angelo will investigate the lawyer and his nephew."

"But I'm working on the widow Emery's case," D'Angelo countered.

A man claiming to be a wealthy merchant had duped the widow. He had paid for a clock worth two hundred pounds by cheque and vanished after taking delivery. It was a simple case of fraud, and the widow was unlikely to receive recompense, yet D'Angelo seemed overly keen to trace the merchant.

Daventry glanced at D'Angelo. "I've no issue with you working both cases."

"Perhaps I might use my newly inherited title to learn more about the countess," Ashwood said. He turned to Miss Hart. "I shall be discreet and respectful of the lady's position. The countess will know nothing of my enquiries into her background."

Miss Hart gave a solemn nod.

"Sloane, that leaves you to visit Doctors' Commons, to question Charles Sloane and anyone else you feel is pertinent to the case." Daventry only had to raise a brow, and Sloane knew what the man meant. Buchanan and Mrs McCready could be considered suspects, too.

"And what of me, sir?" Miss Hart spoke as if she were an appointed member of the Order.

Daventry smiled. "According to Sloane, you have a keen eye for observation, Miss Hart. Might I suggest you use your talents to discover why Mr Golding mentioned the poem by Thomas Gray? It is, without doubt, another clue to finding your legacy."

Abandoning her solemn mood, Miss Hart clapped her hands

with excitement. "If I've time, I shall visit the circulating library today."

"I have a few poems by Gray," Ashwood said, "and shall have a footman deliver them to your home, Miss Hart. Gray is known as one of the Graveyard Poets. It might be relevant."

Having failed to mention the lady was removing to Keel Hall, Evan braced himself for more sly grins and twitching brows.

"Most relevant, my lord. Please have your footman deliver them to Mr Sloane's abode. I'm to reside there until we catch the masked fiend."

The men swapped amused glances but said nothing other than to probe Miss Hart for information about Mr Ramsey and Mr Golding.

Daventry took a moment to pull Evan aside and gave an inconspicuous nod in Miss Hart's direction. "She's far from your usual choice of companion. Original. Spirited. A confusing package of contradictions. You realise you're out of your depth with this one."

"Out of my depth?" Evan snorted. He had been drowning for days. "Since meeting her, I've barely surfaced for air."

CHAPTER 10

PRODUCING a letter signed by a deceased First Lord of the Admiralty caused a stir at Doctors' Commons. It took three days for the admiralty to confirm it was legitimate, for the proctor to consult the archbishop and for them to summon Mr Sloane to collect the special licence.

And while Vivienne's examination of Thomas Gray's poems failed to reveal any answers regarding their legacy, other problems brought a halt to the investigation and their wedding plans.

No one at Charles Sloane's house in Bloomsbury Square would reveal their master's direction. After some poking into his distant cousin's affairs, Mr Sloane discovered the man kept a mistress in Guilford Street near the Foundling Hospital, though she was currently out of town.

Buchanan's visit to Mr Golding's office raised concerns. Twice, he'd arrived to discuss the lawyer's need to attend the wedding, only to find the office locked. The tea seller next door confessed he'd not seen Mr Golding or his nephew for two days.

To complicate matters further, Vivienne found she liked living at Keel Hall. She liked sharing cosy suppers with Mr Sloane, liked their long strolls in the garden, their late-night card games. And although she had woken to the alluring scent of his cologne this morning, he had not visited her bedchamber. Nor had they shared another scintillating kiss.

"So, we have a long day ahead of us." Vivienne watched him eat breakfast, knowing he must have entered her room during the night, wondering why. "Visiting Mr Golding must be a priority."

Mr Sloane dabbed his mouth with his napkin. "We're to visit a costume shop in Holborn after calling on Golding. As I explained last night, the villain bought two identical masks. Hopefully, the shopkeeper will remember the purchase."

During a game of Question and Command, he revealed the intruder had left a plague mask in Vivienne's home. The strange calling card was a means to frighten and intimidate. To prevent her from making an alliance with the gentleman who'd consumed her thoughts ever since their passionate encounter.

"I don't know why Buchanan kept it a secret."

"He said he didn't wish to cause you distress."

She gave a half shrug. "Forewarned is forearmed, is it not?"

"Indeed, though I am just as guilty of keeping it from you."

"Why is that?"

He fell silent as he studied her face. "A man should protect a woman in his care. Fear is not the emotion I want to see swimming in your eyes, Vivienne."

Her heart skipped a beat whenever he uttered her given name. Her pulse soared at the mere allusion to something illicit. "Perhaps we should play another game of Question and Command this evening. So I might discover what other secrets you're keeping."

"You were lucky last night." He cast a sinful smile. "Perhaps I shall be the one asking the probing questions tonight."

"I have nothing to hide." Except for her growing attraction to him.

"Then you won't mind telling me your wildest fantasy."

A thrum of anticipation coursed through her. She enjoyed the teasing banter, enjoyed every second she spent in his company. The thought of returning to her lonely existence in Silver Street filled her with dread. But finding their legacy was all that mattered. All romantic notions were merely fancy.

"Then finish your breakfast and let's be on our way. The sooner we accomplish today's tasks, the sooner we can return home." And based on the problems of the last few days, things were unlikely to go as planned.

"Something's wrong." Vivienne wiped dirt from the downstairs window of Mr Golding's townhouse and peered inside. "This is his home and his business premises. He said nothing about leaving town."

"Based on his odd manner the other day, I think it's wise to pick the lock and search the house." Mr Sloane rooted around in his coat pocket and retrieved a ring of unique shaped keys. "Step closer. I need you to hide what I'm doing in case someone alerts the constable."

Vivienne shuffled closer. "If the constable comes, we can say we're concerned for the gentleman's welfare."

Mr Sloane slipped one key into the lock. "Come closer. Drape your arm around my shoulder and pretend you're whispering lewd words in my ear."

"Sir, I wouldn't know a lewd word if it bit me on the buttock."

Vivienne ran her hand over his broad shoulder, and moved so close his arm brushed against her breasts as he fiddled with the keys.

Mr Sloane cast her a sidelong glance. "How can I concentrate on picking the lock when all I can think about is nibbling your derriere, when all I can feel is the soft curve of your breast?"

Heavens!

The agreement to speak honestly often brought an unwelcome blush to her cheeks.

"You're the one who asked me to play the fawning mistress."

"Continue in this vein, Miss Hart, and I'm likely to make you my mistress before I make you my wife."

Vivienne laughed. It was the only way to banish thoughts of being ravished by Evan Sloane. To banish the vision of him stripping off his shirt to reveal bronzed skin stretched taut over pure muscle. Well, that's how she pictured him. Carved to perfection.

"Continue in this vein, and you can forget about playing our little game. We're likely to spend the night in Newgate."

"Then I had best work quickly, for you will answer my probing questions tonight else you must pay a forfeit and do what I command."

Excitement shot through her like a lightning bolt. With every passing hour, she thought more about this gentleman and less about the case. "Then I suggest you stop talking and focus on the task."

He did. Less than a minute later he opened the door, and they entered Mr Golding's dismal abode.

Mr Sloane tapped his finger to his lips, cocked his ear and listened. Vivienne heard nothing. Not the creak of the upstairs boards, not the hum of conversation, not Mr Wicks' drunken mumbling.

"Follow me and stay close." Mr Sloane padded lightly up the stairs.

Vivienne peered through the wooden railings as she tiptoed behind him. The office door was open, the room a dreadful shambles. Strewn files covered the floor, along with the discarded drawers from the oak desk.

"What if something has happened to Mr Golding?" She gripped the back of Mr Sloane's coat when they reached the landing, fearing they might find the lawyer dead beneath a mound of paper.

"You should wait in the carriage," he said, his voice thick with alarm.

"I'll not leave you." She stood beside him as he assessed the ransacked room from the safety of the doorway. "We should check Mr Wicks' office and the rooms upstairs."

Mr Sloane dragged his hand down his face and rubbed his jaw. "Very well. Based on the fact we visited the office together the other day, we must assume the intruder came for information about our legacy."

Stepping with caution, Vivienne followed Mr Sloane over the threshold. Her heartbeat settled upon finding no sign of the lawyer's blood-soaked body. But the veneer side table with the mechanical drawers had disappeared.

"Someone took the table." She pointed past the overturned bookcase to the space on the far wall.

"Perhaps Golding moved it elsewhere for safekeeping." Mr Sloane sifted through the papers on the desk.

"You won't find the black book. If Mr Golding didn't take it, the intruder did." Vivienne tried to remain positive. Mr Golding had kept the secret notebook for years and wouldn't fail them now. And yet he could have given them fair warning, could have sent a note to Keel Hall or to the office of the Order to inform them of his sudden departure.

"We should leave and alert the constable." Mr Sloane glanced at the ceiling. "Though not before ensuring the man isn't a cold corpse in his bed."

"A cold corpse?" She screwed her eyes shut briefly to banish the terrifying image. "You might have phrased it differently. Now my heart is thundering faster than a Derby contender."

Without Mr Golding, how could they proceed with their plans? These last few days, she had grown more than accustomed to the idea of marrying Mr Sloane.

"Does your heart not race when you're in my company?"

"Rarely," she lied. Her heart thumped wildly just thinking about him, and she had done an awful lot of that lately.

He stepped over the upturned drawers and prowled towards her. "Have you grown tired of me already, Vivienne? Was the kiss we shared so unmemorable you have forgotten how good it made you feel?"

Heat rose to her cheeks. Lust pulsed between her thighs at the sound of his velvet voice. This man was a magician. He could turn fear into desire by uttering a simple sentence.

"It must have been an unmemorable kiss for you, as you've had no desire to repeat the experience. I understand. I lack the skill required to please a man like you."

Indeed, his moods were unpredictable. Only last night, they'd been laughing while playing daring games until he became solemn and subdued. He'd left the room and returned as if nothing had occurred.

"Is that what you think?" He stood so close his breath breezed over her cheek. "The kiss exceeded my expectations on every level." He captured her chin between his long, elegant fingers. "There's a reason I haven't devoured your sweet mouth again, and it has nothing to do with your lack of experience."

The heat from her cheeks journeyed southward to pool in her sex. "Is it because I lack the usual feminine attributes?" Most men didn't want a woman drinking their brandy or beating them at cards.

His gaze dipped to her breasts concealed in a pelisse, though he stripped her naked with his rakish stare. "Trust me. You have everything I need and more."

Then, as quick as a wink, he released her chin and muttered a curse.

"What's wrong?"

"While your arousal is evident in the amber flecks of your eyes, mine is evident in a more prominent place."

Delighted to know she had an effect on him, Vivienne couldn't help but glance at the noticeable bulge in his breeches.

"Avert your gaze, madam, for it feels like the teasing caress of your fingers."

She swallowed past her desire. "Perhaps we should return to the matter at hand." They could continue this conversation tonight while playing the question game. Now, they had more worrying matters to deal with.

"If you mean we should inspect the upper floor, you might have phrased it differently. I need your hand for a more important task than scouring through the discarded debris." As if annoyed at himself for making the lewd comment, he shook his head and resumed a more business-like manner. "But you're right. Let us make a thorough inspection before alerting the authorities."

They visited Mr Wicks' office next. The room stank of liquor, sweat, and stale tobacco. The contents of the shelves lay scattered about the floor. Upstairs, they encountered the same level of carnage. Discarded clothes. Slashed pillows. Hundreds of feathers littering the bed.

"We should be grateful Mr Golding isn't home." Vivienne searched the open armoire only to find more crumpled clothes and an empty valise.

"He can't have left town. His shaving implements are on the washstand." Mr Sloane scanned the room and gave a curious hum. "I've seen enough. We will alert the constable and continue as planned."

Continue as planned?

Did he speak of their wedding or the visit to the costume shop?

"How can we continue when we need Mr Golding to act as a witness?"

Mr Sloane gestured for her to exit the room and he followed. "The villain has us chasing our tails, running this way and that, achieving nothing in the process." His stilted speech conveyed his frustration. "No, we've lingered in the background long enough. It's time to whip up a storm."

The determination in his voice stole her breath. There was nothing more attractive than a man who knew when to take command of the reins.

"What are we to do?"

He placed a hand at her back and guided her to the stairs. "We'll call at the Hatton Garden police office, it's closest, and make them aware of what's occurred here. Then we'll call at the costume shop before returning to Keel Hall. We need the sealed note if we're to visit Mr Howarth. Golding's disappearance is connected to our case, and so we must assume the worst."

What if the poor man had suffered while protecting their legacy?

"We have no need to visit Keel Hall." Did he honestly think she'd leave such an important letter for the intruder to find? "I have the sealed letter on my person."

His curious gaze raked over her from neck to navel. "So you slipped it into your thigh belt."

"No. It's not in my thigh belt."

"You're hiding it in another secret place?" His low voice sounded lascivious.

"I am."

"Can I ask where? Should we encounter a problem en route, I might need to retrieve the important document."

Vivienne suppressed a chuckle. "It's wedged securely between my shift and stays."

Mr Sloane swallowed deeply and dared to glance at her bosom. "For an innocent, you're rather skilled in the art of flirtation. I believe you gain pleasure from provoking me, madam, and won't rest until you have me on my knees."

She found these flashes of vulnerability as captivating as his powerful persona. Who wouldn't want such a masterful man at their mercy?

"The fault lies with you, Mr Sloane, for you have read something more into an innocent statement."

"There's nothing more arousing than your innocence, Miss Hart. Though I wonder how you intend to retrieve the note while sitting in a closed carriage with me."

"I have every faith you will do what is right."

"What, be a gentleman and offer my assistance?"

"No. Close your eyes."

The rich red walls and dazzling array of vibrant gowns in Mrs Mulligan's costume shop would put anyone in mind for a party. Vivienne admired an exquisite Elizabethan dress of orange taffeta teamed with a black velvet gable hood. Swathed in such sophistication, a lady would command everyone's attention.

"Pick something less cumbersome," Mr Sloane whispered from behind. "It would take an age to strip you out of that one, and I would prefer to focus my attention on more pleasurable pursuits."

He was teasing her again, using shameless comments to incite a reaction. Did he not know every word from his mouth stirred her senses? He could list a ship's cargo and make it sound erotic. And the mere fact he stood so close turned her mind to mush.

"A man with your skill surely has nimble fingers."

Vivienne swung around to face him, and her breath caught in her throat. It wasn't the tricorn hat perched rakishly on his head that made her heart thud. Nor was it the black mask covering the upper half of his face. It was the way his sinful mouth curled into a mischievous grin.

"Keep the hat. It makes you look like a marauding pirate." The urge to kiss away his confidence pulsed in her veins. "Discard the mask. I wish to look into my husband's eyes when he's focused on pleasurable pursuits."

The air sparked to life.

Mr Sloane's sharp inhalation made her giddy. He tore off the mask, pinned her to the spot with his indecent gaze. "When writhing beneath me, Vivienne, you won't give a damn what I'm wearing."

Mother Mary! Heat settled low and heavy between her thighs. Her mouth was so dry she couldn't form a word.

Mr Sloane glanced over his shoulder at Mrs Mulligan, who was busy serving the only other customer in the small shop. Then he pressed his fingertip to the top button on her pelisse.

"Do you want to know why I've not tried to kiss you, Vivienne?" Slowly, he circled the button as if it were a sensitive part of her anatomy. "Because the next time you permit me to devour your mouth, we'll not stop there. We'll be lovers before we're husband and wife."

Lovers?

The word spoke to her adventurous spirit.

"I thought fondling innocents was not your forte," she said, hoping to gain ground so she didn't look quite so besotted.

"For you, Vivienne, I would make an exception."

"Good afternoon. Have you come to buy an outfit for a masquerade?" The high-pitched voice invaded the intimate moment. "I've a magazine filled with illustrations if you're looking for something unique."

Mr Sloane whispered through his broad smile, "We shall continue this conversation tonight, Vivienne, somewhere private." Then he gave the woman who wore kohl and rouge and a flamboyant peacock-blue robe his full attention. "I hear this is the only establishment in town selling beaked masks."

"Beaked? You mean the *Pantalone*."

"No, the one I want has a long, hollow beak."

"Ah, let me see." The middle-aged woman reached under the

glass counter and retrieved a pile of magazines. She flicked through the pages of one periodical before tapping an illustration with her pointed fingernail. "Is this what you're looking for?"

Vivienne followed Mr Sloane to the counter. Fear trickled through her veins as she glanced at the image of a hunched figure dressed in a black cloak and sporting the terrifying mask. She had glimpsed the mask last night after Mr Sloane's surprise confession. On its own, it had appeared less startling, had not caused the clawing sense of alarm.

"Yes, that is the costume I wish to purchase." Mr Sloane switched the tricorn hat with his top hat and placed it on the counter. "I'll take the tricorn, too, but I need them both today."

The woman's eyes dulled with disappointment. "Today?"

"We've a masquerade this evening."

Mrs Mulligan raised her chin. "Ah, you're going to Lord Newberry's costume ball."

"Newberry?" Vivienne mused. The name sounded familiar. Yes, the countess had taken great delight in discussing her costume, though had informed Vivienne masquerades were not for innocents. Well, after the wicked way Mr Sloane devoured her mouth, she hardly fell into that category. "Yes. Lady Hollinshead is to attend, though I'm sure she mentioned going as Cleopatra."

A sly smile played on Mr Sloane's lips. "Did I not say we should have purchased our costumes weeks ago?" He bent his head and beckoned Mrs Mulligan closer. "A masquerade is a place where a lady might satisfy a fantasy. My wife needs a costume to enhance her natural beauty, to cause a stir."

Vivienne's heart skipped to her throat. Excitement left her shaking. Not just because she longed to attend a masquerade, but because she liked hearing Mr Sloane call her his wife.

Mrs Mulligan straightened her shoulders as if ready for a challenge. She eyed Vivienne's figure. "Something delicate, ethereal. Something to boost a lady's confidence."

"Money is no object."

Mrs Mulligan's eyes shone like polished gems. "I'll need a few hours."

"I shall wait."

Vivienne thought to remind him of their need to visit Mr Howarth. "But we have an urgent appointment across town."

"We can call on him tomorrow. Based on what we've discovered today, it might be best to visit under cover of darkness."

No doubt Mr Sloane feared someone would follow them to Mr Howarth's premises and the man might vanish into thin air, too. Besides, attending the masquerade would allow them to cross the countess off the suspect list.

"Is there something specific you wish your wife to wear, sir?" Mrs Mulligan asked while rifling through the magazine.

"My wife is free to make her own decisions. She may choose whatever her heart desires."

Vivienne hadn't a hope of listening to her heart when it galloped like a wild horse. Mr Sloane was as skilled at sentiment as he was tongue tangling.

"And what of you, sir?" Mrs Mulligan said. "A wife should complement her husband. It will be difficult to match anything with a plague doctor."

"What about a corsair? Would that make your job easier, madam?"

Vivienne liked the idea of him embracing his ancestry. And seeing Mr Sloane in pirate garb would surely cause his cousin discomfort, presuming Charles Sloane attended the masquerade. But then the countess had claimed it was to be the social event of the year.

"Much easier, sir. I have the perfect coat in mind." The woman turned her attention to Vivienne. "Shall we retire to the salon and discuss your ideas? I shall lock the shop so we're not disturbed."

Mr Sloane cleared his throat. "Just one more question, Mrs Mulligan. Might you have a plague mask I can purchase?"

The shopkeeper shook her head. "Alas, someone purchased three such masks, and I have yet to receive the replacements."

"Three?" Mr Sloane frowned. "That's an excessive amount for an unusual mask."

The woman shrugged. "The fellow was half-cut when he bought them, slurring and stumbling about the place. He fell into the console table and knocked over my fancy gilt clock." She laughed. "Happen he got home and couldn't remember how he came by them."

"Did he give his name?" Mr Sloane said abruptly.

Mrs Mulligan seemed suddenly suspicious.

"You must put my husband out of his misery," Vivienne said. "He's wagered fifty pounds on the fact he can purchase a plague mask before the masquerade." She tapped Mr Sloane on the arm. "Mr Mallory is determined to win the bet and must have purchased every mask in town."

"The gentleman placed an order for two more masks." Mrs Mulligan removed a leather tome from under the counter and turned to the relevant page. "Oh! No, I'm afraid you're mistaken."

"Mistaken?"

"His name isn't Mr Mallory. It's Mr Wicks."

CHAPTER 11

"I CANNA RECALL SEEING the lass so excited." Buchanan joined Evan in the hall. "Seems she wants to keep her costume a secret, though I heard Mrs McCready say she'll catch her death in the flimsy gown."

Anticipation burned in Evan's chest. The wait was killing him. For twenty minutes he'd paced back and forth at the bottom of the marble staircase, dressed in his corsair costume—grey coat with gold buttons and trim, an open-necked shirt and a brown leather belt thick enough to carry the weight of three pistols.

"If it's flimsy, I doubt she's coming as an Elizabethan courtier."

Whatever the costume, Evan would make her come tonight. It was impossible to suppress his desire, impossible not to gather her into his arms and plunder her pretty mouth. They'd be married within a week. Why postpone the inevitable?

Buchanan heaved a sigh. "She's barely raised a smile since her mother died."

Evan wondered what was worse. Never knowing a mother's love or feeling its loss so intensely.

"But I thank ye for showing her life is worth living." The Scot raised his hand. "I know ye'll go yer separate ways when this is over, but she's happy now, and that counts for something."

Buchanan's statement roused a host of questions, roused emotions too complicated to consider when consumed by lust. And the sudden appearance of Vivienne Hart at the top of the stairs did little to calm Evan's mental chaos.

"Sorry to have kept you." She floated down, her silver slippers barely touching the steps. "I forgot to bring the silk cloak the countess gave me and had to wear this old thing."

Evan hadn't a clue what Miss Hart wore beneath the thick wool cloak, but the teasing braid dangling over her shoulder held him riveted. As did the smile so brilliant it could light the night sky.

His gaze drifted to her earlobes, free of adornments. And while he longed to take each one into his mouth and suck softly, old feelings of inadequacy surfaced.

"Wait here. I shall be but a moment." Evan darted past her and mounted the stairs in his heavy cavalier boots, returning a few minutes later clutching a black leather box. He stood before her and raised the lid to reveal two pairs of earrings. "It's difficult to know what to choose without seeing your costume, but pearls and diamonds complement any gown."

Miss Hart's eyes widened as she studied his offering, though she looked at him more than she did the sparkling jewels. "It's kind of you to think of me, but I cannot wear another woman's earrings."

Her clipped tone said she had misunderstood. Like the new stockings she'd discarded in favour of Lamont's dandified clothes, she assumed they belonged to a lover.

"They were my mother's earrings, Vivienne." Hell. A lump formed in his throat. "They've been in this box for thirty years. It would please me if you wore a pair this evening."

"Your mother's?" She pursed her lips so tightly her nostrils flared. She looked at him, at the box, dabbed tears from the corners of her eyes and blinked almost as many times as she swallowed. "I—I would like that very much. Pearls would be perfect with my gown."

Evan offered her the box. He lacked the dexterity to remove something so precious without showing signs of his inner torment. Words failed to describe the strange combination of emotions as he watched her slip on the earrings.

Fitchett appeared, the wrinkles on his weathered face deepening into a smile upon noticing the pearls. "Turton insists on driving tonight, sir. He said he'd die of boredom if left in his sickbed."

"Turton is to refrain from all strenuous activity for two weeks." Thank the Lord the same didn't apply to Evan. He wasn't sure how much longer he could resist Miss Hart's charms.

"Morris agreed to accompany him should he get into any difficulty, sir."

Evan nodded. "Did Daventry send the invitations?" Having discovered evidence of Lord Newberry's wicked misdeeds, Daventry often bribed the peer to do his bidding.

"Morris has them, sir. And Miss Hart's mask is in a box in the carriage."

Hmm. The mask might hold a clue to her costume. But Evan didn't long to peer inside the box the way he longed to peer inside Vivienne's cloak. The mere thought of the woman made him hard of late. Indeed, he was rather glad he wore a knee-length frock coat, else the thirty-minute drive to town would be embarrassing with a cockstand.

Lord Newberry knew how to host a lavish party. Carriages barged and jostled their way for a coveted place in a queue that stretched around Cavendish Square and as far as Henrietta Street. Doors opened and slammed as impatient guests, dressed in elaborate costumes, took to parading through the streets. A Turkish prince, a Greek goddess, and a monk passed the carriage window.

"Come, we should follow the crowd," Evan said, eager for Miss Hart's uncloaking. "The sooner we accomplish our task tonight, the sooner we can go home." And amongst other reasons for spending time alone together, they had the problem of Mr Wicks' involvement to address.

Miss Hart pulled her cloak tighter across her lap, though he glimpsed a cerulean blue skirt. "So, our first task this evening is to find the countess and inform her of our betrothal. Are you sure that's wise?"

"We need to dangle the bait if we're to separate the guilty from the innocent. We're going to tell her we've been secretly meeting for months and have fallen in love. That I've secured a special licence and we will marry within the week."

Daventry had sent his man to watch Miss Hart's house in Silver Street. Both the countess and Mr Ramsey had called. Both had resorted to hammering the knocker, banging the window and rattling the sash. Both had questioned the widow living next door. Neither had appeared at Bow Street fraught with worry, keen to report her missing. Neither had visited the lawyer's office in Long Lane.

"She won't approve."

"You're of age. You don't need her permission or her approval."

"She will insist I return home until after the wedding." The anxious hitch in her voice was unmistakable. "I cannot tell her I am staying at Keel Hall."

"No." Evan didn't give a damn what the countess thought, but it took one malicious whisper to ruin a lady's reputation, to ruin it for good. "We will say you're staying with Ashwood. She cannot complain if you're a guest of Lord and Lady Hawkridge."

And considering Ashwood and his wife had agreed to attend the ball and play chaperone, it sounded plausible.

Miss Hart winced. "But she will be hurt, hurt I've not confided in her."

"Whatever happens, you cannot mention the contract." Did the countess know about the pact made between two privateers? Did she know about the cache of pirate gold? Either way, Evan's task was to protect Vivienne Hart, and the less anyone knew of the hidden treasure, the better. "We're in love. That's all she needs to know."

Her gaze drifted over his face, curious yet caressing. "I know how it feels to be in lust, Mr Sloane, no notion what it feels like to be in love."

He knew next to little of the emotion. Nothing of paternal

love, or the deep, abiding attachment shared by lovers. Nothing but what he'd read in poems. Nothing but the brotherly bond he shared with his colleagues.

"We will muddle through somehow."

A sudden knock on the carriage window had Evan reaching for the blade hidden in his boot, but it was Ashwood who yanked open the door.

"You'll not find the masked rider while cooped in a carriage." Ashwood was dressed in a black domino, while his wife Eva clutched a crook and wore the garb of a shepherdess.

"It's a masquerade, Ashwood, could you not be a little more inventive with your costume?"

"Says the man dressed as a pirate." Ashwood doffed his tricorn. "It's the best I could do at short notice, though at least we have matching hats." His gaze drifted to Miss Hart, and he offered a warm greeting. "I'm one of the best enquiry agents in London, Miss Hart, though I am at a loss to put a name to your costume."

"It's a simple gown, not really a costume. I am not one for extravagance, my lord, and lean towards the understated."

If it was a simple gown, why all the secrecy?

Ashwood offered his hand to Miss Hart, though his gaze dipped to her silver slippers. "Perhaps understated is best. At a masquerade, the more ostentatious the dress, the more one blends into the background."

Evan reached for the blue velvet box on the opposite seat, itching to remove the lid. He alighted, waited while Ashwood introduced Miss Hart to his wife, and then handed her the box.

"Leave your cloak in the carriage. There's always a crush at the cloakroom." Equally, they might need to make a quick exit. And Evan wanted to see Miss Hart's costume before other men had the pleasure. "If we're separated, I'll need to identify you amid the horde. I know I'm not looking for an Elizabethan courtier."

"Based on the gold strands threaded through Miss Hart's hair, I would wager she's come as a Greek goddess," Eva Ashwood said.

Ashwood laughed. "Based on the glint in Sloane's eyes, she's Aphrodite."

"Peitho is the goddess of seductive persuasion," Eva challenged.

A blush as red as a berry stained Miss Hart's cheeks. "I am neither Aphrodite nor Peitho, but I suppose I cannot hide beneath this cloak forever."

She opened the box and removed an exquisite handheld mask decorated with blue and green spangles that sparkled like the surface of a sunlit sea. He should have known she would pick something alluding to their shared heritage, to their grandfathers' love of the ocean.

Eva gasped. "It's beautiful, Miss Hart."

"Mr Sloane said to choose whatever my heart desired."

Ashwood cast Evan a knowing look. "I'm sure he had no thought for himself when he made the generous gesture."

Oddly, he'd thought of nothing but making her happy. Now, imagining the bounty of delights hidden beneath her cloak left every muscle tense with anticipation.

He took the empty box and placed it on the carriage seat, held her mask while she unbuttoned her cloak and slipped it off her shoulders.

Holy hell!

Evan gaped at the woman whose luscious figure robbed him of rational thought. Dressed in a satin cerulean blue gown with a silver diaphanous overskirt that shimmered in the muted light, Miss Hart looked like a delicate nymph burst from the sea. His hands throbbed with the need to explore every curve. His stomach muscles clenched hard. Oh, how he longed to capture this mermaid in true pirate fashion and plunder her senseless.

"Now I see why Mrs McCready feared you'd catch your death." He'd likely expire, too, if his heart didn't settle. "Though you look beyond beautiful, Vivienne."

Her shy smile turned luminous. "I told Mrs Mulligan my husband believed a mermaid had saved his grandfather from drowning. That the least I could do was play to his fantasy."

Oh, this woman played to every wild and wicked fantasy. "If I thought you'd come to my rescue, madam, I'd gladly throw myself in the Thames."

Ashwood chuckled. "Newberry has a fountain. It might be safer to start there."

"It's not as rank or as murky." Eva Ashwood laughed as she gripped her husband's arm and led him towards Newberry's mansion house.

Evan threw Miss Hart's cloak into the carriage before escorting his nymph to join the queue of flamboyant revellers.

Being a man with a reputation for hosting extravagant events, Newberry sought novel ways to amuse his guests. Tonight was no exception. Amid the vast array of glowing candelabra and champagne fountains were the most bizarre group of entertainers the *ton* had ever seen.

Miss Hart tugged Evan's arm as he led her past the nun with a monkey perched on her shoulder. "That monkey can do card tricks. He picked the ace of spades from the pack."

"I imagine the card is marked," Evan said cynically.

"And he made a shilling disappear."

"The creature is skilled at stealing snuff boxes and pocket watches, too. By the end of the evening, his mistress will have more than a decent bounty."

Miss Hart touched the pearl earrings dangling from her lobes and gave a relieved sigh. "I heard someone say there are fire eaters and snake charmers outside."

Evan snorted. "The air chokes with the stench of perfume. One accident with a lit torch and the entire room would be ablaze. Can you imagine the chaos if a snake suddenly darted from its basket and took to the dance floor?"

She glanced at him and lowered her mask. "I must sound like a naive debutante, one easily impressed by freakish exhibitions."

He touched her hand. "I have a rather jaded view of these events. Years of overindulgence leaves me weary." Strange that he had been unaware of the fact until now. The only thing holding his interest was the captivating woman beside him.

They pushed past a group trying to knock a jester off a hobby horse and followed Ashwood to the grand marble fireplace.

Ashwood glanced up at the large portrait of the pompous

Lord Newberry. "No one wants to stand here for fear the painting is too heavy for the rail."

Eva laughed. "The painting has to be huge, for it reflects the depth of the man's conceit." She looked at Evan. "Mr Sloane, you're not wearing your mask."

"Charles Sloane never misses a masquerade, though I'll have a devil of a time finding him in the crush. Someone keen to fuel our mutual hostility will alert me to his presence."

Miss Hart lowered her mask again, drawing his gaze to the soft swell of her breasts. "Perhaps we should separate and search the mansion house. I shall look for those dressed as Cleopatra, and you can search for your cousin."

"Second cousin," Evan reminded her, for he wished to distance himself from the peer. "But based on the assumption someone wants to steal our inheritance, I would prefer to keep you in my sights."

Masquerades were hunting grounds for debauched devils. He'd not have his sea nymph sneaking about the corridors, drawing the attention of every licentious rogue.

Miss Hart glanced enviously at the ladies twirling about the dance floor. "While everyone is here for pleasure, we're here to conduct an investigation."

With his growing need to make this woman happy, Evan wished he could forget about the case, too. "Once we accomplish our task, there might be time for a waltz."

The sudden hitch in her breath, and the vibrant sparkle of her eyes, proved oddly satisfying. "Then we should start our search in the refreshment room where we can at least partake in a glass of champagne."

"Unmarried ladies take lemonade," he teased. If they made love later this evening, he would have her dizzy with desire, not sparkling wine.

"Tonight I'm a mermaid, and mythical creatures do as they please."

"Oh, I intend to discover exactly what you find pleasing." The sooner they found the countess and made their announcement, the sooner he could take his nymph home.

Cleopatra proved a popular choice of costume. Lady

Farringdon had squashed her large frame into a gold silk dress. Mrs Finsbury had discarded her black wig and wore her cobra crown perched on top of golden locks. While in the refreshment room, Ashwood noticed another Cleopatra saunter past the door. This time, the woman's slim frame and elegant bearing suggested it could be the countess.

Evan handed Ashwood his champagne flute. "Wait here. I'll follow the Egyptian queen and see where she's heading."

"I'm coming with you." Miss Hart swallowed the last sip of champagne and placed her flute on a passing footman's tray. "We should make the announcement together."

"We will note your direction and linger in the background, in case we're needed." Ashwood grinned at his wife. "Let's find a discreet alcove so we may keep watch."

When in his wife's company, Ashwood would struggle to notice a herd of elephants stampeding. The more time Evan spent with Vivienne Hart, the more he understood his friend's obsession.

"We shall reconvene here in twenty minutes." Evan placed his hand at Miss Hart's lower back and guided her into the hall.

The heat of her body warmed his palm. It was impossible to concentrate on the figure in gold who stopped in the corridor to pass pleasantries with a sailor. All thoughts led back to the same pressing question. How would he survive another night without making love to Vivienne Hart?

Then the countess glanced along the corridor, forcing Evan to pull Miss Hart into an alcove. Their bodies collided. She grabbed hold of his shirt. Obscene thoughts bombarded his mind. The need to devour this woman's mouth gripped him like an opium addiction.

"Vivienne," he whispered as he pressed her soft, pliant body to the wall, let her feel the length of his growing erection.

Her breath caught. "Mr Sloane, I ..."

"Tell me what you want, Vivienne. Tell me what you crave."

The swell of her breasts rose to greet him. "I want ... I want you." She held her mask in place and touched her lips to his—a kiss so gentle, so sweet, so damn arousing.

His cock jerked in response.

Mother of all saints!

He smoothed his hand over her hip, reached around to grip her bottom.

Lust, the overwhelming need to push into her warmth and thrust to the hilt, robbed him of all logic and reason. Perhaps it was the taste of champagne on her lips or the lawless air of the masquerade that left him playing out a host of erotic fantasies in his head. He traced her lips with his tongue, ready to plunge deep—until a cough from behind brought him crashing back to reality.

Evan dragged his mouth from Miss Hart's and turned to meet Ashwood's mocking stare. "Your quarry is on the move, Sloane. Might I suggest you save the pleasantries for later?"

CHAPTER 12

STRANGE HOW A CHASTE kiss could awaken one's primitive desires. Strange that when deeply attracted to a man, a lady forgot about propriety and thought of nothing but her carnal cravings. The pulsing between Vivienne's thighs was so intense she didn't give a fig why Cleopatra had slipped into the library with a Roman emperor.

"Might the emperor be Lord Hollinshead?" Mr Sloane whispered as they stood outside a door on the first-floor landing. "Might they seek a private moment to indulge their whims?"

Vivienne watched his mouth move, remembering the earthy taste she found so compelling, remembering the gentle stroke of his tongue across her lips, just how delicious—

"Miss Hart? Might the emperor be the countess' husband?"

"What? Oh, no. I highly doubt it." Lord Hollinshead was a known philanderer who kept more mistresses than horses. "Surely you've heard the gossip. They live in separate houses and rarely attend the same functions." The countess had persuaded Vivienne's mother to move to London to ease her dreadful loneliness. "The lady hates her husband with a vengeance."

"Does she have a lover?"

One did not pry into such a powerful lady's affairs.

Vivienne was about to reply, but Mr Sloane touched his finger to her lips. "Hush. I can hear raised voices." Yet he made no attempt to listen.

Fixated on her mouth, and with a look one might describe as salacious, he breached the seam of her lips with his finger, ran the tip slowly over the wet flesh inside.

Her nipples hardened at the sensual invasion. Her legs trembled as she waited for him to slip deeper. She gave in to her urges, flicked her tongue against his finger, bit down on the tip.

"Minx," he mouthed, fixing her with his ravenous gaze. "Let me come to your bedchamber tonight. Let me show you the power of my tongue."

Vivienne swallowed deeply. Climbing into bed with this pirate seemed more than appealing. What harm could it do? What reason did she have to hold on to her virtue? And wasn't it better to make love to a man she desired than to suffer the fate of most ladies her age?

"You're lying!" came the feminine screech from beyond the door. "I demand you put a stop to this at once."

"Madam, what my rakehell cousin does is his affair. For years, I've strived to avoid any association with the scoundrel and couldn't give a hoot who he marries."

"Will you not at least confirm the rumour is true?"

Vivienne leant closer to Mr Sloane and lowered her voice. "That's definitely Lady Hollinshead. Only two people could have told her about our decision to marry."

"Three. Ramsey, Golding, and the drunken sot Wicks."

"Maybe now is the time to begin our performance."

Mr Sloane straightened. "As my betrothed, you will need to align yourself with me, not the countess. And having Charles Sloane here means we can lure them both with the bait." He stroked her cheek with the backs of his fingers. "They have to believe we're in love and mean to marry."

"Do you honestly think either of them would be interested in pirate treasure? They don't need the money. What possible motive could they have for stealing our bounty?" And was the countess not trying to prevent the marriage?

"The legacy might not be money, but damning information or a dreadful secret. That's motive enough to prevent our alliance.

And Charles Sloane must know of the contract. Perhaps he's swimming in gambling debts, one creditor away from drowning. Most of what he owns is entailed."

But surely the information gained at the costume shop shed new light on recent events. "Is Mr Wicks not the one who fired shots at the carriage, who hurried to Keel Hall to destroy the painting?"

Mr Sloane arched a brow. "The clerk can barely walk straight, let alone ride in the dark while firing two pistols."

"Could his sotted-fool routine not be an act to divert suspicion?"

He pondered the point until the frustrated countess cried, "Do not belittle me. I heard it from a reliable source."

"Come, let us join the party before one of them leaves." Mr Sloane clasped Vivienne's hand and barged into the dimly lit library before she could protest. "What have we here? Cleopatra consorting with an envoy of Rome? Are you seeking to bring about the destruction of an empire, or just poking your noses into my affairs?"

The Roman emperor cursed. He tore off his gold mask and glared at Mr Sloane. "As I have just explained to Lady Hollinshead, marry who the devil you please. Thankfully, in her infinite wisdom, our great-grandmother sought to divide the family. So those of us with blue blood might avoid any association with our dissolute relatives."

Mr Sloane laughed. "And yet Lady Boscobel-Sloane raised my father and left him a huge portion of her estate. It must cut to the bone to know I'm wealthier than you, despite the fact my grandfather was a marauding pirate."

The viscount, who was a wisp of a man compared to his cousin, glared down his patrician nose. "Money does not make you a gentleman. Your mother was a governor's daughter. Your lowly status is evident in the sordid work you do for Lucius Daventry."

The atmosphere turned volatile, the threat of danger as frightening as Mr Sloane's thunderous glare. "Do not dare speak about my mother. Not if you want to live to see tomorrow."

"Saving innocent children from blackmailing monsters is far

from sordid," Vivienne spat. The need to defend Mr Sloane took command of her senses. "The fault lies with you, not Mr Sloane. Men of privilege ought to right society's injustices instead of endlessly pursuing pleasure."

"Miss Hart!" The countess put her hand to her throat as if struggling to breathe. Her cheeks looked deathly pale against the stark black wig. "Mind your manners. You're speaking to a viscount." Despite her heritage, her accent was devoid of the Scottish burr, a burr she occasionally let slip.

"I have spent the last three months minding my manners, my lady, but I cannot permit anyone to disrespect the man I'm to marry."

She glanced at Mr Sloane, who did a remarkable job of appearing touched. Vivienne would fight his corner even if they weren't putting on a show.

The countess scanned the delicate gown hugging Vivienne's frame like a silk glove. "Please tell me this is a terrible dream and I will wake in a cold sweat, praising the Lord and counting my blessings." She pressed her gloved fingers to her brow. "This cannot be true. Not after your dear mother left you in my care."

Vivienne had passed the age of majority years ago and did not need a guardian. But she supposed the lady had taken her under her wing and sought to introduce her into society.

"I am extremely grateful for your kindness, my lady. Indeed, when I met Mr Sloane two months ago, I didn't imagine our relationship would blossom so quickly."

For the first time in history, Cleopatra looked ready to swoon. Lady Hollinshead gripped the rosewood writing desk. "Are you with child, my dear? Has this devil violated you? Can you be sure he will go through with this marriage, and it is not a ploy to annoy his cousin?"

"Second cousin," Mr Sloane corrected, for he was equally keen to distance himself from his relative. "And if a man had made those derogatory remarks about my character, I'd shoot him dead."

"Do you not entertain courtesans, Mr Sloane?"

"Like most unmarried men, I did until I fell in love with Miss

Hart. And while I long for the day when we might cement our union, I would never disrespect the woman set to be my wife."

The countess groaned. "Oh, this is dreadful."

"Then perhaps you should have paid more attention to the daughter of your friend instead of leaving her alone to watch the gaiety from her chair. Indeed, why did you not find her a suitor from your long list of respectable acquaintances? Not once has she graced the dance floor. According to Buchanan, she hasn't received a single offer to ride out."

Vivienne couldn't help but feel somewhat inadequate when she considered the lack of male attention. And when had Mr Sloane taken to questioning Buchanan about her private affairs?

"Well?" Mr Sloane prompted.

After an episode of excessive swallowing, the countess found her voice. "It's an extremely complicated situation."

Vivienne frowned. This was the first time the countess had suggested there might be a problem. "Complicated? I don't understand." Or perhaps she did but didn't want to believe the countess was as prejudiced as the rest of society.

"Isn't it obvious? You've no dowry. You're but a cousin to the current laird, and your paternal grandfather—"

"Second cousin," Vivienne interjected, grinning at Mr Sloane. "What you're trying to say is Lucian Hart's choice of career means I fall beneath acceptable standards."

The lady raised her chin. "Many gentlemen frown upon your grandfather's seafaring background. Edinburgh society would suit you so much better."

The viscount laughed. "So, the lady's ancestor was a pirate, too. Did this fellow escape the noose? Did he go unpunished because he had connections to the aristocracy? Did you inherit a fortune despite being the offspring of a criminal?"

A darkness fell over Mr Sloane's fine features.

A darkness of satanic proportion.

"A criminal? Livingston Sloane served the Crown. I have proof." Evan Sloane gritted his teeth. "Next time we meet, I shall stuff the document down your throat and watch you choke." He cricked his neck. "Beware. I intend to inform everyone of the false charges made against my grandfather. I intend to ensure you're made to grovel for the mistake."

Vivienne should have been petrified, but Mr Sloane radiated a raw masculinity she found highly arousing. Indeed, she was keen to bring the conversation to an end. Keen to ensure Mr Sloane kept calm, for the viscount was no match for the virile gentleman clutching her hand.

"My lady, might I ask how you learned of my betrothal before I had a chance to tell you personally?" Did the woman have anything to hide? Would she confess?

Consumed with her thoughts, it took the countess a moment to reply. "Mr Ramsey came to see me, concerned by your sudden announcement. We have called at Silver Street more than a handful of times these last three days."

"I've struggled to sleep since the intruder tore through my home, and needed a brief respite." The countess believed the blackguard was an opportunistic thief and knew nothing of the mask left behind.

The lady's face turned ashen. "Blessed Lord! Tell me you are not this gentleman's guest."

"I am Lord and Lady Hawkridge's guest and will reside there until the wedding."

The countess appeared mildly appeased. "You'll need help with your trousseau. Your mother would have insisted I take on the role. And it would be better for everyone concerned if you stayed with me in Russell Square."

Vivienne might have found the kind gesture touching. But she noted a hint of desperation in the woman's voice, feared the countess would resort to manipulation in the hope of changing Vivienne's mind.

An inner war raged.

You need to align yourself with me, not the countess.

Mr Sloane's comment raced through her mind. And as much as she was grateful to the friend who had nursed her mother during those final hours, a feeling deep in her chest said she could not completely trust the countess.

"Buchanan and Mrs McCready remain my loyal companions. And Mr Sloane has opened an account with a fashionable modiste. Besides, we are to marry in a matter of days." Vivienne took it upon herself to taunt Charles Sloane. "A marriage between descendants of Lucian Hart and Livingston Sloane is what our grandfathers wanted. An alliance will reap untold rewards."

"I daresay all pirates keep to a code."

Upon witnessing his cousin's sneer, Mr Sloane took a single step forward. It was enough to make the fop retreat. "Should I discover you're prying into my affairs, I shall take a cutlass and gut you like a fish." He bowed to the countess. "We shall post an announcement in the broadsheets. You're welcome to visit my wife at Keel Hall. I trust you enjoy the rest of your evening."

Without further comment, and keeping a tight grip on Vivienne's hand, Mr Sloane led her from the room and down the crowded staircase to join the exuberant throng.

The first strains of a waltz reached her ears.

"Dance with me, Vivienne." Mr Sloane drew her towards the large double doors leading to the ballroom. "Else I'm likely to storm upstairs and rip that popinjay's head off his shoulders."

Music drifted through the hall, teasing her with its sensual rhythm. All thoughts turned to the dance, to the feel of his warm hand on her back, the nearness of his body, the intoxicating scent of his cologne. Every nerve tingled with anticipation until a buxom lady in the garb of a serving wench blocked their path.

"Sloane, I've been searching for you all night. I believe this dance is mine." She stared at Vivienne through the eye slits of a silk mask. "The fairy can wait her turn. Old friends take precedence."

"Mrs Worthing." Mr Sloane removed the woman's wandering hand from his chest. "I'm afraid I must decline the invitation and correct your misconception. The lady is a sea nymph, and soon to be my wife."

"Wife!" the wench scoffed. "Wife! Oh, you're a devil of a tease. I suppose I can wait. Let the fairy have her dance. Meet me outside afterwards, and we shall find a secluded corner of the garden so you can tease me some more."

Jealousy slithered through Vivienne, hissing wicked taunts. It took every effort not to pull the blade from the gentleman's boot and press the point to Mrs Worthing's throat. But words spoken with calm assurance carried a deadlier blow.

"Clearly you know little of sea nymphs, Mrs Worthing." Vivienne spoke with renewed confidence. "Mr Sloane has no control here. I lured him with the promise of a wild adventure. Now the man is besotted, infatuated, and has no desire to bed any woman but me. Ask him if you doubt my word."

Mrs Worthing sneered. "You know what they say about sirens, Sloane. An old crone lurks beneath the vision of beauty. Better the devil you know, I say."

"That might be true of sirens." Mr Sloane looked at Vivienne and his gaze softened. "But I've fallen in love with a sea nymph. Every other woman pales in comparison."

Vivienne's pulse thumped in her throat. Oh, he was so good at this game, so believable she might get lost in the fantasy. What would it be like to be loved by this man? To be worshipped above all others?

Mrs Worthing gave a half shrug, and one breast almost escaped its confines. "You'll be bored within a week. Visit me if you're looking for someone to plunder." And with that, the woman turned her back and was soon lost amid a sea of heads.

Despite the raucous laughter and boisterous antics of the crowd, Mr Sloane's mood plunged off a precipice into an abyss. Grave was the only way to describe the harsh look spoiling his handsome features.

"Are we to dance?" Vivienne asked, hovering at Mr Sloane's side as if they were both lost in the darkness. People were staring. Some took to whispering. Some nodded in their direction. "Mr Sloane?" she muttered through clenched teeth.

"Dance?" He shook himself from his reverie. "No. We should leave, leave now. We need to find Ashwood."

The next ten minutes passed in a blur. His friends were equally surprised at his insistence they leave the masquerade. Bluntly, he explained they had completed their task for the evening and had no need to remain. Mr Sloane demanded his friends escort Vivienne to the carriage and instruct Turton to wait on Henrietta Street. He would join her there shortly.

A heavy silence marred the journey to Keel Hall.

Suspicion clouded Vivienne's thoughts. But whenever she examined the conversation with Mrs Worthing, she came to the same conclusion. Mr Sloane was plagued by regret. The thought of marriage and losing his liberty must be the reason for his depressing disposition.

"You're quiet," she said when she could no longer bear the tension.

He continued to stare out of the window at the sprawling blackness of Little Chelsea. "We have much to do tomorrow," he said as if that were the reason for his disquiet. "And it's late."

Perhaps she might have ignored him, yet she couldn't help but wonder if he'd gone in search of Mrs Worthing during the fifteen minutes he'd spent alone at the ball. What had he told the woman? That he would tire of his wife within a week? That he would seek her services as soon as he was finished with this dreadful business?

"Late? Does that mean we won't take a drink in the drawing room or play our little game?"

He swallowed. "Not tonight."

The pang of disappointment was nothing compared to the sharp stab of jealousy. So this did have something to do with Mrs Worthing. Annoyance surfaced—though she had no right to be angry. Not when he'd made it clear he didn't want to marry, didn't want to have anything to do with the contract. Not when he'd been coerced into keeping his ancestor's vow.

So why did she feel the usual jolt of electricity when he clasped her hand and helped her from the carriage? Why did he look like a man starved of air when his gaze dropped to her mouth? Why did he linger in the hall and struggle to say good night?

If ever there was a perfect time to play a game of honesty, this was it.

"Go to bed," she said, slipping off her cloak before Fitchett hurried to attend to them. "I'm in need of something strong to drink and might mix my own concoction."

"We have an early start tomorrow, a busy day. I suspect the masked rider will do something wicked to scupper our plans."

They were to meet at the office of the Order to receive an

update from Mr D'Angelo, as well as visit Mr Howarth, make arrangements to marry and see if the Hatton Garden constables had located Mr Golding.

She shrugged. "All the more reason to relax and gather my thoughts. Good night, Mr Sloane." She walked away so he couldn't see the desperate loneliness etched on her face, the loneliness that left her chest empty, her hopes hollow.

"Vivienne."

"Yes." She stopped and glanced over her shoulder.

"It's unwise to be alone together, to drink when spirits lower one's inhibitions."

She laughed. "Do you fear I might prance around barefooted?"

Green eyes with the allure of polished jade settled on her face. "You know what I'm trying to say."

No. She had no idea. All thoughts of a romantic evening had abandoned her after the mild tussle with Mrs Worthing. "Perhaps a glass of brandy might loosen your tongue. Or perhaps the reality of our situation leaves a bitter taste in your mouth that makes everything unpalatable. Either way, I bid you good night again, Mr Sloane."

He paused. "Good night, Miss Hart."

Miss Hart? Not Vivienne?

She fought the sickening churn of rejection and continued to the drawing room. Despite leaving the door open in invitation, the clip of Mr Sloane's boots on the marble stairs confirmed his retreat.

CHAPTER 13

THE BITTER TASTE in Evan's mouth had nothing to do with Vivienne Hart. This crippling feeling of malcontent had nothing to do with abiding by a contract made seventy years ago. No. Evan's rude awakening came from the realisation he'd been living a lie.

Strange that he had spent his life fighting against the failings of his ancestor, proving his valiance, showing the world he was no cowardly pirate and had courage abound. In truth, his need for casual relations made him as weak as every other man.

Having seen the destructive power of love—how his father had lived in a constant state of mourning—the thought of being dependent upon one person had left Evan avoiding commitment.

And then Vivienne Hart had hammered on his door amid a raging thunderstorm to play havoc with his rationale. Seducing him with the prospect of an adventure. He'd been enticed by her bravery, her tenacity and cavalier attitude, not by hidden treasure or the prospect of vengeance.

Miss Hart deserved the moniker Valiant. She had defended him in front of Charles Sloane. Stood beside him like the king's own guard, ready to fight to the death. She trusted him. With resounding confidence, she had placed her beating heart in his hands.

And how had he repaid such loyalty and devotion?

By dragging her into a lewd conversation with an old paramour.

By dragging her down to his low level.

She deserved better. Yet despite finding the strength to walk away from her downstairs, he couldn't calm his craving. He couldn't let her think him indifferent to her charms. He couldn't let her settle into bed, believing he didn't care. Hence the reason he sat in a chair in the corner of her bedchamber, hidden in the shadows. Waiting.

He remained alone with his thoughts for half an hour, had dismissed the maid who came to stoke the fire, light the lamp and turn down the bed.

The rattle of the doorknob sent his heart shooting to his throat. It was laughable that a man with his experience should feel nervous about being in a woman's bedchamber, but such was the power of Vivienne Hart's allure.

Evan watched the figure enter the room, hoping it wasn't Mrs McCready with her penchant for snooping. Fitchett mentioned he'd found the servant examining the portraits in the drawing room. And Evan was sure he'd seen her walking the corridors late last night, too.

It wasn't the cranky old crone. He knew it was Vivienne Hart when she braced her hands on her hips and scanned the room.

"How odd."

"Odd the lamp isn't lit?" he said from the depths of the dark recess. "Or odd the maid isn't here to undress you?" That task was unreservedly his. Indeed, his voice held the smooth drawl of a man intent on seduction.

Miss Hart didn't gasp or stumble back, terrified. "Odd this isn't the first time I've been accosted by the smell of your cologne in this room."

He stretched languidly and crossed his legs at the ankles to ease the ache in his loins. "I've been waiting for some time."

"You entered my bedchamber last night while I slept."

"Is that a statement or merely conjecture?" He threw a pack of playing cards onto the bed. "Pick a card, Vivienne. Let's see who will be the question master and who will bare their soul."

"It seems I have the devil's luck, sir. Are you sure you want to play?"

"The law of averages suggests you will confess a secret at some point. You can pick my card. I have the utmost faith you will do what is right." It was time she knew she had his trust and respect.

He felt the spark of excitement in the air before hearing her light laugh. "Very well. Be warned, this is a game of truths. Play only if you're brave enough to speak from the heart."

"It's also a game of forfeits. Play only if you're willing to do as I command."

The hitch in her breath fed his growing desire.

"Perhaps I'll be the one issuing commands," she said. "In the absence of a maid, I might have you light the lamp and pull back the coverlet."

And he would do both willingly, for he would have every inch of her naked body bathed in light when he lowered her down onto the bed.

She removed her gloves, though did not slip them down slowly to seduce him into submission. She tugged them off as if braced for a challenge. He liked that. He liked the fact she aroused him without the fake artifice. And while she shuffled the cards like a novice, she drew with the skill of a cardsharp.

"The ace of spades." She flashed the card, though it was impossible to see it clearly against the dim firelight. "There is little point drawing a card for you. Do you concede?"

"An ace? Madam, let us hope you're not about to rob me of my pocket watch while my attention is diverted." Another ace would force her to draw again, but he wasn't playing to win the game of questions. He was playing for a far greater prize. "But yes, I concede."

"Excellent." She paused while deliberating, yet he knew the question she longed to ask. "Why did you enter my bedchamber last night without seeking permission?"

The truth filled him with the same warm—yet confounding —tenderness he'd experienced last night. "I was drawn here, drawn by a feeling I cannot explain. But the need to see you sleeping peacefully after the stresses of the day brought surprising comfort."

She touched her hand to her throat but didn't speak.

"Draw again, Vivienne."

After some fumbling with the cards, she pulled two from the pack. "Ten of diamonds. You have the seven of clubs. It's my turn again, Mr Sloane."

Evan rubbed his thighs. "Let me save some time. You want to know why I left you alone in the drawing room and came upstairs. Why I didn't devour your mouth when I've hungered for you all day."

She stepped closer and gripped the bedpost. "Have you? Have you hungered for me all day?"

"Is that your question?" he teased. "For it is unlike you to ask something which is so blatantly obvious."

"A woman is often plagued with doubts."

"Then why do you think I came upstairs?" He doubted she had the measure of the situation. Indeed, he had only just come to the logical conclusion himself.

"Seeing Mrs Worthing tonight brought a marked change in you." She sat on the edge of the bed, shoulders slumped, still holding the post as if expecting devastating news. "You must miss entertaining your friends, miss the freedom that comes with doing as you please. Know I will not outstay my welcome. Soon, I shall be gone, and you can continue as before."

Gone!

The word hit him like an uppercut to the jaw. Gone. It meant to be left alone, lost and hopeless. Gone. Nausea bubbled in his stomach. His lungs screamed for air, yet he was still breathing.

Evan sat up straight. "Loneliness can make a man behave indelicately. A man might make excuses for the incorrect choices he makes when his heart craves companionship."

"I know what it's like to be lonely. I'm telling you I understand. You wish to surround yourself with people, and I am in the way."

"I wish to surround myself with you, Vivienne, no one else." He wanted her bare skin pressed against his, her hands smothering every aching muscle. He wanted to bury his face in her hair, his cock so deep in her body he would never feel alone again. "I seek a meaningful connection with my wife and am not interested in tupping a harlot."

The crackle of the fire echoed the sparks of sexual tension in the air.

She pushed to her feet. "I am not your wife yet, Mr Sloane."

"That's a mere formality." He stood, prowled towards the nymph shimmering in the muted light like the surface of the ocean. So enticing. So damn inviting. "Pick a card, Vivienne."

Fate would grant him a boon.

Her fingers shook as she shuffled the pack. She fanned them in her hands, forced him to choose. Evan drew the king of hearts—a gift from the gods. When she pulled the eight of hearts, he was almost knocked off his feet by a rush of euphoria.

He smiled. "Eight signifies new beginnings." Making love to Vivienne Hart would be a novel experience. "And now I believe it's my turn to ask a question."

She bit down on her bottom lip, and he resisted the urge to pull her close and suck on the plump flesh. "Then ask it."

He spent a few seconds raking his gaze boldly over every delicious curve, over the soft swell of her breasts rising rapidly to torment him.

"Do you want to make love? Do you want me to pleasure you in ways beyond your wildest imagination? Do you want to ease my loneliness, Vivienne, let me ease yours, let me prove I'm not a bore in bed?"

The glazed look of desire in her eyes said she did.

"You asked three questions, Mr Sloane."

"All requiring one answer, Miss Hart." He could not take her to bed without having her consent. "Unless you wish to pay a forfeit and do what I command."

Her tongue appeared, licking the corner of her mouth, driving him wild. "What would you have me do?"

Lascivious visions burst into his mind. He'd have her on her knees sucking him to completion. He'd have her spread out before him like a feast while he gorged on every morsel. But those were pleasures reserved for a woman comfortable with intimacy. He would have to begin slowly. Arouse her to the point she was no longer abashed.

"I sent Randall to bed. I want you to play valet and undress me, Vivienne." He'd removed his coat and belt. There wasn't much for her to do.

Her eyes widened as she glanced at his shirt, a flimsy barrier to his nakedness. "I can be rather clumsy, not at all seductive, and am likely to remove your clothes as if you're an obstinate hospital patient."

Evan couldn't help but smile. "Let me make it easier."

He strode to the bedchamber door, turned the key in the lock, sat on the cushioned stool by the dressing table and yanked off his cavalier boots and stockings.

"Undress me in the way that pleases you," he said, coming to stand before her. "If you wish to wrestle the shirt from my back, so be it."

She studied him as if he were a complex puzzle.

"Don't be shy. You're the woman who stormed into my home, pulled a contract from your thigh belt and told me I was obliged to marry you."

She laughed, and her shoulders relaxed. "I doubt I'll ever forget the look of horror on your face."

"And now I wear a different look, one I see reflected in your eyes, a longing to join our bodies and bask in pleasure." He paused. "If this isn't what you want, we don't—"

"No. No, it is what I want."

Relief coursed through him. "Then strip me naked, Vivienne."

She found a burst of courage from somewhere. Those delicate fingers he hoped would squeeze his buttocks as he thrust long and deep, settled on his hips and tugged the shirt from his breeches.

He bent his knees and raised his arms while she drew the garment over his head and dropped it onto the bed.

The muscles in her throat worked tirelessly as she stared at his toned physique. "Most men who indulge their desires, who live life to excess, have a paunch."

"Daventry insists we box and fence weekly. Courage alone is not enough to tackle the villains in the rookeries."

She reached out, smoothing her hands over the broad expanse of his chest, tickling the dusting of hair, trailing her fingers down over the rigid planes of his abdomen.

Evan sucked in a sharp breath. He'd been caressed and fondled many times, never like this, never with hands that explored every contour with utter fascination.

Innocence proved arousing.

His cock throbbed with approval.

"Be warned. When you slip off my breeches, my erection will spring free." He heard her nerves in every prolonged breath. "I'm already desperate for you, and you're still fully clothed. How does it feel to have a pirate at your mercy?"

"Exhilarating."

"Then free me from my constraints."

With brows knitted together in concentration, she undid the buttons on the waistband. Taking a deep breath, she drew the garment gently down over his hips, down to his ankles. The stealing glance at his erect manhood left her wide-eyed, impressed more than fearful.

"Do you like what you see, Vivienne?" He was stark naked and aroused beyond belief.

She gulped. "I find it all rather curious."

"Curious?" That was certainly a unique way of describing a man's solid shaft.

"Yes." She took to staring then, examining the length and girth. "Fascinating, in fact. May I touch you?"

He laughed in shock. "Love, you may do whatever your heart desires. I am but a slave to your whims. A servant to your pleasure."

The first tentative touch of her fingers on his cock drew a hissed obscenity from his lips. He fought the urge to tell her how to hold him, what to do. The anticipation of that first firm grip, that first glide back and forth, almost made him come in her hand.

"It's a strange contradiction." She wrapped her fingers around him, moved her hand in experimental strokes. "The sheath is so soft, yet you're remarkably hard. The slightest movement makes you moan."

"You hold the power, Vivienne. The power to bring me untold pleasure. The power to turn me away unsatisfied." To sweep out of his life as quickly as she came. To leave him unloved and alone.

"Power is a formidable thing." Her hot gaze licked his torso, though he noted a flash of tenderness that usually had no place in illicit liaisons. "But I would prefer to share the responsibility. I wish to be at your mercy, too."

He glanced at the gown bathing her body in an incandescent sheen, and couldn't wait to see it a crumpled mess on the floor.

"Then let us begin by stripping you out of that dress."

With surprising gentleness, he stroked her cheek with the backs of his fingers, brushed her hair from her face, ran his thumb over her bottom lip. Who knew a sweet sigh of content-ment could melt a man's heart? Who knew a man could undress a woman slowly while sporting a throbbing rod of iron?

He took his time, peeled away the layers as if she were a gift conjured by his ancestor and delivered from his heavenly plane. She breathed deeply when he removed her stays, filling her lungs, though soon she would be breathless again.

"Your skin is like porcelain." He pressed his lips to her nape before slipping her chemise up over her bare thighs, over her hips and head.

He stepped back, surveying the beauty of her womanly form, every gentle curve taunting him. The ache in his cock was nothing to the ache in his chest. He would most likely spend the second she turned around. Yet while her breasts were equally magnificent, the longing in her eyes sang to his soul.

She reached out to him first, sliding her hand over his bare chest and up around his neck, melding her naked body to his. He locked her there, his hand flat against her spine, his erection pushing against soft flesh.

"Are you sure you want to give me your virtue, Vivienne?" The irony being it was a far more precious gift than anything one would find in a pirate's chest.

"There is no man I trust more than you." The minx kissed his neck, inhaled the scent of him and sighed. "And I doubt I shall ever have these overwhelming feelings again."

He vowed she would, swore a silent promise to make love to her every night from here on in.

But it was time to stoke passion's flames, and so he captured her plump lips in a searing kiss, explored the wonders of her mouth with his inquisitive tongue, for he had never tasted a woman as intoxicating as Vivienne Hart. Never thought the mating of mouths could make his heart swell as large as his manhood. Never expected the first slide of his fingers against her slick wetness would drag a guttural groan from *his* lips.

"Touch me," she panted against his mouth. "Touch me there again, Evan."

Hell, he wasn't sure what aroused him more—the instant shiver that came from hearing her speak his given name, or the pant of approval as he massaged the sensitive nub. They should retreat to the comfort of the bed, but he liked the way his nymph moved against his hand, rolling her hips like the gentle undulations of the sea.

"Shall I make you come like this, Vivienne?"

Her head fell back, exposing the elegant column of her throat. "Your words, your voice, they're as stimulating as your fingers. Oh! Don't stop, Evan."

Stop? He'd rather fifty lashes with a birch.

She reached down between their hot bodies and stroked the length of his cock. Damn. Her untutored touch was beyond divine.

"I need to be inside you, love." This would be a quick affair, he feared. They had the whole night to work up to an encore. "Don't be afraid. Trust me to take care of you."

"I do, I do trust you."

He scooped her up into his arms and carried her to bed. She tried to protest when he kissed his way down between the valley of her thighs.

"Trust me, love," he whispered, though she surrendered with the first flick of his tongue.

As long as he lived, he would never forget the way she gripped his hair, the way she anchored his mouth to her sex and convulsed. There was nothing staged about her whimpers, nothing fake. She cried his name as if he were a knight come to her rescue, the hero of her tale.

The moment he settled between her thighs, he felt a stirring in his chest as fierce as the one gripping his cock. Indeed, when she wrapped her legs around him, opening herself for his inevitable invasion, his only thought was of her.

"If you want me to stop simply say so." He kissed her cheek, her chin, her lips. "We can lie together, talk if that is your wish."

Fool! Never had he uttered such tender words. Never had he tried to talk a woman out of making love. But Vivienne was right. There was a crude term for what he'd done in the past, a term that in no way defined what was about to happen here.

Please say you want me.

She responded by smoothing her hands over the muscles in his back, arching into him. "I want my first time to be with you, Evan. Don't worry. I hear the pain is often exaggerated."

He wouldn't know.

But he knew how to make her want him, how to tongue her mouth the way he'd tongued her sex. It didn't take long for her to pant his name, to rock her hips and beg him to fill the emptiness.

He obliged. Hell, she was so tight, so warm and wet, so divine. The way she hugged his cock proved maddening. So maddening he almost forgot about her virtue as he moved in and out of her body. She moved with him, drawing him deeper with each moan of encouragement.

"Do it now," she breathed upon sensing his sudden hesitance.

He pushed past her maidenhead with one hard thrust.

She gasped, took a few seconds to catch her breath before reassuring him all was well and urging him to continue.

He might have spent time lavishing her breasts, frolicking and feasting, but the intensity of their passion, the urgency for release, had him rocking into her like a lovesick buck.

Vivienne Hart made him feel like a virgin.

She did not lie there demanding pleasure. She hugged every inch of his body, kissed the bulging muscles in his arms, stroked him, looked deep into his eyes as she took every hard thrust. She made him feel like a king amongst men, made him feel worshipped and adored.

Then she did something else new and novel—she cupped his cheek as she found her release, touched him tenderly as she milked his manhood and squeezed him tight. Hell, he managed to withdraw in time, but he wanted to fill this woman with his seed, pour everything of himself into her, leave her soaked, dripping with the evidence of his devotion.

CHAPTER 14

HOWARTH'S MATHEMATICAL, Optical and Nautical Instruments shop employed two staff. One middle-aged man, dressed impeccably in black and sporting a sturdy pair of spectacles, demonstrated how to use an octant and sighting telescope to his customer. Behind another oak counter, a young fellow with fashionable side-whiskers had numerous quizzing glasses displayed on a velvet-lined tray. Thankfully, the elegant lady inspecting the objects decided she would consult her husband and return forthwith.

After placing the items back inside the glass cabinet behind him, the fellow addressed them directly. "Good morning. May I be of assistance?"

Vivienne chuckled to herself. She wondered what the man knew of magnetism. Could he explain how Evan Sloane compelled her with his indeterminable force? How he wielded an invisible power that left her aching for his touch, longing to join him in bed?

Evan stepped closer to the counter, and she took a moment to admire his magnificent form. "We wish to speak to Mr Howarth," he said, unaware of her silent appraisal. "It's a matter of some urgency."

The man's expression turned apologetic. "I'm afraid he's occupied, making a pair of spectacles for a client who is to arrive shortly. If you would care to come back this afternoon, I can schedule an appointment."

Vivienne gave a discreet cough. "Might you tell him we are worried about a friend? Tell him Mr Sloane and Miss Hart are here at Mr Golding's behest."

Evan presented his calling card. "It's a matter of life and death."

The assistant appeared disturbed. A scan of Mr Sloane's card had him hurrying through the door at the end of the counter. He returned with a look of surprise and an invitation for them to join Mr Howarth in his private workshop.

One would expect the workshop of a maker of optical instruments to be full of tools for grinding and turning lenses, with measuring sticks and scientific apparatus. But they were shown into a dark, sumptuous room lit by candlelight, a room filled with curiosities and old tomes, a room carrying the smell of herbs and aromatic oils which grew more potent as they passed the display of unusual glass bottles.

An elderly gentleman, the age of Mr Golding, pushed out of a worn leather chair behind a cluttered desk. "Sloane and Hart. Good heavens. I never thought I'd see the day." He wiped his hands on his black apron and brushed a swathe of silver hair from his brow. "Do you have any idea how long I've waited?"

"Seventy years?" Vivienne suggested.

Mr Howarth laughed. "Not quite, my dear, but my father knew Livingston Sloane and Lucian Hart and left me with the task of safeguarding the treasure."

"Treasure?" Evan inhaled deeply and then glanced at the glass tubes in the rack on the desk. "Please tell me our ancestors weren't opium dealers."

"Opium? Lord, no." Mr Howarth's eye's glinted with recognition. "Ah, you can smell milk of the poppy. I'm an apothecary by trade, Mr Sloane, but I swore an oath to continue my father's legacy, and so Mr Jameson and Mr Austin deal with all matters of mathematics and optics."

Vivienne frowned. "Your assistant said you were making a pair of spectacles."

"Howarth is a trusted name when it comes to optical equipment and the like, Miss Hart. We must give the illusion I am skilled with a lens." He leaned closer and tapped his nose. "And though I imagine your ancestors have you darting this way and that, you're not here to purchase a compass."

"What do you know of the contract made between Livingston Sloane and Lucian Hart?" Evan spoke in the suspicious manner of a Bow Street constable. Evidently, he wished to draw information from Mr Howarth, not tell him their most guarded secrets.

"A direct descendant of Livingston Sloane is obliged to marry a direct descendant of Lucian Hart. It is a debt owed after Lucian risked his life to save his enemy."

"His enemy?" Vivienne didn't hide her shock. She glanced at Evan Sloane, the man who'd made her body sing with pleasure. "I thought they were firm friends."

Mr Howarth nodded. "They were, after the incident that almost cost Livingston his life."

"Do you know why they were enemies?" Vivienne wondered if it might be pertinent to the case.

"Perhaps *enemy* is too strong a word. They were rivals, rivals seeking the same goal until they both realised serving their country was all that truly mattered." He shrugged. "That's what my father told me. He said the men discovered a shared hatred for the aristocracy, for the hypocrisy rife in high society."

Evan's deep exhalation carried his frustration. "We agreed to abide by the contract. We followed a set of instructions written by our ancestors but relayed through Mr Golding. But now the gentleman is presumed missing, his office ransacked. I confess he expected something sinister to occur, which is why he wrote a letter and insisted we come to you."

Mr Howarth's expression turned grave. "Greed is a plague. A blight that scourges the hearts of men. Your ancestors believed only worthy beneficiaries should inherit. Not everyone agrees."

Vivienne wondered again about Charles Sloane. Resentment radiated from every fibre of his being. Had he not alluded to the unfairness of Evan inheriting indirectly from Lady Boscobel?

"Do you know who would wish to harm Mr Golding?" He seemed like such a sweet man. Whatever wickedness had befallen him had to stem from his knowledge of the contract. "Do you know who might wish to harm us?"

Mr Howarth suddenly stepped forward and gripped her hand. Evan looked ready to grab him by the throat and throttle him, but the gentleman's concerned mutterings eased the tension.

"Be wary of everyone, my dear, everyone. This is a test of loyalty. A test of integrity. A test that will push you both to the limits of your sanity."

She might have thought the man overly dramatic had it not been for the devil in the plague mask. The fact the villain had not shot at them again or found another means to attack them proved worrying.

"Everyone knows Livingston amassed a personal fortune. Everyone knows he left nothing but land in his will. It's a matter of public record, available to read for the price of a shilling."

"How is it you know so much about my grandfather?" Evan said in the quizzing tone of an enquiry agent. "How did your father know Livingston Sloane? Be trusted by him to keep something so important?"

Mr Howarth shrugged. "I seem to recall they met by chance in a tavern. Both had parents who tried to force them in certain directions. But Livingston helped my father finance his first optical instrument shop. Helped Golding's father, too. Yes, Livingston Sloane believed all men might rise to greatness if given a helping hand."

Vivienne stole a glance at Evan Sloane. Chin raised and wearing a satisfied grin, he appeared rather proud of his grandfather. The excited flutter in her chest had nothing to do with Livingston's benevolence. She cared only about easing Mr Sloane's pain.

Mr Howarth took a moment to study Evan Sloane, too. "I met your grandfather a couple of times as a boy. You have inherited his confident bearing. The question is, have you inherited his generous heart?"

On the subject of hearts—and the fact Evan Sloane had captured hers—it was time to press on with their investigation and discuss their wedding.

"Mr Golding said he must witness our marriage before we can receive the clues to finding our legacy. We cannot proceed until we find him." Vivienne withdrew the sealed letter from her reticule and handed it to Mr Howarth. "Should anything unto-ward happen, Mr Golding urged us to give you this note."

Taking the letter between bony fingers, the gentleman hurried to the lamp on his desk and examined the seal. He took hold of the quizzing glass dangling from a gold chain around his neck and studied the red wax.

"Yes, this bears the correct mark." He broke the wax and peeled back the folds, the lines between his brows deepening as he read.

"Does the note reveal anything of Golding's fears?" Evan asked.

"I'm afraid not. Rest assured, there are a few places where I might look for him."

"Assuming he has not met a tragic end."

"Just so. Just so." A weary sigh left the man's lips. "Well, I am instructed to inform you there has been a change of plan. There is no need for you to marry, and it seems pointless if Golding cannot bear witness. No. We will proceed as if the deed has been done."

No need to marry?
No need to marry!

Vivienne clutched her hand to her chest. It took tremendous effort not to stumble back in shock. No need to marry? My, she felt the pain of those words like a stab to the stomach. She had got used to the idea of waking next to Evan Sloane each morning —if only for a short while.

"Pointless?" Anger and disbelief warred in Evan's clipped tone. "But if we do not marry, I cannot honour my grandfather's debt. I cannot ... I cannot—" He broke off, his wide eyes searching her face, gauging her reaction.

Mr Howarth looked almost apologetic. "On that, I cannot comment. I am simply instructed to give you your wedding gifts."

"Do you not want to check Golding's office, confirm we speak the truth?"

"The fact you've asked the question tells me I can trust you, Mr Sloane."

Mr Howarth folded the letter. He dangled the end over the lit candle in the brass stick on his desk. Like the prospect of becoming Mr Sloane's wife, the paper disintegrated, shrivelling to nothing but blackened ash.

Mr Howarth dropped the remnants on the floor and stamped violently to extinguish the flame. Then he reached into the mouth of a skull positioned on a plinth and removed a key. The key belonged to a trunk on the far side of the room, and the man returned to present Vivienne with a fan.

"A fan?" Disappointment marred her tone.

Of what use was it to their investigation?

She spread it with a sharp snap, fanned her face before stopping to examine it in detail. The sticks looked to be ivory, the painted scenes small vignettes, each one depicting the theme of love and courtship. It smelt old and musty. Lord knows why Lucian Hart had left her such a gift.

"And I have something for you, Mr Sloane." Mr Howarth enlisted Evan's help to lift a large painting of fruit off the wall. "I trust you've brought your carriage."

Evan appeared equally crestfallen. "I often wonder what goes through an artist's mind when he paints mundane objects."

"One must read the symbolism," she said. "Fruit might represent fertility or the decay that comes with age. A pineapple might signify wealth, an apple the sins of the flesh."

Her cheeks grew hot as she recalled just how sinful they had been last night. Though was it a sin to show him how much she cared?

Mr Sloane smiled. "Then I might commission a painting of an apple cart."

"While this is all very interesting," Mr Howarth interjected, "the wedding gift lies beneath the painting of fruit. Might I suggest you attend to the matter in the privacy of your home?"

She met Evan's eyes. Their silent exchange held the same burning excitement—an eagerness to find another clue.

Mr Howarth removed his apron and draped it over the desk chair. "Now, I suppose I should get myself over to Long Lane and see what Bonnie has to say about my friend's disappearance."

"Bonnie?" Mr Sloane spoke first, though Vivienne was about to ask the same question.

"She runs the Old Red Crow. The woman knows the comings and goings of all those living in the lane." He blew out the candle in the stick and the one in the lamp. "Is there anything else I might help you with?"

"You have Mr Sloane's card," Vivienne said. "Please let us know the moment you find Mr Golding." Alive hopefully. Not that they needed him to witness a wedding, but she hoped he had not met a tragic end on their account.

The gentleman took his coat and hat off the stand and ushered them out of the workshop that looked more like a necromancer's spell room. They'd barely stepped out onto the pavement when he bid them a good day and hurried along Oxford Street.

Noticing them standing outside, Buchanan climbed down from atop the carriage and crossed the road. "Let me help with that, laddie, lest ye drop it on yer toes."

"Buchanan, I'm a man of thirty, not a laddie of ten."

Vivienne pursed her lips. "It's an endearment. It means he likes you."

"Aye, I mean nae offence, sir." Buchanan took hold of the painting. "I thought the shop sold compasses, nae paintings of fruit."

Vivienne glanced at Evan, feeling torn between her loyalty to Buchanan and the man who was her lover, not her husband. "It's a gift for Mr Sloane. A gift from his grandfather." Though it pained her, she was economical with the truth. She did not mention the hidden clue or the fan she'd thrust into her reticule.

"I'd have thought a seafaring man would have given ye a painting of a ship battling a violent storm, nae a basket of fruit."

"One must look for the symbolism, Buchanan." Evan grinned at her as he took hold of her arm and helped her cross the busy thoroughfare. After Buchanan had placed the picture inside the carriage, Evan said, "Might I ask you to do something?"

"Aye, sir. I'm here to help."

"Did you see the gentleman who left the shop with us?"

"Aye. The elderly man in the burgundy coat."

"I need you to follow him, see what he does when he reaches Long Lane. A man of his age won't walk to West Smithfield. Take a hackney and visit the Old Red Crow. Find out what you can about Bonnie, the proprietress. We shall reconvene at Keel Hall."

Mr Sloane went to thrust coins into Buchanan's hand, but the Scot refused. "I've money to pay for ale and the fare. I'd best be off if I mean to catch him." And with that, Buchanan pulled his greatcoat across his chest and hurried along the road.

"Hart Street, Turton." Evan helped Vivienne into the carriage. The second he closed the door and settled in his seat, he mentioned the topic she was hoping to avoid. "Vivienne, about last night. I—I assumed we would marry. I wouldn't have seduced you had I known ... known—"

She laughed, though as ridiculous as it was, a large part of her felt deeply saddened. "While I have no wish to diminish your masculine pride, sir, you were equally seduced. What happened last night stemmed from a mutual attraction. And I certainly have no regrets. Though it sounds as if you do."

He reached over the gilt picture frame—a barrier wedged between them—and grasped her hand. "I regret nothing."

She snatched her hand away. Touching him added to her confusion. "Then there is nothing more to say on the matter." Thankfully, it was but a five-minute drive to Hart Street. Once there, the conversation would turn to the case, not the chaos of emotions whirling around in her chest.

"We will discuss this latest development once we're home," he said, watching her constantly.

"Keel Hall is your home, not mine. It is foolish to pretend otherwise."

"Damn it, Vivienne. It's not my fault Golding instructed Howarth to give us these gifts without proof of a wedding. It is not my fault our ancestors made the pact."

He was right. They were both mere pawns in a game. "No, it is not your fault, but let's focus on the case and forget about this confounding attraction that exists between us."

"Forget?" His voice lowered to a whisper. "Forget the way it felt to be inside you? Forget the way you urged me to drive harder, deeper? Forget the fact I have never felt so connected to a woman?"

"Yes."

The carriage jerked to a halt outside the townhouse belonging to Lucius Daventry, used as the premises of the Order. Silence enveloped them like a thick shroud, making it hard to breathe, hard to speak. They remained silent as they alighted, remained silent when they entered the house and found the other agents seated in the drawing room.

They were not silent enough.

"Evidently, you've encountered a problem." Mr D'Angelo spoke with keen discernment. "If this melancholic mood is an insight into married life, I thank the devil for my bachelorhood."

Mr Daventry lowered his newspaper and glanced at the painting Mr Sloane had placed against the wall. "Is there a reason you've bought a picture of a fruit basket?"

"That's what married men do." Mr D'Angelo's Italian brown eyes glinted with amusement. "They turn into old maids. Next, you'll find he's swapped his brandy for fruit punch, his stallion for a lame donkey."

Mr Cole shook his head. "You have a pessimistic view of marriage, D'Angelo."

"I have a pessimistic view of life, Cole. Still, when a man buys a painting of—"

"He didn't buy the painting." Vivienne couldn't bear all this talk of marriage. "Mr Howarth gave us the wedding gifts left by our grandfathers. The fruit basket is merely hiding a clue to our legacy."

Their curiosity aroused, all four men straightened.

Mr Daventry frowned. "But I thought the man needed Golding's sworn testimony as proof of your marriage?"

"We gave him the sealed letter from Golding." Mr Sloane's sharp tone roused some confusion with his colleagues. He failed to mention they did not need to marry. "Apparently, the lawyer changed the plans."

"As an agent of the Order, one must adapt to changing

circumstances." Mr Daventry folded his newspaper and placed it on the low table between the sofas. "Such things rarely faze you, Sloane, yet your agitation is plain for all to see."

A deep-rooted need to defend Evan Sloane took command of Vivienne's tongue. "Nothing about this is easy. A man might remain objective when helping a stranger. Not so when every new piece of information challenges his beliefs."

Knowing glances passed between the men.

"Then let us focus on solving this case." Mr Cole relaxed back on the sofa. "I can tell you that Mr Ramsey is engaged in an affair with the owner of the Old Red Crow."

Vivienne was not surprised. Mr Ramsey had made no secret of his love for her mother, though the feeling was not at all mutual. Mr Ramsey made no secret of his love for all women.

"With Bonnie?" Evan asked.

"Yes. He visits at least three times a week, has done for the last six months. Ramsey lavishes the woman with expensive gifts and has run up extensive debts in various shops around town, most notably perfumeries and chocolatiers."

Vivienne swallowed deeply. The news supported her theory that Mr Ramsey was a consummate deceiver. A cad.

"Then perhaps there's something else you should know about him." A blush as hot as furnace coals warmed her cheeks. "In his usual tactile way, Mr Ramsey suggested I need a mature gentleman to take care of me, to provide the necessary comforts."

Evan Sloane muttered a vile curse.

"He made similar advances to my mother."

Mr D'Angelo snorted his contempt. "These lecherous sorts take advantage of anyone they deem weak."

Vivienne agreed. "We might assume he learnt about the legacy from my father. That what he desires is to wed me and get his clammy hands on the treasure."

Mr D'Angelo consulted his small notebook. "Bonnie is a rampant sort. Mr Wicks visits almost daily and spends time in her private rooms."

"Or is he visiting Ramsey, and Bonnie is the facilitator?" Mr Sloane rubbed his sculpted jaw. The deep sound of his curious hum sent a shiver from her neck to her navel. "So Wicks purchases the masks, while Ramsey plays the intruder to frighten Miss Hart."

"Then who fired shots at your coach?" Vivienne asked.

"It's easy to hire a thug from the rookeries, though most are skilled with blades, not pistols. Hence the reason Turton escaped with nothing but a minor injury."

Mr D'Angelo flashed a confident grin. "You might be right. The owner of the tea shop in Long Lane said Wicks has been acting strangely since his mother died. He gave me the woman's name, and I discovered she left her house to her brother, Mr Golding, not her wayward son."

No wonder the man had turned to the bottle.

"Mr Ramsey must have followed me to the lawyer's office," she said. Or he might have noticed her when leaving the inn. "He formed a partnership with Mr Wicks so they might share the bounty."

"It certainly seems like a logical deduction," Mr Daventry agreed. "Now, we must make plans to prove or disprove the theory."

The more she thought about it, the more she believed Mr Ramsey was a cunning devil capable of all kinds of atrocities.

All they had to do now was set a trap to catch both men, solve the clues, find their legacy, and that would be the end of the case. Then she would be free to leave town, to start a new life in the far reaches of Scotland, far from the gentleman who had stolen her heart.

So why did she feel sick to the pit of her stomach?

Why did she have to fight back a barrage of tears?

CHAPTER 15

"I HATE to be the one to upset the apple cart, but I have news that might point to another potential suspect." Ashwood paused when Mrs Gunning entered with fresh coffee and a plate of macaroons.

D'Angelo flashed the housekeeper a charming smile. "You know the way to a man's heart, Mrs Gunning. There's nothing like the sweet taste of almonds on one's tongue."

Evan had tasted something far sweeter, something much more satisfying. Since waking this morning, he'd thought of nothing but pressing his mouth to Vivienne Hart's soft skin. Then Howarth said marrying was pointless, and she seemed reluctant to continue their affair. And it was an affair. Nothing could change the fact they were lovers.

Evan drew his mind back to their present dilemma. "Have you discovered something about Lady Hollinshead?" Ashwood had been tasked with making enquiries into the countess' background.

Vivienne was about to take a bite of her macaroon when she hesitated and placed the biscuit back on her china tea plate. "But the countess is a lady of high moral virtue."

"That may be," Ashwood said, "but she is desperately unhappy in her marriage. I have it on good authority the earl has cut off her funds. She told him she has served her time and wishes to return to Scotland. He reminded her who rules the roost."

Vivienne's shoulders sagged. "The earl treats her terribly. He blames her for not bearing his children, taunts her with his many mistresses. Thirty years is far too long to remain married to an ogre. My mother always hoped the countess would find the strength to leave."

"It seems she has opted for Boston, not Scotland. She sent her lady's maid to purchase passage on *The Maybury*, leaving from Liverpool one week hence."

"Boston? Strange she made no mention of it." Vivienne looked worried, not annoyed. "While her situation is terribly sad, what has it to do with the shots fired or the damaged painting?"

"She pawned a brooch and a necklace to pay for the tickets," Ashwood replied. "How will she fund a lavish lifestyle across the water? Being a good friend of your mother, maybe she knows about the contract, knows Sloane and Hart hid treasure, and you're close to finding a fortune."

A shiver ran the length of Evan's spine, though it had nothing to do with the fact the countess might be a cunning thief. "You said tickets. She's not going alone?"

"I believe she's taking her maid."

Vivienne snorted. "I doubt she'll get far. Lord Hollinshead has spies everywhere. The countess told me so herself. And if she's leaving next week, how does she mean to steal our legacy?"

"That's something we need to discover." Daventry turned his attention to the painting propped against the wall. "Sloane, focus on following the clues and discovering your grandfather's intention. We will continue to pry into all the suspects' affairs. We will meet here daily until the matter is resolved."

D'Angelo hummed and narrowed his gaze. "So, if you have your wedding gifts, must you still marry? And if not, is it wise for Miss Hart to remain at Keel Hall? Surely the longer she is there, the greater the risk of discovery."

The devil. Trust D'Angelo to focus on the one point certain to cause distress. And based on Vivienne's flush of embarrassment, the reason Evan wanted her at Keel Hall was evident.

"There is more to this than finding treasure," Evan countered. "Our lives are in danger. And we've the matter of a vow, a contract." And the host of unfamiliar feelings plaguing his mind and body. "We will do as Daventry said, follow the clues and see where they lead us."

D'Angelo's teasing grin said he had the full measure of the situation. "Then are we permitted to see what's behind the basket of fruit?"

Daventry pushed to his feet. "I think it prudent they examine the painting privately. Someone may have followed them here. Should the fiend catch a glimpse of a map, he may attack their carriage on the quiet road through Little Chelsea."

"Perhaps one of us should follow behind," Cole suggested. "Ensure they arrive safely."

"Agreed. D'Angelo will go." Daventry bowed over Miss Hart's hand when she stood. "Report here tomorrow with any new developments." Then he bid the men good day and took his leave.

D'Angelo stole a macaroon off the plate and popped it into his mouth before helping Evan carry the painting to the carriage while Ashwood engaged Vivienne in conversation.

"Tell Turton to drive like the devil. I have an appointment in town in an hour and cannot be late." D'Angelo pushed the painting between the seats and brushed dust off his coat and hands.

"An appointment? You should have told Daventry to send someone else."

D'Angelo glanced quickly behind. "Then I would have to tell him I'm conducting a personal investigation."

A personal investigation!

Evan knew what that meant. D'Angelo lived to avenge the death of his parents. If his meeting involved romping beneath the bedsheets with a buxom widow, the fellow would have a lascivious glint in his eye.

"Tell me you're not risking your neck, scouring the rookeries on a hunch. Wait until I've dealt with this matter and I shall accompany you on your crusade."

"Sloane, I'll not have you gamble with your life. Any fool can see what's happening between you and Miss Hart. It's only a matter of time before I'm left alone again. The orphan. The bachelor. It matters not."

Bitterness filled D'Angelo's heart.

The poison tainted his mind, tormented his soul.

"We're like brothers, D'Angelo. The bond we share cannot be broken. My relationship with Miss Hart changes nothing between us. Promise you'll wait until I can assist you."

D'Angelo gripped Evan's shoulder in a masculine gesture of affection. "I'll not drag you into this when your heart is engaged, when you have the prospect of a bright future. Not when you've spent all these years alone, too. But I swore an oath. An oath to find the devil who shot my parents. An oath to find the bastard who murdered an unarmed woman in front of her young son."

He wiped his face as if it were still smeared with his mother's blood.

D'Angelo wore his pain like a second skin—hidden beneath the expert cut of his clothes, beneath his masculine charm and devil-may-care attitude. To the trained eye, it was there in every sleek movement, every mocking grin.

"Let me help you."

"No. Not when I plan to fight with every breath in my lungs. Not when I'm determined to fight to the death."

Evan sat before the fire in the drawing room, waiting for Vivienne to fetch the fan given as a wedding gift by a grandfather who'd died years ago, for a marriage that hadn't taken place.

The thrill of anticipation was marred by the fact he couldn't shake D'Angelo's comment from his mind. Few men had the strength to die for a cause. Few men had witnessed such a tragedy and managed to remain sane.

Vivienne returned, dressed in the simple blue gown she had worn to dinner, when they had talked about everyone and everything aside from what had occurred last night. Wasn't he supposed to forget he'd made love to a woman he cared about?

"I brought the book of Thomas Gray's poems." Clutching the

book to her chest, she sat in the chair beside him. "We might stumble upon a connection once we decipher the clues."

"Golding mentioned the poet for a reason." Evan gestured to the two glasses on the side table positioned between the chairs. "I had Carter mix your drink. If it's too strong, I can pour you a glass of sherry."

She smiled, though it failed to reach her eyes. She'd been subdued since Howarth made his damning declaration. "The last one scorched my tonsils."

"You mentioned trying a whipkull—the nectar of a Viking warrior. Is it not a better way to drink rum?"

"You remembered."

"How could I forget?" Strange how he remembered nothing of his previous romantic encounters, yet recalled every precise detail of the time spent with her.

Any fool can see what is happening between you and Miss Hart.

Well, he was glad D'Angelo could, as he hadn't a damn clue.

She captured a glass and sipped the creamy liquid. "Hmm. It's extremely sweet. So sweet, I can hardly taste the rum. To a novice, I daresay it could be quite lethal."

"You mean I might need to carry you to bed."

She stole a glance at him but looked away. His gaze never left her.

"Perhaps we should play a game while I have an advantage," he said, for he could not forget the feel of her soft, pliant body, could not forget she aroused his mind as much as his manhood.

"Have we not got a more important task to attend to?"

"What's more important than lovers bearing their souls?"

She rolled her eyes but did not contradict him. "At least you're honest. It seems we were destined to be lovers, never man and wife."

"When it comes to relationships, honesty is the jewel in the crown." He decided to avoid the topic of marriage. She was right. They did not have time to argue or wallow in regrets. "The gem that leaves most people gawping in awe."

"You mean too many lovers keep secrets."

"Too many lie and deceive."

She looked at the small leather-bound book in her lap. "Can I ask you something?"

"Ask me anything."

Her gaze drifted from the book to him, though it took a moment for her to find the courage to speak. "What did you say to Mrs Worthing during those fifteen minutes you were alone at the masquerade? Did you dance? Did you—"

The questions shocked him. "I didn't see Mrs Worthing, or dance with her, or do anything one might deem inappropriate. I used the time to speak to a few men I know—Lord Fox, Mr Trenton-Parker, amongst others."

Their eyes met. The flash of vulnerability said she cared.

"I wanted them to see me alone, Vivienne. You made the mistake of lowering your mask when you spoke to Mrs Worthing." He'd made the mistake of revealing too much. "Gossip spreads like wildfire. She'll be the first to strike a flint and spark her own version of the tale. I didn't want anyone presuming we had consummated our union. It would have been the obvious assumption had we danced."

"I would have clung to you like a love-sick fool." A sweet chuckle escaped her. "Having spent too much time watching the proceedings, I lack experience in the dancing department, too."

She lacked nothing when it came to lovemaking.

"And while I'm considered somewhat exceptional on the dance floor," he said, "I'd have been a quivering wreck the second I took you in my arms."

The air thrummed with sexual tension.

Was she remembering the moment he pushed deep into her body?

Was she imagining him doing so again?

She snapped open the old fan and waved it before her flushed cheeks. Yes, her mind was engaged with illicit visions. Perhaps they should see what lay behind the painted picture of fruit and then move to more pleasurable pursuits.

"May I look at the vignettes on the fan?"

Vivienne handed him the delicate object. "They're scenes of love and courtship."

Evan studied the white-wigged figures dressed in clothes

fashionable seventy years ago. One vignette showed the couple dancing. One showed them sitting beneath a tree, the gentleman reading while the lady listened. One showed the gentleman bowing over his lady's hand, ignoring the scantily clad women bathing in the lake behind.

"Interesting," he said, for a harem of naked women could not tear him away from Vivienne Hart.

"Perhaps you should get on your knees and examine the gift from your grandfather."

Evan thought to tease her. Livingston Sloane had sent him a sea nymph bursting with intelligence and passion. No other gift could compare. "I'll get to that once I've discovered what lies behind the painting of fruit."

He stood, took the painting hanging in the space left by Livingston Sloane's portrait, and placed it on the floor before the hearth.

Vivienne came and knelt beside him. The nearness of her body made it hard to concentrate on the task, but he took his knife and set to work prising the stretcher bars away from the frame.

"I thought there might be a label on the panel—the name of the artist." She kept her hands clasped in her lap and watched intently. "But then your grandfather wouldn't want you following a false trail."

"No, clearly it's not important." The wood groaned and creaked against Evan's assault, but he freed the stretched canvas from the gilt frame, leaving the painted board of a fruit basket still in place.

They both gasped when Evan turned the canvas around to reveal the same painting of Livingston Sloane that had hung to the left of the mantelpiece since he was a boy.

"How odd," she said, drawing his mind back to the moment she entered the bedchamber, and his world changed for the better. "It's identical. The table, the window, the date, they're all the same."

"Not entirely the same." He pointed to the open book. "Now we know the name of the poem."

Vivienne squinted. *"Elegy Written in a Country Churchyard.* It's a poem about death. How might a person be remembered? How some are forgotten while others live on in people's memories?"

"I'm not familiar with it." He avoided anything morbid. "Ashwood will have an opinion. He's fond of poetry, though usually of the more amorous sort."

Vivienne captured the book from the chair and flicked to the relevant page. She sat reading while Evan stared at the familiar image of his grandfather, looking for other unique differences. An obvious one made him jerk his head back.

"The compass points northeast." And there was something different about the landscape beyond the window. He tugged the bell pull and had Fitchett bring his best magnifying glass from the study. "You've not heard from Buchanan?" he asked when the butler returned.

"No, sir, though his first note said not to expect him back until morning."

That was another odd thing. Howarth must have left London in his search for Golding. Thankfully, Vivienne confirmed it was Buchanan who'd written the note, else Evan might have suspected the masked rider was somehow involved.

"And what of Mrs McCready?"

"Gone for a long walk in the garden, sir. She complained about supper, about the house being dusty, about the fact she should be in Silver Street, not stuck in the devil's lair."

"Nothing out of the ordinary, then."

"No, sir."

"Mrs McCready can be rather dramatic," Vivienne said as soon as Fitchett left the room and closed the door.

"While Buchanan's talents are obvious, I struggle to see why you entertain the grouch."

"Mrs McCready is loyal to a fault. She served as my mother's companion for years and loved her dearly. Her moods stem from her longing to go home, that's all."

"Back to the Highlands?"

"Yes."

And Vivienne would accompany the woman once this was all over, unless he persuaded her to stay. Perhaps their inheritance was worth a small fortune, enough for her to remain in town.

Holding that thought, Evan resumed his study of the painting, peering through the looking glass, moving it back and forth to sharpen his focus. He noticed a couple sitting under a tree amid the sprawling fields and did not recall seeing them in the original painting.

"Might I look at the fan again?" He took the proffered fan and considered the vignettes. "Well, I'll be damned."

Vivienne immediately closed the book. "What have you found?"

"If I'm not mistaken, everything leads to Highwood, my country estate." Evan pointed to the vignette on the fan. "The house in the background is identical to the old Elizabethan mansion. And it's northeast of here."

"Why would it lead there?"

"Highwood was a wedding gift to Daniel Sloane and Jane Boscobel. When Livingston's older brother Cecil inherited the viscountcy and the Leaton estates, Lady Boscobel decreed Highwood would go to Livingston's heir—my father."

Vivienne thought for a moment. "Presumably, that's why Charles Sloane is annoyed. He believes it should have gone to the eldest son."

According to Charles Sloane, a pirate's offspring didn't deserve to own anything. "Highwood was not entailed, so Lady Boscobel could do as she pleased."

They both stared at the painting, lost in thought.

"Something doesn't make sense." Vivienne glanced at the sash window before continuing. "Lady Boscobel's actions suggest she loved Livingston despite his nefarious antics. Yet she refused to acknowledge the contract, told Lucian Hart she had disowned her son."

Evan grew up wondering if the mother and son had shared a bond. Livingston and his wife, Maria, had returned to Highwood weeks before both dying of a fever. And Lady Boscobel had welcomed them, had agreed to raise their son. Why?

"Wealthy people seek to protect their assets. Perhaps she didn't want Lucian Hart thinking he could make a claim on the estate. But Livingston is buried in a mausoleum there."

"A churchyard in the country?"

"Not quite. He's buried on the estate. The fact Thomas Gray's poem is about death leads me to think we should make the forty-mile journey to Bedfordshire."

Vivienne glanced twice at the window, though the curtains were drawn. "I cannot shake the sense we're being watched. I had the same feeling when we entered Mr Howarth's shop, and again when we left the office of the Order."

Evan gripped her hand and squeezed it gently. His pulse raced. "I've felt the same for days, but you're safe here." He leant closer and pressed a reassuring kiss on her lips. He longed to touch her, touch her anywhere, touch her everywhere. "No one will hurt you while I've breath in my lungs."

She stared at his mouth, inching closer as if drawn by his magnetic pull. "But soon I must leave here, Evan."

"Let's not think about that now. We've the gift of today. Despite what you said, I cannot forget how good you make me feel, Vivienne, how good we are together."

His words inflamed her. She reached for him, her hands sliding wildly over his chest, around his neck, her fingers tugging at his hair. Then she kissed him in a maddening way that had them pushing aside the painting, had him seizing her around the waist, crushing her to his chest.

They were on their knees, locked together, their tongues deep in each other's mouths, mating in a fierce frenzy, as if time were precious and they hadn't a second to lose.

Hell, he'd never been so aroused.

Every muscle in his body was as hard as his cock. He gripped her buttocks, massaging in such a way as to tease her sex. Damn, he yearned to push inside her, craved that first thrust.

She tore her mouth away, fixing him with hungry brown eyes. "I need you, Evan. I need you now. Do you understand?"

He understood. She needed to feel full with him, needed to satisfy the insatiable ache, needed to feel this invisible yet tangible thing that existed between them, this thing he couldn't explain.

"We must be quick."

"Just hurry."

He sat on the floor, his back against the sofa, his placket

open, his cock a rod of iron. Vivienne gathered her skirts to her waist and came to sit astride him as he instructed. She sank down so slowly he almost flooded her with his seed.

Her head fell back. Her mouth fell open.

He'd already fallen, fallen hard days ago.

"Show me how well you ride, love—gallop, canter, you choose."

"Let's start with a teasing trot." She came up on her knees, moaned as she sheathed him to the root.

He didn't care how she rode him. He reached under her skirts, found the sensitive nub, caressed, teased and tormented until she convulsed around him, crying out in ecstasy.

With some urgency, he pulled out of her body, came by his own hand.

They sat there, breathless. Yet he knew from the look in her glazed eyes she would want him again before the night was through. He wanted her, too. He wanted to do everything, walk, talk until the early hours, play games, solve cases, probe her body, her mind.

A sudden knock on the door had him wiping his hand on his shirt in a panic, left them both hurrying to straighten their clothes and look reasonably presentable.

"Enter," he called, aware the scent of sated lust hung in the air.

Fitchett appeared. "Forgive me, sir, but it's a matter of the utmost urgency. You asked to be informed when I heard from Mr Buchanan."

"Has he returned?"

"No, sir. A boy arrived in a hackney. He brought a note." Fitchett stepped forward with the salver. "Buchanan paid the boy's return fare."

Evan took the note and read it quickly. "We need to head to town."

Vivienne gasped. "Tonight? Is everything all right?"

"Yes, we're to meet Buchanan in Lambeth, south side of Walcot Square. It appears he's found Golding and Wicks."

CHAPTER 16

W ALCOT SQUARE CONSISTED of two rows of terrace houses facing a communal green, though Vivienne wondered why it was considered a square when it resembled a triangle.

"You're certain both men are in the house?" Evan addressed Buchanan in a hushed voice, despite the fact they stood hidden in the shadows.

"Aye. I met both men when I escorted Miss Hart to the office a few weeks ago. It's them. Golding answered the door to the fellow in the burgundy coat. He went inside, left two hours later. Then Wicks left and took off towards Kennington Road."

"But he came back," Vivienne confirmed.

"Aye, stumbling about the street and singing a country ballad. Golding ushered him inside and slammed the door. That was about an hour ago."

Vivienne glanced at Evan, though it was difficult to concentrate when remembering the wanton way she'd claimed his body. Indeed, she would rather be astride him in front of a roaring fire than standing in the dark on a cold, damp night.

"So," she said with a shrug. "What's the plan?"

With his mouth curled in a wicked grin, Evan looked like Lucifer's prodigy. "We'll hammer on the door until someone answers. One's past seventy, the other a drunken lout, I doubt they'll run." He looked at Buchanan. "You'll remain with us."

"I canna wait to hear why the canny old devil lied."

"Mr Golding hasn't exactly lied, Buchanan. He might be hiding here in fear of his life."

"You must be cold, Buchanan, and I'm desperate to get home to my bed." Something in Evan's tone hinted there was space for her there, too. "Let's get this over with."

They strode across the square, opened the wrought-iron gate of Number 8, and mounted the five stone steps. Evan banged the black door with his clenched fist, raised the brass knocker and slammed it against the plate. No one came.

Vivienne inhaled. "Someone is home. I can smell stewed cabbage."

"Och, the devil just peered through the gap in the curtains."

Evan knocked again.

They heard the scuffle of feet, raised voices and barked orders, before Mr Golding called, "Wait! Wait! I'm coming!" He opened the door and craned his neck to look over Evan's shoulder. "Hurry. Come inside before every fortune hunter in London knows you're here."

He ushered them in quickly, closed the door and slid the bolt across.

Vivienne followed the lawyer into the front room. "We've been so worried. Out of our minds wondering what happened." She sat in the chair closest to the hearth as directed, glad of an opportunity to warm her hands, though the thought left her picturing Evan Sloane's muscular chest. "We feared you'd met a grisly end."

"Forgive me, my dear." Mr Golding gestured to the sofa, and the old thing creaked when Buchanan and Evan dropped into the seat. "We had no option but to leave Long Lane."

"I gave you my card," Evan snapped. "You could have let us know you were safe. Had we not gone to visit Howarth, we would still be wandering aimlessly in the dark."

Mr Golding's weary sigh carried the weight of a seventy-year burden. He sat in the wingback chair opposite Vivienne and shook his head.

"You must understand. My father swore to follow the instructions set by Livingston Sloane and Lucian Hart. I swore to repay my father's debt and do the same. My loyalty is to them first and foremost. It was a condition I remove myself from Long Lane, so you couldn't find me."

Evan's jaw firmed. "Our ancestors underestimated our talents."

"I don't suppose Livingston considered the fact his grandson would be an enquiry agent. Not when your father was raised by one of society's grand matrons."

"Like Livingston Sloane, I do what I please. I do not bow to society's hypocritical demands."

"A philosophy that would have made him proud."

Evan's mood altered—his annoyance replaced by a sad introspection. Vivienne thought she knew why.

"It's strange we should feel deeply connected to men we've never met." She considered her mother's serene temperament, her father's need for praise. "I share Mr Sloane's loathing of rigid rules. A trait I must have inherited from my grandfather."

Evan managed a smile. "I imagine he would be equally proud, Miss Hart."

"All the more reason to continue playing their game."

"To prove we have their mettle?"

"Yes."

Buchanan sat forward and glared at Mr Golding. "So, was the office ransacked before ye left or after?"

A blush tainted Mr Golding's wrinkled cheeks. He winced. "I'm afraid my aim was to make you fear the worst. We made the mess, you see, made it appear—"

"Why?" Evan demanded. "For what possible reason?"

Again, Mr Golding looked pained. "To make it difficult for you to marry. To see if you had the gumption, the initiative, a deep-rooted desire to abide by the contract and follow the clues."

Evan muttered something damning beneath his breath. "My newfound respect for my grandfather diminishes by the second."

"They're testing us, Mr Sloane. Making sure we've inherited their wisdom, their integrity, before we inherit their wealth. What the eyes do not see, the heart cannot follow. From beyond the grave, they're creating facades, putting up barriers, dangling bait, all to see if we're worthy."

Evan's smirk spoke of contempt. "Did they not stop to consider the fact you might have been killed by the masked intruder, by the devil shooting at you in the dark?"

He had a valid point—but the comment roused her suspicions.

Was it not Mr Wicks who purchased the masks?

The odd groaning noise came from Mr Golding, not the old sofa. "You were never in any real danger, not from the masked figure."

Not in any danger?

Suddenly everything fell into place.

Vivienne gritted her teeth, recalling how terrified she'd been when the carriage overturned in the field. "Your nephew purchased the plague masks from Mrs Mulligan's costume shop. He followed me to Keel Hall because it was your idea I go there." Her temper flared. "Mr Sloane is right. I could have been killed in that accident just so you could follow instructions."

"Forgive me," Mr Golding pleaded. "The drunken fool was supposed to fire into the air, not at the coachman."

"You! You destroyed the painting of Livingston Sloane!" With a face like thunder, Evan shot to his feet.

"No, no, no. I took the painting for safekeeping, threw some old bits of wood into the fire to make it seem as if someone wanted to steal your legacy." Mr Golding started shaking. "Please. Please. If you will just calm your tempers and listen. Please. I doubt my heart can take any more stress."

"Stress!" Evan spat. "My life has been an utter nightmare since learning of the contract."

A sharp pang in Vivienne's chest made her catch her breath. It had been far from a nightmare. She'd had the most wonderful time of her life.

Evan suddenly caught himself. His eyes locked with hers.

She tore her gaze from his, pressed her lips together to halt her tears.

"Let me tell you everything," Mr Golding pleaded, oblivious to her inner torment. "Then you may continue as planned."

Evan dropped into the seat. She could feel him watching her, staring, but she focused on Mr Golding. "Let me save you the trouble. You told me to go to Keel Hall and discuss the contract with Mr Sloane. You and your nephew followed me there. Being a gentleman, you knew Mr Sloane would insist his coachman take me home. Then, while your nephew shot at us, you entered Keel Hall and took the painting."

"Yes. I'm ashamed to say that is how it happened."

"Yet you couldn't have known we would have an accident, or that Mr Sloane would ride to our rescue. How would you have taken the painting otherwise?"

Mr Golding dragged his hand down his face. "We surveyed the house, knew the window was often left open, knew to wait until the coast was clear. I had terrible trouble climbing under the raised sash and had to give the jarvey three sovereigns for his help."

Vivienne had no sympathy.

"How did you know where to find the painting?"

"You told me the butler let you into the drawing room to examine the painting of Livingston Sloane."

Heavens! She had told him that.

"You must understand, my dear, when you first came to me with the contract, my heart leapt at the prospect of helping you secure the legacy. I feared Sloane and Hart's scheme would die with me, and it would have all been for nothing."

"You wished to ensure I played my part," Evan said coldly. "That's why you took the painting. As the grandson of a pirate, you knew I would never let anyone steal my bounty."

"I had to bring you together. I had to make sure you found the treasure, else I would have tossed and turned in my grave for all eternity."

It was Buchanan's turn to lose his temper. "So one of ye devil's broke into the house in Silver Street, made a hell of a mess and left a plague mask to frighten the lass to death."

An icy chill ran down Vivienne's spine.

She'd spent sleepless nights waiting for the devil to return.

Fear had taken her to Mr Golding's office.

Desperation had taken her to Keel Hall.

Mr Golding cradled his head in his hands. "The intruder was the impetus needed to give Miss Hart the courage to visit Mr Sloane."

Buchanan muttered in Gaelic. "The sooner I get the lass out of this miserable place and back to the Highlands, the better."

The thought of sitting amongst the heather, of paddling her feet in the burn, seemed so appealing. Tears welled. Sad, that her heart would always belong to the man who might have been her husband.

"Then let us solve these clues, Buchanan, so you can take me home."

"Aye, lass."

An awkward silence ensued, made more difficult as she battled her emotions.

"Don't think for one moment you're safe now." The lawyer's grave comment cut through the stillness. "You must take every precaution. Greed lives in the hearts of men. Find the treasure and then return to me in Long Lane."

"And why should we trust a word you say?" Evan said bluntly. "Your nephew spends a lot of time at the Old Red Crow, and not just to fill himself with ale. Why not call him in and ask him about his relationship with Bonnie?"

"Because he's three sheets to the wind and of no use to anyone. But he visits Bonnie to drown his sorrows. Who am I to deny his quest for peace?"

The comment must have resonated because Evan paused for thought.

"Mr Ramsey is an old family friend who knew my father." The mere mention of the man made Vivienne's skin crawl. "He also visits Bonnie, and pesters me weekly, insinuating my life would greatly improve if I were his wife. His debts are mounting, as is his need to find the means to pay. Now tell me that is a coincidence, Mr Golding."

Mr Golding's chin dropped. He gripped the arms of the chair with his bony fingers and pushed to his feet. "Excuse me a moment while I discuss this with my nephew."

The second the lawyer left the room Buchanan spouted threats.

"I swear I shall string Ramsey up from the scaffold and let the crows poke at his flabby flesh. Did I nae tell ye, lass, to stop inviting the lech into yer home? And as for that drunken devil upstairs, why I'll shove his head in a whisky cask and wait till there are nae more bubbles."

Evan Sloane seemed disinterested in Buchanan's ramblings. "Miss Hart." His intense gaze pinned her to the chair. "When I described this unfolding nightmare, I spoke of our frustration. My comment in no way reflected the nature of our relationship."

Did he have to speak so openly in front of Buchanan? Yes, the man knew they were supposed to marry, but knew nothing of their amorous liaisons.

"Pay it no mind, Mr Sloane. You were right. Mr Golding and his nephew have pushed us to the limits of our patience."

As if on cue, the shouting started above stairs. She hoped Mr Wicks had stumbled whilst in a drunken stupor, and the loud bang was not him assaulting his uncle.

Evan glanced at the ceiling. "Perhaps I should intervene."

"It might be prudent."

Evan pushed to his feet, but the slow plod of footsteps on the stairs made him hesitate.

Flustered, Mr Golding hobbled back into the room. "It seems this Ramsey fellow knows you've been to visit me numerous times and has asked Bonnie to probe my nephew for information. He swears he's told her nothing about the contract or the delicate nature of our business."

"Bonnie's a rum old lass. I can tell ye that." Buchanan grinned. "Aye, she'd have told me anything I needed to know in exchange for a few shillings and my company this evening."

Mr Wicks was hardly discreet in his drunkenness. Drunken fools had loose tongues. No doubt Bonnie extracted enough information to please Mr Ramsey. After all, Mr Ramsey was the one bringing gifts.

"We must assume Wicks was too inebriated to recall the conversation," Evan said, coming to the obvious conclusion. "I caution you against telling your nephew anything about our business in future."

Mr Golding's shoulders sagged. "I'm tired, Mr Sloane, weary, and seek a quick end to this matter. There's little more for me to do or say. I suggest you attempt to find your legacy with the clues given. When you do, return to me in Long Lane, and I shall read the last entries in the notebook."

The lawyer was scared. Fear clung to him like a starving urchin. She had seen it that day in his office, and it gripped him now. He'd manipulated events because he wanted this business done quickly.

"You're hiding here," she blurted. "It's not just about the instructions in the notebook. You're frightened. You believe someone has discovered you have knowledge of the clues, and now you know that man is Mr Ramsey."

"Money is the devil's currency, Miss Hart. It makes good men do wicked things. If this Mr Ramsey knows of my involvement, I suspect he will come knocking."

"Perhaps you should remove to Keel Hall until this is all over," Evan suggested.

"There's no need." Mr Golding lowered his voice. "Should anything untoward happen, you must visit the optician." He paused and caught his breath. "We should part now. The rest is up to you."

They left the house wiser than when they entered.

In the coming days, you'll not know who to trust.

When Mr Golding uttered those words in his office, Vivienne hadn't imagined he might be referring to himself. By rights, she should be angry, livid, but his actions stemmed from desperation. The same urgency to get this matter over with now compelled her.

Vivienne and Evan waited in the carriage on Kennington Road, while Buchanan scouted the area to ensure Mr Ramsey hadn't followed them to Lambeth. Within seconds of them settling into their seats, Evan mentioned the subject tormenting both their minds.

"Vivienne, let me explain what I meant earlier."

"Honestly, there is no need. You were happy until I arrived amid a thunderstorm to turn your life upside down." And all because Mr Golding had encouraged her to deal with things promptly.

"I wasn't exactly ha—"

"I would never have held you to the contract if it wasn't for finding our legacy. I thought our lives were in danger. I didn't know it was Mr Wicks who'd donned a mask and ransacked my home." Yet despite all the trauma and turmoil, she wouldn't change a thing. She'd suffer again for one kiss from Evan Sloane's skilled lips.

"Vivienne, I didn't lie earlier. The struggle for the truth has been wrought with problems. But I see our relationship as separate to the case. Indeed, I hope things continue once we've found our lost legacy."

She'd like nothing more than to spend her life wrapped in his arms, but it was a fantasy. Everything had changed.

She had fallen in love with him, this spectacular specimen of a man who stole hearts, not bounty. These strange emotions had to be love. The longing, the profound ache, excitement, desire, her preoccupation with his happiness—the list was endless—the willingness to make sacrifices.

"Evan, I don't regret anything that's happened between us, but I cannot be your mistress. And we would have been fools to marry because of a contract. I know that now." Knowing he'd married her out of duty would hurt more than being apart.

"What are you saying?"

She fought the urge to slide across the carriage and ease the tension from his shoulders, soothe the frown lines from his brow. "That we should do as Mr Golding says. Concentrate on solving this quickly. Forget everything else."

"Forget? You're rather fond of that word." He remained silent for a time, his gaze focused on the window. "Will you not stay with me tonight?"

"I think it unwise to do—"

"Please, Vivienne." He settled those hypnotic green eyes upon her. "Come to my room. Have the bed. I'll take the chair. Just stay with me."

She smiled. "We'll be writhing between the sheets within a minute of you closing the door."

He managed a smile, too. "You thrust the scroll into my hand

and said you trusted me. Let me keep my word. Let me prove your trust is not misplaced."

How could she resist such a heartfelt plea?

"I suppose it cannot hurt." Everyone knew it was better to surrender to a pirate. "But I'll not have you sleeping in the chair. You may lie on top of the coverlet." She sighed. "I doubt I shall get a wink of sleep."

"You can sleep during the long carriage ride. Tomorrow we journey to Highwood."

CHAPTER 17

HAVING SPENT the night in bed, facing each other while still fully clothed, talking about things Evan would never dare mention to his friends, let alone a woman, they both slept on the journey to Bedfordshire. But Vivienne's insistence that Mrs McCready and Buchanan travel with them was the main reason Evan had closed his eyes.

He had not sent word to Highwood, informing them of his impending arrival. Consequently, the air in the grand hall thrummed with nervous tension. Mrs Elkin, like most experienced housekeepers, spoke with calm aplomb when firing instructions to the staff. Maids curtsied and footmen bowed before hurrying to attend to their tasks.

"While the maids prepare the rooms, perhaps you'd like to take tea in the drawing room, sir. I've taken the liberty of putting Miss Hart in the east wing, her companion in the chamber next door."

"Thank you, Mrs Elkin."

Drat! His apartment was in the west wing, hence the reason the housekeeper had placed an unmarried woman far from his reach.

"I shall speak to Cook, sir, prepare menus for the coming days and have them brought to you within the hour."

Evan smiled. The woman wanted to know how long he

planned to stay but would not ask directly. "Excellent. We will dine at seven o'clock. That should allow a little more time to prepare. No need to go to too much trouble as we must head back to London in a day or two."

The next few hours passed quickly. While Vivienne took a nap, Evan met with his steward, Mr Bradmore, who wished to take advantage of his master's sudden appearance and discuss the plans for the new tenant cottages. The steward would have rambled on about estate business all afternoon had Evan not promised to return in a week.

Under the guise of taking Miss Hart on a tour of the gardens, Evan escorted Vivienne on the mile walk to the memorial grounds—a row of depressing mausoleums housing the graves of Daniel and Livingston Sloane, amongst others.

"Is Lady Boscobel buried here?" Vivienne glanced at the weathered tombs, pointed to the only one with a bouquet of hothouse flowers in a stone vase to the left of the entrance.

Evan nodded. "My great-grandmother died at the grand old age of ninety-four, the year after I was born. Mrs Elkin changes the flowers weekly as a mark of respect."

"Which one is Livingston's resting place?"

"The one guarded by the statue of a wanderer." He gestured to the figure of a robed man clutching a staff, perched above the entrance to a gloomy mausoleum. "Livingston and Maria are buried there."

"It doesn't seem right to disturb his grave."

No. Evan had been plagued by similar thoughts all morning. "It won't hurt to enter the tomb. All the clues point here—the painted vignette of the house, Gray's poem of death, the compass leading us northeast of London. Equally, the mausoleum lies northeast of the house. We've every reason to believe this is where he hid the treasure."

Vivienne stared pensively at the entrance, lost in a sad, wistful dream. "While it must be obvious to you that finding any treasure would ease my financial burden, it was never about the money."

Evan closed the gap between them. The need to hold her and

kiss away her melancholy took command of his senses. He clasped her upper arm and drew her around to face him.

"It's never been about the money for me."

It started as an amusement, a way to ease his boredom. It started as a need to prove his worth to a deceased relative he'd never met, to correct misconceptions, to right a wrong. And yet none of those things mattered now.

She laughed and glanced at her surroundings. "No, clearly you have no need of pirate gold. Your sense of duty brings you here. In that respect, you possess a quality your ancestor lacked."

He took a moment to consider her words.

Duty? He had no loyalty to the man who had them chasing their tails. Livingston had lived by his own code, a code some might consider selfish. Despite being born into privilege, he turned his back on his family. Perhaps his return to Highwood, his desire to have his mother raise his child, was a way of correcting his mistakes. The prodigal son returning to the fold.

"The irony is I pride myself on the fact I avoid commitment, and yet I stand here as master of this estate, a commitment I take seriously. I stand here as an agent of the Order, committed to work I value and deem necessary."

She touched him lightly on the cheek. "The difference is, those things are within your control. You avoid things you cannot control because it scares you to think you might try your best and still lose something precious."

"Life is cruel. Like my father, I avoid anything that might cause pain."

"And yet what counts is not the material things we leave behind. What counts is who we loved and who loved us in return."

His heavy sigh was a sort of exorcism—an expulsion of false beliefs.

The darkness left his body, leaving a newfound clarity.

"I encourage D'Angelo to mask his pain, to use women and drink and vengeance as a means of coping. When our task is over, I must help him find another way to banish his demons."

Vivienne came up on her toes and kissed him gently on the mouth. "Love is the only thing capable of freeing Mr D'Angelo from his torment. Love is the key to the shackles that bind him to the past."

"Then there's no hope for him."

"There is always hope."

Evan stared at her, his heart swelling, his body infused with a warm glow, though he struggled to label the feeling. "Before we continue our quest, may I say how much I respect and admire you, Miss Hart." He wished he'd crossed the ballroom and asked her to dance, wished he'd turned to her in Gunter's and commented on the fact they'd both chosen pineapple mousse.

Her smile failed to reach her eyes. "I have always admired you, Mr Sloane. Even when you dumped me in a carriage in my stocking feet."

He laughed, though he was troubled by the unspoken words hanging in the air between them, troubled by the words craving a voice, nagging at his conscience.

"Then I pray you still admire me when I make you hold the coffin lid while I examine the contents." There, light-hearted banter banished the need to speak from the heart.

She seemed suddenly fearful. "I'll do it, of course. As long as you do not disturb his remains."

"The clue to our legacy may be apparent when we enter the tomb."

"There's only one way to know."

The solid stone door moved with surprising ease. One would be mistaken if they expected to find the pungent smell of rot in the air, or an atmosphere permeated with damp and decay. No. Evan inhaled nothing but a cold, sterile emptiness.

"It's freezing in here." Vivienne snuggled into her pelisse and rubbed her arms. She scanned the rectangular stone tomb, ran her gloved hands over the carved figures of a bearded man and a young woman lying next to each other, holding hands. "Livingston and his wife are buried together?"

"Yes." Evan stood for a moment and let the strange wave of loss pass over him—the stark realisation nothing was permanent. "I've never been in here, but I know my father visited often."

He braced himself to answer her next obvious question.

"Is your mother buried here?"

Nausea roiled in his stomach. "She is in a tomb with my father, one almost identical to this."

Vivienne did not reply, but sidled up to him and slipped her hand into his. He clutched it, taken aback by the immeasurable sense of peace.

He was in love with her.

He was certain—as certain as a man who'd never known love could be. But a mausoleum was not the place to make a declaration.

"There's an inscription." Keeping a firm grip of his hand, she studied the plaque. "*Kindred souls in heart and deed.* I rather like that."

Perhaps the inscription was their legacy.

The knowledge that love lived beyond the grave.

"It will be impossible to move the tombstone." He'd need Buchanan's help, would struggle even then. "Clearly, Livingston did not intend for us to look inside. We should examine the carvings."

"There's little to examine. Maria is holding a fan in her left hand, and Livingston looks to be holding a compass in his right hand."

Evan leant forward and studied the compass closely. "There are no markings on it, but it points south." He led her outside and glanced out over his lands. "The only point of interest south of here is the lake."

"Livingston liked the water. Let's walk there."

They walked through a small copse down to the lake.

"If you stand between the lake and these trees, you can see the house." She took to mumbling then, muttering about the book, reciting parts of the poem from memory. Evan watched in awe, consumed by nothing but the intense rush of emotion he'd managed to name.

After minutes of pacing back and forth, nibbling on her bottom lip, she gasped. "Evan, I know where we should look. We need to dig beneath that beech tree." She pointed, her hand trembling. "The couple on the vignette sat beneath a tree, reading a book. When we look at the vignette on the fan, I'm sure we'll find it's identical."

Evan studied their surroundings, noting she had a point.

"You think they're reading Thomas Gray's poem?"

She hurried over to him and captured his hands. "Gray's poem is about how people are remembered, about their successes and failings, about hiding truths. Will people remember him stretched beneath the beech tree? When he's gone, will they notice his absence?"

"And if we find nothing?" Would Livingston have him digging up the entire estate?

She shrugged. "We go back to the mausoleum and begin again. What have we to lose?"

Perhaps it was the frisson of trepidation, or the unsettling feeling they were being watched, that made him say, "We should work under cover of darkness. We'll return late tonight with a lantern and spade."

And after the information he'd gained from his steward, he'd come armed with a loaded pistol.

To dinner, Vivienne wore a simple dress of deep emerald green. Against the soft glow of firelight she looked delicate, so dainty. Yet Evan had never met a woman with her strength and determination.

He watched her eat, consumed with strange thoughts. Love was like a potent drug, stirring a man to imagine himself a devoted husband, a father to a brood of healthy children, the master of a house filled with love and laughter. Happy.

Still, the sense of foreboding sat like a brick in his stomach. Perhaps he was trained to expect misfortune. Perhaps a man who had never uttered the word *love* had every right to be concerned.

He led her from the dining room, telling the footman they would stroll around the garden before returning to take refreshments in the drawing room.

"You told no one we were coming down to the lake?" he asked, draping her cloak around her shoulders as if she were a child in need of coddling. He stole any opportunity to touch her now. "And you have the fan?"

"No one knows of our plans tonight." She placed her hand on his chest, finding a reason to touch him, too. "And you've already asked me about the fan."

"Yes," he breathed. The need to carry her to bed outweighed the need to dig a hole in the darkness. "Let's pray we resolve this matter tonight." He had every reason to believe they would.

She smiled, though sadness lingered in her brown eyes. "I've enjoyed every second of our adventure."

He hoped this was the first of many. "Some devil may still attempt to scupper our plans."

"Do you not think we should tell Buchanan?" she whispered.

"Buchanan is no fool," came his cryptic reply, for he did not wish to lie. "Come, let's hurry while the night is clear. The moon is out and will cast a modicum of light, although Mrs Elkin said to expect a storm."

She arched a teasing brow. "Later, we should play a game of questions. I shall pick the winning card, then knock on your door, soaked to the skin, and demand to know what you really thought of me the night we met."

He touched her again, stroking her cheek in such a way the servants would know they were lovers. "Let me save some time. I found you as fascinating then as I do now."

Her eyes brightened. "I find you equally fascinating."

"Me, or a certain part of my anatomy?"

"Everything about you." And there it was—the sudden flash of desire—the sign that said one kiss would lead to a night of rampant passion.

Hell.

The wait would be the death of him.

"Let me come to your room tonight." Never had he sounded so desperate. "There's something important we need to discuss in the privacy of your bedchamber." He was already imagining her thighs clamped around his hips, their sweat-soaked bodies writhing in pleasure.

"If you mean to seduce me, Mr Sloane, you must do better than that."

Being a man who embraced a challenge, he lowered his head. "Let me tell you a secret, something I've longed to tell you all day. Let me whisper the words as I make you come, Vivienne."

Her sigh was more a hum of anticipation.

She stepped back and grinned. "Then let us return to the lake and get this business over with. I'm keen to release you from this heavy burden."

The mere mention of release played havoc with his imagination. "I'll dig three feet, that's all. If we find nothing, we shall resume our search tomorrow."

At this rate, they'd be staying a week at Highwood.

A week of nightly visits to her bedchamber.

A week of pure bliss.

Yet he knew the devil would appear tonight.

They hurried to the lake, their breathless pants and obvious excitement hinting at the amorous interlude to come. Once there, Evan lit the lantern and studied the painted scene on the fan.

"Tell me where to dig," he said, for he had lost interest in this particular adventure. Playing Livingston Sloane's game had become tiresome. But it would be over soon.

Vivienne picked up a twig and dragged it over the damp grass. "X marks the spot. Dig here. Shall I hold your coat?"

"It's too darn cold. Just keep the lantern aloft."

She did as instructed, though her chattering teeth and intense gaze made it hard to focus.

"All this exercise will wear you out." Evidently, she was tired of this game, too, and sought more thrilling entertainment. "Your biceps look like they might burst through the seams of your coat."

"Have no fear," he said, throwing a spadeful of soil to join the mound on his right, "nothing will keep me from your bed. Later, you can massage my aching limbs—all of them."

The sudden thud of the shovel hitting something other than earth drew a shocked gasp from Vivienne's lips. It reminded him of the day in her garden when discovering the truth about his grandfather consumed his thoughts. Now, his love for this woman informed every thought and deed.

Vivienne crouched over the hole in the ground, moving the

lantern this way and that, attempting to gain a better view. "It sounds like you've hit a box, but all I can see is a sack. Quickly, Evan. Use your hands to haul it out."

Evan thrust the shovel into the ground next to the pile of soil. Between them, they wiped away the loose earth to reveal a box wrapped in a coarse linen grain sack.

"It's identical to the one covering Lucian Hart's tea chest." Evan brushed his hands and sat back on the grass before removing the box from the sack.

Vivienne held the lantern while he examined the tea chest similar to the one in which Lucian had stored his letters. "There's a key in the lock."

He turned the key, his heart thumping hard in his chest as he anticipated finding hidden treasure inside. A velvet pouch full of rubies. Rare gold doubloons. Disappointment struck when he lifted the lid and his gaze settled on white fur.

"It's rabbit skin," he said, confused until he pulled the item out of the box. "Livingston wrapped his letters in rabbit skin."

"Oh!" Vivienne dropped down beside him and placed the lantern on the ground. "Rabbits are a symbol of good luck."

"It's fair to say luck played no part in any of this. We've been hunting for treasure worth a king's ransom and found a pile of grubby letters. And were it not for your keen insight, we might never have found the tea chest."

She shrugged and held out her hand. "Having gone to all this trouble, we may as well read them."

He agreed. "It will be proof Livingston wasn't a pirate. But why we had to follow clues when he could have left them with Golding is anyone's guess."

They sat silently on the cold, damp grass, reading the letters, although some parts were illegible.

Vivienne tapped his arm to get his attention. "This one is from Lord Anson, thanking Livingston for risking his life. It seems he single-handily boarded a French vessel and stole back Government secrets. I wonder if that's when my grandfather came to his rescue."

"These are more letters confirming Livingston served the Crown."

"It's the truth alluded to in Gray's poem. How might a man be remembered, as a pirate or a loyal servant to his country?"

Still, the heavy weight of disappointment anchored him to the ground. He peeled back the folds of another letter, read the first few lines before his mouth dropped open.

"Hellfire!"

Vivienne came up on her knees, panicked. "What is it?"

Evan covered his mouth with his hand while he reread the damning words. "Now I know why Livingston had us chasing our tails. He needed to make sure this letter didn't fall into the wrong hands. He needed to know whoever found it could be trusted."

"Evan, will you tell me what it says before my heart gives out."

He swallowed numerous times before finding his voice. "My grandfather discovered the name of the traitor who sold Government secrets to the French. It's a list of dates and locations where the transactions took place. The name of the French spy who moved in society and his English counterpart." Evan glanced at the back of the letter, at the blank paper devoid of an address or wax stamp. "It's a letter written to Lord Anson, but never sent."

"Do you recognise the name of the traitor?" She clutched her hand to her chest. "Please. Tell me it's not my grandfather."

"It's not your grandfather. Like you, Lucian Hart was honest and loyal to a fault." Releasing a weary sigh, he glanced at the name again. "Should this information be made known, there's no telling—"

Sensing a presence behind him, Evan stopped abruptly and glanced over his shoulder. A figure moved out from the small group of trees, out of the shadows. Moonlight glinted on the barrel of the pistol he held aimed at their heads.

"Which is why you're going to give me that letter," the devil in the plague mask said. The click of the hammer pierced the night air. "Don't force me to shoot Miss Hart."

CHAPTER 18

THE FIGURE STOOD SWAMPED in a black greatcoat. A wide-brimmed hat pulled low over a plague-doctor mask. From his height and build, from the arrogant clip in his tone—a self-assurance born to all aristocrats when held over the font and anointed with holy water—Evan knew the devil was Charles Sloane.

"'Ere, put the letters in the box, place it on the floor and step away." Charles attempted to alter his accent, but a long stint in the workhouse couldn't rid this man of his breeding.

"You may as well take off the mask, Charles. No doubt, it's hard to breathe." Evan glanced at Vivienne and whispered, "Don't be afraid. Just do as I say." He took the small tea chest and opened the lid. "Place the letters inside."

Her hands trembled as she folded the letters and quickly placed them in the chest. "If we give you the box, what then?" she said. "You've one shot in that pistol, and you might miss your target."

"Then I shall be sure to aim at you, Miss Hart. Sloane won't give chase. He won't leave you to die alone."

Though his tone lacked conviction, Vivienne clutched her cloak to her chest and failed to suppress a whimper.

"Remove the mask, Charles." Evan kept his temper. "I cannot take you seriously while staring at that ridiculous white beak."

And he wanted to look the blackguard in the eyes when he broke his nose and knocked him on his arse.

As expected, the comment roused the viscount's ire. "You should damn well take me seriously." He jabbed the pistol in Evan's direction. "I'll not hesitate to shoot."

Evan doubted Charles Sloane had ever taken a life. Agents of the Order thought twice before shooting murderous blackguards. A coddled fop was unlikely to pull the trigger. Still, Evan could not risk losing Vivienne.

"There's a reason Livingston buried the incriminating letter in a box beneath this tree. He could not betray his brother. Just as Miss Hart has always known about the contract, you've always known the letter naming your grandfather Cecil Sloane as a traitor was hidden somewhere on this estate."

Charles threw his hat to the ground and tugged off the mask that made him look like a sideshow clown, not a man intent on murder. The burning question was, how had the devil come by the mask?

"My father made me swear an oath to find that damn document, to make sure it never saw the light of day, to destroy the lies written by a pirate to gain his mother's sympathy."

His mother's sympathy?

Past events became clearer.

Lady Sloane reverted to her maiden name to distance herself from Cecil, not Livingston. She must have known Livingston served the Crown, must have begged him to keep his brother's secret. It certainly explained why Evan owned Highwood, why he had inherited the lion's share of her fortune.

"You were right when you said Lady Boscobel wanted to divide the family. But it had nothing to do with Livingston. She wished to separate the son who served the Crown from the son who turned traitor."

Charles took a step forward, his agitation evident. "Livingston lied, lied, I tell you. My grandfather inherited the viscountcy from his uncle. Why in blazes would he want to betray his country?"

Evan recalled the vast sums of money listed in the letter. "If we examine the Leaton estate accounts, we can prove whether Cecil was innocent or guilty. He was already married when he inherited the crumbling seat in Cheltenham. So where did he get the money to restore the property to its former glory?"

"Lady Boscobel-Sloane gave her support," Charles snapped.

The fool. He'd said exactly what Evan hoped. "Excellent. Then there will be a record of the transaction amongst the accounts."

Panic flashed in the viscount's eyes. "Just give me the damn box. What does it matter now?"

If it didn't matter, Charles wouldn't be waving his pistol.

"There are other letters naming your grandfather," Evan lied, "though we've yet to find them. Shoot either of us, and the agents of the Order are instructed to search for the hidden documents. What will you do, Charles, slaughter every one of them? Become a murderer as well as the grandson of a traitor? Is it not better to lower the pistol and accept we cannot change the past?"

Like a cornered animal, Charles Sloane bared his teeth and growled his frustration. "You know how it works. One word of this and I shall be shunned from society."

"That depends on the man. Even the grandson of a pirate can command respect."

Charles snorted. "Give me the damn box."

Evan considered all that had happened since this adventure began. Why had Livingston constructed a mysterious game of secrets? What was his objective, his goal? Vengeance? No, he chose not to send the letter incriminating his brother. And why sign a contract and expect strangers to marry? Evidently, he trusted Lucian Hart to raise respectable offspring.

Kindred souls in heart and deed.

Livingston Sloane's blood flowed in Evan's veins. The man standing opposite was also his kin. It was up to Evan to decide if they remained estranged, or if he could do something to heal the rift. Charles Sloane was not to blame for his grandfather's choices. Evan had spent years coming to the same conclusion about his own fate.

However, Charles was responsible for aiming a pistol at their heads.

"I'm keeping the box, Charles, but shall give you the letter incriminating your grandfather, on the condition you answer my questions. The first being, where did you get that mask?"

"The mask? Does it matter?"

"It matters."

Charles shrugged. "A gentleman by the name of Ramsey came to see me. He had information to sell. He's the one who told me you were following clues to a chest of pirate treasure."

Damn Wicks and his drunken mouth.

Damn Bonnie and her loose morals.

Vivienne muttered her condemnation. "Mr Ramsey gave you the mask because he knew we'd been shot at by a plague doctor."

"He sold me the mask given to him by his informant, said it would be the perfect disguise."

"Bonnie!" Vivienne huffed. "Someone needs to teach that woman a lesson." She directed her annoyance at Charles Sloane. "I suppose you followed us here from London."

Charles hesitated. "I—I knew Livingston's clues would lead you to Highwood. I'm staying locally at—"

"The coaching inn in Potton," Evan declared. "This is a small village, Charles. My steward received word you were in the area."

While Charles cursed, Vivienne looked aghast. "You knew he was here yet didn't tell me."

"Bradmore wasn't completely certain." Evan had carried the guilt of it all day. "But I didn't want you pulling a pocket pistol from your thigh belt and getting yourself killed. You should be pleased. My first thought was to lock you in your bedchamber."

He'd rather suffer an argument than lose her.

"Surely you suspected someone would follow us here, Vivienne. Someone determined to steal our treasure. And we did find treasure. To Charles, the letter is worth a king's ransom."

"My mind has been so consumed with solving the clues, I've thought of little else."

Had she not thought of their heated kisses and passionate romps? Had she not thought these feelings they shared ran deeper than mere admiration?

"We wouldn't be standing here had you not made your intelligent deductions. Charles would have gone to his grave, knowing one day someone would stumble on the truth."

Charles gave a mocking snort. "If you were expecting me to make an appearance, why dig in the dark? Why not arm yourself and lie in wait?"

Because Evan was tired of playing games—unless it was one of questions and commands, he would never tire of that—tired of racing about like a Bedlamite.

"I have a blade in my boot and could hit you between the eyes before you took aim. But Buchanan would likely shoot you first."

Evan gestured to a point beyond Charles' shoulder.

The Scot stepped out from the trees. "Aye, just say the word, and I'll put a lead ball between his brows."

"But I don't need to pull a blade, Charles. And Buchanan doesn't need to fire his pistol. No, I estimate in three seconds you'll be on the ground, injured and disarmed."

It took two seconds for Evan's words to penetrate his cousin's brain. Then the fellow jumped in fright. Too late. For the last few minutes, D'Angelo had been moving stealthily towards them.

D'Angelo moved like a panther in the darkness, fiercely sleek, determined and deadly. His black eyes held a vicious hunger, a need to savage every man who posed a threat. He pounced. A few swift punches and Charles lay bleeding on the ground, D'Angelo hovering over him brandishing the pistol.

"Am I to shoot him, Sloane? We could weigh him down and throw him in the lake, let him rot there until he's but a slimy bag of bones."

Playing along with D'Angelo proved entertaining. "I cannot murder my own cousin. And if Livingston Sloane wanted vengeance, he would have named the traitor."

"Please!" Charles wiped blood off his nose and held up his hands in surrender. "I came for the letter. Just the letter. I cannot cope with the stress, the worry."

D'Angelo kicked the lord. "The last thing you need is this

coxcomb spreading gossip about your grandfather, or jumping out of the shrubbery and threatening the woman you love."

Vivienne inhaled sharply.

Evan felt the heat of her gaze moving tirelessly over his person. Now was not the time to drop to his knees and surrender to these confounding emotions.

"Let me kill him." D'Angelo's growl was almost feral. Make no mistake. If D'Angelo wanted this man dead, a battalion of trained soldiers couldn't stop him. "Let me end this so you may live your life in peace. No one will find his body. We will spread gossip, say he's obsessed with an opera singer and followed her to the Continent."

"Aye, let me shoot him," Buchanan said, playing his part in this little charade. "The hounds here look like they might rip a man to pieces and gorge on the remains."

Despite D'Angelo's ferocious glare, Vivienne was intelligent enough to know both men were bluffing. Still, she decided to even the odds and play along.

"Can you not see the viscount merely wishes to save his family name? As you said, he is not responsible for his grandfather's misdeeds. Can you not show mercy?"

"Mercy?"

"Please!" Charles howled.

"Very well. I'll give you the letter naming Cecil as the traitor." Regardless of their estrangement, tarnishing the Sloane name would result in repercussions for Evan, too. "But I will keep the rest. I intend to erase the stain from Livingston Sloane's name and prove he served the Crown. And Charles will help if he wants me to hold my tongue."

Charles clutched his broken nose. "I'll do anything, anything you say if you let me burn that letter, if you help me find the other incriminating documents."

Evan tutted. Did this coward not have an ounce of sense?

"There are no other documents, Charles. Not to my knowledge. I was playing for time. Now, come inside and let Buchanan fix your nose. You must have been out here for hours and could do with a stiff brandy."

D'Angelo offered his hand and hauled Charles to his feet. "I'll keep the pistol." He grabbed the lord firmly by the arm. "Let me escort you to the house, tell you what happens to those who cross the gentlemen of the Order."

Buchanan followed behind, telling the viscount what Highlanders do to the ballocks of men who betray their kin.

Clutching the box under his arm, Evan turned to Vivienne and slipped his free arm around her waist. She came to him, melding her body to his as if it were as natural as taking a breath.

"Am I forgiven for not mentioning my suspicions regarding Charles?"

"We agreed to be honest."

"While I doubted Charles had the strength of mind to pull the trigger, I feared you might fire a pistol and force his hand. It was a selfish decision on my part. Selfish because I don't want to lose you."

Her mouth curved into a smile. "When we play our game of questions in my bedchamber later, I might demand to know why."

He bent his head and claimed her cold lips, warming them quickly, thoroughly, with the same skill he'd employed in Golding's office.

"As I'm likely to lose the game, I shall have to tell you my darkest secrets, my deepest fears." He would say the words he had not uttered to another living soul.

"I think an honest conversation is needed."

"And a little game of forfeits. Maybe the odd command or two."

Touch me. Thrust harder.

They kissed until their pulses soared, until their bodies ached to join.

"Are you disappointed?" He whispered against her mouth. "Disappointed about finding letters, not gold or jewels?"

"No." The word was a resigned sigh. "As we said, this has never been about money. It's been about us."

It had stopped being about money and duty the moment their mouths met in Golding's office. "I need to talk to Charles and escort him back to the coaching inn in Potton. Then I'll wash and change and come to your chamber."

She cupped his cheek. "I'll be waiting."

Hands clasped tightly, they walked back to the house.

They entered the hall to the sound of Charles Sloane's pained groans emanating from the study.

"Stop yer damn complaining," came Buchanan's frustrated roar. "I need to click the bone into place and yer whining like a wee lassie."

"Perhaps I should knock the devil unconscious," D'Angelo teased.

Evan came to a halt at the bottom of the stairs and handed Vivienne the small chest. "I have the letter for Charles, but keep this in your bedchamber." He turned the key in the lock, then slipped it into his waistcoat pocket. "You can't open it without me. And now I have every reason to prowl the corridors at night."

She glanced left and right before coming up on her toes and kissing him in the reckless way he'd come to love. "Don't be long."

"Love, keep kissing me like that and I shan't go at all."

"Och, there's dirt all over yer pretty dress, and grass stains on the knees." Mrs McCready put her hand to her brow and almost expired. "Thank the Lord yer mother isn't alive to see ye looking like this."

"I can dress myself, Mrs McCready."

Vivienne was used to her fretting, but the woman insisted on dragging a thick nightgown over Vivienne's head. Were it not for Mrs McCready's unwavering loyalty, the fusspot would feel the sharp edge of Vivienne's tongue.

"Do ye want to end up in bed with a fever? What lass in her right mind goes walking in the cold at this late hour? I'll put an extra blanket on the bed. That should help warm yer bones."

If there was one thing Vivienne could guarantee, it's that she would not be cold tonight. The heat of Evan Sloane's bare skin was enough to stoke her inner flames.

"I'll keep the fire going for a while, lass. Get into bed and drink yer toddy."

Anyone would think Vivienne was a child, not a grown woman involved in an illicit affair. Besides, she had downed the drink before undressing, all in the hope of getting rid of Mrs McCready quickly. Perhaps she should go in search of Evan's room, for the woman had ears like a hawk.

"I've drained the last drop. The glass is empty." Vivienne climbed into bed, desperate to be rid of her companion. "And I plan to settle beneath the covers and sleep until ten tomorrow." She imagined being thoroughly exhausted after issuing Evan with a host of erotic commands.

"Then let me nip downstairs and get you another restorative. I lost yer mother to a fever, and I'll nae do the same again."

Vivienne suppressed a sigh, her annoyance subsiding. How could she be angry when Mrs McCready acted out of love?

"Very well. I'll take your medicine if it will make you happy."

The instant Mrs McCready hurried from the room, Vivienne's thoughts turned to Evan Sloane. Excitement and fear mingled together to cause all sorts of odd reactions. The wait for him to come to her room, the anticipation of their lovemaking, left her body trembling.

She shuffled lower in the bed and drew the blankets over her shoulders.

Maybe it was fear, fear of the case being over, fear of losing someone she loved, that made her stomach roil. Maybe it was the stresses of the day that made her lids feel so heavy.

Mrs McCready returned with a root decoction, a bitter-tasting tonic mixed with milk and spices. "Finish this, then I'll leave ye to sleep."

Vivienne sipped the tonic, for she'd cast up her accounts if she drained the teacup quickly. Mrs McCready took to fussing, draping Vivienne's cloak around the chair by the fire, moving back and forth to the window, tugging down the sash even though the window was closed, rearranging the curtains to keep out the draught—then peeping out again.

The restorative served as a relaxant.

The more Vivienne watched the woman, the more her eyelids grew heavy. Mrs McCready approached the bed and stared intently. She took hold of Vivienne's wrist and checked her pulse. Then she muttered her frustration and pulled back the blankets.

"Come, lass, I fear that drink is having some strange effect. Let's get something on yer feet." She grabbed Vivienne's ankles and thrust on a pair of satin slippers. "Take my hands now, and let's have a wee walk about the room."

It took three attempts to stand. The floor rolled like waves, affecting her balance. Her limbs were heavy, as if she'd been swimming against the tide for hours and had only just managed to scramble back to shore.

"Och, I put too many logs on the fire. Yer body feels like a furnace. There's nothing to do but take a wee walk around the garden."

Thinking and processing the woman's words proved difficult now. Vivienne let Mrs McCready wrap her in a cloak, but was too confused to ask what had happened to the tea chest full of letters, for it was no longer on top of the dressing table.

"We'll take the servants' stairs. Nae point in troubling anyone."

They passed a footman in the corridor running adjacent to the kitchen. Vivienne could barely keep track of the conversation, but the servant went about his business as if it were normal to find a woman staggering below stairs in her nightgown.

They left the house without a lantern. Cold air curled around her lower limbs as they ambled towards the shrubbery where Mrs McCready picked up a valise.

She wanted to tell Mrs McCready that she couldn't walk another step, wanted to flop down on the grass and sleep for an eternity. She wanted to ask why they were creeping about, why they'd turned left and were heading towards the road. But forming the words proved an impossible feat.

"Come, lass, we're nearly there. Just a few more steps and all will be well again. I promise ye that."

But Vivienne sagged, too tired to do anything but rest her weary head.

Mrs McCready took to complaining until a man in a great-coat appeared. He helped drag Vivienne to a carriage parked on the dark road.

The carriage door flew open, and Vivienne heard familiar voices before closing her eyes and falling into a dark abyss.

CHAPTER 19

"I WOULD SUGGEST we sit in the drawing room until dawn and finish my best bottle of brandy, but—"

"There is a certain lady in the house who commands your attention," D'Angelo said. "You were like an automaton going through the motions tonight, mending bridges with your cousin while your thoughts were elsewhere. It's as I suspected. You're in love with Miss Hart."

Guilt flared. Evan didn't want to leave D'Angelo to tackle his demons alone. And he could feel his friend distancing himself, moving further away, disappearing into the darkness. It reminded him of how Cole had been when life seemed hopeless. But while Cole had sought to destroy no one but himself, D'Angelo was likely to bring about an apocalypse.

"I believe so. I've never felt this way about a woman, but then Vivienne is unlike anyone I've ever met." Evan draped his arm around D'Angelo's shoulder. "Come, let's have a quick night-cap, and you can tell me why your knuckles were bruised before you punched my cousin."

D'Angelo winced as he formed a fist and examined the cuts and purple marks. "It's nothing. Go to bed. No doubt Miss Hart is frantically awaiting your return, and you know we'll not stop at one drink."

Evan might have dragged his friend to the drawing room, but

he'd been gone for almost two hours and the invisible thread binding him to Vivienne was already stretched thin. The need to see her, talk to her, to have her hands roam wildly over his body, proved too powerful to ignore.

"You'll stay tonight?"

"Perhaps."

"Now the matter of my grandfather's legacy is solved, let me help you with your case. Stay tonight. We'll go riding in the morning and can discuss whatever mischief you're making."

D'Angelo made no reply, but the sudden chime of the long-case clock filled the silence. Each toll sounded like an ominous warning—a sign Evan should save his friend from walking a dangerous path.

"I admire what you did tonight," D'Angelo eventually said. "You brought the Sloane family together when you could have wrought untold havoc, had your vengeance."

Love changed a man—made him more forgiving.

"Why should Charles pay for his grandfather's mistake? We work to protect the innocent. I'd be a hypocrite to act differently."

"Innocent? The lord pointed a pistol at Miss Hart."

"You know of my skill with a dagger. If I thought he had any intention of hurting her, I'd have buried a blade between his brows long before you appeared from the shadows."

Buchanan entered the hall, rubbing his hands together to chase away the cold. "Och, yer housekeeper was right about the storm. The heavens are weeping tonight." He removed his felt cap and patted his mop of grey hair. "Well, laddie, do we nae deserve a drink to warm our bones?"

D'Angelo laughed. "Laddie? I may be the youngest here, Buchanan, but I pray to God you're referring to Sloane."

"It's an endearment," Evan said. "It means he likes me."

D'Angelo patted Evan on the back. "Well, laddie, go and speak to Miss Hart about the letters while I help Buchanan empty your crystal decanters. I'm sure he has many tales of Highland lasses to keep me entertained."

Buchanan shrugged out of his greatcoat and hung it on the coat stand. "I've stories that will make yer hair curl." Buchanan followed D'Angelo to the drawing room. "Let me tell ye about Marion. Och, when she grabs yer by the bahookies ye canna shake her off. Claws like a wildcat."

Evan heard D'Angelo's hoots of laughter above stairs. Thank the Lord for Buchanan. Shame Evan didn't feel the same way about the whiny Mrs McCready. Indeed, he wondered if the woman would be stuck to the adjoining wall, her ears pricked and honed.

Perhaps it was best to visit Vivienne while still fully clothed, give her the directions to his room and have her come there. The old crone was likely to do something to spoil their plans.

He knocked lightly on Vivienne's door, whispered her name, but braced himself to face the devil's spawn keeping guard next door.

Vivienne didn't answer. It was almost eleven. Maybe both women were asleep in bed. Still, he turned the doorknob and slipped into the dimly lit room.

The fire had burned to nought but glowing embers. The candle in the lamp was but a stub. An ache in his gut told him something was wrong before he glanced at the unmade bed, before he strode to the armoire and found it empty. Despite a thorough search of the room, he could not find the tea chest containing his grandfather's letters. But he found a glass of milky liquid, some sort of tonic or restorative. One sip revealed a sickly concoction of milk and spices and something else, bitter like bark tea, bitter to hide the taste of laudanum.

Panic rose to his throat.

If this were a case, he might assume the worst, believe Vivienne had lied and manipulated events, believe she'd read something to make her steal the chest and disappear into the night.

His innate trust in her said otherwise. No. This amounted to something other than a lover's betrayal.

He hurried to Mrs McCready's door and hammered loudly before barging into the room. It was empty, too.

Hoping Vivienne had taken the chest and crept to his apartment, he sprinted to the west wing. No. No sign of the woman who must have left the house, who must have been taken against her will.

"D'Angelo! Buchanan!" Evan raced downstairs. He skidded across the hall and burst into the drawing room.

Both men looked at him, the laughter in their eyes dying.

"What is it?" D'Angelo was on his feet.

Evan could barely catch his breath. It was as if his heart were being crushed in a vice, crushed and squeezed until his chest was so tight he might pass out.

"It's Vivienne," he managed to say. "She's not in her room. Her clothes are gone, along with the tea chest. Gone. I have a terrible feeling. A coldness in my bones."

Buchanan jumped up from the chair. "Have ye checked with Mrs McCready?"

"She's not in her room." Evan dragged his hand down his face. "Charles couldn't have returned to the house, not without passing us on the road."

"No, Charles seemed sincere when he agreed to help you clear your grandfather's name. Trust me. Like a bloodhound, I can sniff out deceit."

The need for action burned in Evan's veins. He should charge out into the night, search the lanes, the fields, the mausoleums, everywhere, but he knew he had to focus on thinking logically.

While Buchanan went to inspect Mrs McCready's room, Evan summoned the butler and had him call every member of staff to the hall.

"I have reason to believe Miss Hart has been abducted from the house. I want to know if anyone saw her this evening, saw anything untoward."

"Yes, sir." The butler bowed and left to attend to the task.

"Let's examine the facts," D'Angelo said. He was always calm and composed when dealing with other people's problems, more a wild, bloodthirsty predator when dealing with his own. "What reason would anyone have for kidnapping Miss Hart? It cannot be another love interest for the woman is a wallflower."

"She is not a wallflower."

"You told Cole she was a wallflower and a pest."

Evan huffed. "That was before I knew her."

"So, she may have another suitor."

"No! This isn't helping."

D'Angelo began pacing, for he always thought best when walking. "Let's assume Charles wasn't the only person following you. Someone else came for the treasure, perhaps expecting to find a chest full of gold. So why burden themselves with a hostage?"

Evan tried to focus through the mental chaos. "No one entered the house. There are too many rooms, too many servants. Attempting to locate the chest would have posed a risk of discovery."

"Then the answer is obvious." D'Angelo stopped pacing. "Mrs McCready stole the chest and somehow persuaded Miss Hart to leave." D'Angelo paused. "Or it happened the other way around."

"You know damn well Vivienne has not left of her own accord." Evan's faith in her was steadfast. "Mrs McCready has taken her, but they won't get far on foot."

Buchanan returned, quickly followed by the butler and a footman.

"James has something important to tell you, sir. He saw Miss Hart with her companion over an hour ago."

"Describe exactly what happened. Leave nothing out."

The footman nodded. "I passed them near the kitchen, sir. The lady's companion said her mistress was unwell and they were taking a turn about the garden."

"Did you not think it odd?" Evan couldn't hide his frustration.

"The lady looked unwell, sir. Her companion said she was likely to cast up her accounts and so I left them to their walk." James' face twisted in panic. "Sir, I mentioned it to Flora, and she agreed to check on Miss Hart when the lady came back from her walk."

Evan assured the footman it was not his fault and dismissed the servants. He turned to Buchanan, "Miss Hart is an excellent judge of character. Why would she speak of Mrs McCready's loyalty when the woman is a cunning devil?"

"Och, Mrs McCready is a nag, but she loves the lass. Whatever's going on here, she means her nae harm. And she wouldna want the laird to think she betrayed his kinsfolk."

"Then why take the chest?"

Silence ensued.

They all stared absently, their minds engaged in finding a motive for the woman's despicable actions.

D'Angelo spoke first. "When Miss Hart brought the contract to you, she desired two things. That you find the intruder who broke into her home, find the treasure and share the bounty. Perhaps Mrs McCready believes Lucian Hart's granddaughter deserves to keep the reward."

"Vivienne doesn't care about money." She cared about honesty, about finding the truth. She craved love, not jewels. "Her main reason for solving the clues was so she could sleep soundly at night."

He'd never sleep soundly again if anything happened to her. He would be an empty shell like his father. It was too late to save himself from the crippling heartache, too late to stop the wave of grief.

"Bloody hell!" He punched the air. "I need to do something, damn it! We're wasting time."

"Be patient," D'Angelo said. "There's no point darting to town when they might have gone in the opposite direction."

"Mrs McCready would head for the Highlands."

"They've no money, no transport."

The sudden knock on the drawing room door brought Evan's agitated butler. "Sir! Sir!" The ageing man tried to walk gracefully with his salver but could not contain his excitement. "We have news, sir. A groom from a coaching inn near Tempsford has come with a note."

Tempsford? That was 5 miles north.

They could not have made it that far on foot.

Evan took the note and peeled back the folds with shaking fingers. Panic turned to relief the moment he laid eyes on the name scrawled at the bottom of the page.

"Well?" D'Angelo said impatiently.

Evan took a second to catch his breath. "It's from Ashwood. He received information the countess was leaving London and had a mind to follow her. It seems Mrs McCready and Vivienne are heading north in the matron's carriage. He thinks they'll head west once they reach Huntingdon, head for Liverpool."

Excitement flashed in D'Angelo's dark eyes. "No horse can match Arion's speed and stamina. Take him. Have your groom saddle two of your fastest horses for Buchanan and me."

"They'll have covered more than ten miles by now." Buchanan shook his head. "Why didna this Ashwood fellow stop them?"

Because when villains panicked, they became irrational. Ashwood would bide his time, pounce only when it was safe to do so. "Ashwood will likely wait for us to arrive before making a move. But have no fear. He'll find a way to stall them."

The argument dragged Vivienne from her forced slumber. She barely remembered a thing since slipping into bed and taking the sickly milk drink. Had no memory of climbing into the carriage, but recalled stumbling out onto a grass verge and casting up her accounts.

Mrs McCready had rubbed Vivienne's back in soothing strokes, but she'd been sick until her stomach muscles hurt. Perhaps that's why she seemed a little brighter now. Perhaps she'd vomited the wickedness she'd drunk to keep her under this witch's spell.

"Ask your coachman. He must have a knife in his pocket."

Vivienne's skin slithered at the sound of Mr Ramsey's voice. She peered beneath half-closed eyelids and watched the exchange.

"We will open the treasure chest when we stop to change the horses in Huntingdon." Lady Hollinshead stared down her nose at the gentleman seated beside her. "Rest assured. You will be rewarded for your efforts before we leave for Boston."

"Good. None of this would have been possible were it not for me."

The countess sighed. "And I am grateful you brought it to my attention. It's hard to believe Douglas' drunken comment led us to this—abducting his own daughter."

It took every effort to suppress a gasp. Had Mr Ramsey

always known about the contract? Did his regular visits to the house stem from a desire to pester Vivienne's mother for information?

Mr Ramsey glanced at the tea chest in his lap and snorted. "Douglas said it was a treasure worthy of a prince of Egypt. Looking at this old thing, one might think there's nothing inside but a pauper's pennies."

Vivienne held back a mocking chuckle. In his drunken state, her father had revealed part of her family's clue. Had he made an intentional mistake in saying prince instead of pauper? Had he known Mr Ramsey was a conniving devil or had he been too drunk to care?

"I think we should open it now. I'll take my share. You should have no problem reaching Liverpool. No one will notice Miss Hart is missing until after breakfast."

Oh, but they would. Evan would come to her chamber, eager to share his secrets. By now, he must surely know she was missing.

Then another thought struck, one that brought on a bout of nausea. What if he thought she'd abandoned him? Now the treasure amounted to nothing but a pile of old letters, he might think she had no interest in pursuing a relationship. And he would feel so dreadfully alone again.

Mrs McCready gave a discreet cough. "But the treasure belongs to the lass. I thought we were to use it to help her settle in Boston."

"And we will," the countess replied. "We will. But I have it on good authority the chest is full of precious gems. It won't hurt to let Mr Ramsey have his share. After all, he's the one who first told us about the clues and the contract."

Which fool told the countess to expect priceless gems?

Mr Ramsey shook the chest but did not hear the rattle he expected. "They must be secured in pouches. I promised my informant a ruby for her loyalty. We wouldn't have known the full value were it not for her probing Mr Wicks."

Bonnie!

Had Mr Wicks told Bonnie the chest was full of gems?

This time a snort escaped her, but she passed it off as a snore.

Mrs McCready drew the blanket over Vivienne's lap and checked her pulse. "We shouldna do anything with the box until the lass wakes. I promised her mother I'd always take care of her, and I'll nae break an oath."

"I promised to take care of her, too. Why do you think we're going to all this trouble? We cannot have her marrying Mr Sloane. Lord, I'd rather push a cart around Covent Garden than let that rakehell get his hands on the treasure." Lady Hollinshead visibly shivered. "No, I shall take control of her fortune and ensure she never wears a tatty gown again."

"But the lass is of age and can control her own inheritance."

"Really, Mrs McCready, for a mature woman you're incredibly stupid. Look at the terrible mess she's made of everything. Cavorting with a degenerate who will rob her blind. I'm sure Miss Hart will be grateful we arrived when we did."

It was not difficult to determine Lady Hollinshead's motive. Her greedy eyes glinted at the mere mention of treasure. Oh, she would pretend to take care of Vivienne while stealing a large portion for herself.

"Besides, you can stop with the holier-than-thou attitude. You've played your part in this, too. You listened to their conversations, studied the clues. You determined they would find the treasure at Highwood. You sent word we were to follow you to Bedfordshire. Arranged the rendezvous point and told us to come back tomorrow if they hadn't found the treasure."

Mrs McCready broke into a sob. "Because ye promised to help the lass, make sure she didna marry that devil."

The countess shrugged. "And I have."

The carriage slowed and pulled into the yard of a busy post-house.

Mr Ramsey shuffled to the edge of the seat. "Well, I'm famished. I'll hurry inside and order supper. You must wake Miss Hart, help her from the carriage while they change the horses."

"We cannot do it on our own," the countess complained.

"We cannot take her into the inn in her nightgown. It will look mighty suspicious."

"We shall have to leave her alone in the carriage. I shall tell the postmaster she's sick. There will be no issue when he learns I'm a countess."

Vivienne listened to them concocting their plan. Somehow she was going to steal the tea chest and make a hasty escape. Somehow she would find her way back to Evan Sloane.

CHAPTER 20

VIVIENNE'S first opportunity to escape came when the three other occupants of the carriage alighted. Mr Ramsey hurried through the rain into the inn, leaving the countess and Mrs McCready to explain the unfortunate nature of their sick passenger to the postmaster.

She could have simply climbed out of the vehicle, cried that she had been abducted. But she still felt a little woozy from the toddy and tonic, and a hysterical woman in a nightgown might be carted off to the nearest asylum.

Equally, the countess had taken possession of the tea chest, gripping it to her hip like a beloved babe. And Vivienne would not return to Evan without the precious letters.

As luck would have it, the yard was in chaos. Post-boys hurried about carrying luggage, lugging mail bags to protect the contents from the sudden storm, helping injured passengers hobble back to the inn. An armed guard barked orders while all stable hands darted left and right, not knowing which way to run. The accident had occurred half a mile away, and the post-master insisted on retrieving his horses and the mail before he could think about hiring post-horses.

"Do you know who I am?" the countess complained when the postmaster informed her the inn's private parlour was now a storeroom for mail. "It's late, and I insist you change my horses at once."

"Beggin' yer pardon, my lady, but you'll have to wait."

The countess did wait. Rain pelted the windowpanes. An hour passed during which Vivienne pretended to be asleep while her abductors squashed into the carriage and ate supper, for it was far too rowdy and uncivilised in the coaching inn.

More coaches and riders entered the yard, seeking shelter or fresh mounts. All were told the same story, all made to wait.

Needing to drain his bladder after consuming a flagon of wine, Mr Ramsey disappeared into the white stone building and did not return.

"No doubt the fool is gorging on beef stew and has the serving wench dancing to his tune."

"Och, he's been some time, my lady. Perhaps he's unwell."

"Good riddance." The countess huffed. "I say we leave without him and he can forfeit his share."

"But Mr Ramsey threatened to tell the earl of yer plans. And we've five days before the ship sails. We canna risk getting caught."

"Mr Ramsey will sell the information, regardless."

"Shame ye only purchased three tickets. It might have been better to take the loose-tongued rogue, too."

Three tickets? But Mr Ashwood had mentioned only two.

The countess stared at the box as if it held the answer to her prayers. "Well, I'm tired of waiting. I shall instruct the coachman to head to the next inn. The horses are rested, and we should make the five miles without incident."

"What about Mr Ramsey, my lady?"

"I must use the inn's facilities if we're to continue on our journey. I'll not stoop behind the carriage. I shall see if he's sprawled across a table in the taproom." The countess gripped the tea chest. "Wait here. Give our charge a few drops of laudanum. Just in case she wakes."

As soon as they were alone, Vivienne opened her eyes.

She turned to Mrs McCready. "My mother would be ashamed of you." Tears welled instantly. "Drugging her daughter and stealing her away in the night. And to think I sang your praises, told Mr Sloane your loyalty knew no bounds."

Mrs McCready's eyes widened in horror. It took her a moment to catch her breath. "Och, no, lass, no. Yer mother wouldna have wanted to see ye married to a scoundrel. But there's nae need to marry him now. Ye can claim all the treasure for yerself once we're away from these shores." She clutched Vivienne's hand. "We're off to Boston."

Vivienne snatched her hand away. "I'm not going to Boston, and neither are you. The countess bought two tickets, though I've every reason to believe the second one is for the tea chest. You're being duped."

Mrs McCready frowned. "But the countess loves ye like a daughter."

"Then it's a blessing she has no children. The countess wants the treasure. She has waited patiently this last year, waited for me to take the contract to Mr Golding."

Vivienne thought back to the last moments with her mother. From her sickbed, she implored Vivienne to find Evan Sloane. Evan Sloane would protect her. She had made no mention of the countess. Indeed, Vivienne recalled seeing a look of panic in her mother's eyes when the countess entered the room. Panic Vivienne had thought stemmed from a fear of death.

"I'm in love with Mr Sloane. I trust him with my life." Indeed, she could not imagine a life without him. "My mother urged me to trust him."

"But he's using ye for the treasure."

Vivienne laughed. "There's nothing in the chest but a pile of old letters."

"Letters?" Mrs McCready's mouth fell open.

"Yes, letters. The countess hasn't the means to fund a life in Boston. You know she brought nothing to the marriage, and the earl will cut off all means of support. You're sending me to my doom." Vivienne watched the woman sag in the seat as realisation dawned. "Trust me. When Mr Sloane catches up with us, there'll be hell to pay."

Mrs McCready choked on a sob. "I meant nae harm. I was trying to save ye, lass."

"Then if you wish to save me, you will help me steal the letters, help me return to Highwood."

"Aye. I will. It's the least I can do for the mess I've made."

A sudden bang on the carriage window tore a gasp from them both. A man pressed his nose to the misty glass and gave a wide grin.

"Buchanan!" Vivienne flung open the door and threw herself into his embrace. "Merciful Lord! How did you find us?" Tears rolled down her cheeks. Relief pumped through her veins.

He hugged her tightly. "There now, lassie. All's well. Yer gentleman rode like the devil to get here. Yer'd be mighty proud of his horsemanship." He released Vivienne and turned on Mrs McCready. "And as for this witch. Happen the laird will be keen to hear about her treachery."

Mrs McCready trembled. "Forgive me, Buchanan. I meant nae—"

"Tell that to the laird." He muttered something in Gaelic before focusing on Vivienne. "Come now, lass, they're all waiting inside."

Buchanan escorted them across the muddy yard and into the crowded inn. People were too busy tending those injured in the accident to notice a woman wearing a nightgown beneath her cloak. He led her upstairs to a bedchamber with a beamed ceiling and a small poster bed, then went to speak privately with Mrs McCready.

Mr Ramsey and Lady Hollinshead sat perched on the sagging mattress, while Lord Hawkridge—or Mr Ashwood as he preferred—Mr D'Angelo and Evan Sloane all stood with their arms folded, glaring at the deceitful devils.

"Evan!" Vivienne ran into his open arms. She didn't care who saw them embrace, who saw him stroke her hair, brush his thumb over her cold lips, clutch her to his chest.

"Are you all right?" His tone brimmed with concern, but there was no mistaking the steely edge. "Are you hurt?"

"No, just a little tired, and I have a terrible headache."

"This is ludicrous!" the countess cried. "Move aside and let me leave, else I shall send for the magistrate. Innkeeper! Innkeeper!"

Mr D'Angelo chuckled. "And what will you tell him? That you abducted a woman from her bed so you might steal her jewels?"

The countess raised her chin. "Nonsense. I have simply come to the aid of my friend's daughter. Mrs McCready said the girl was sick, being drugged by Mr Sloane so he might do away with her and keep the treasure. What crime have I committed?"

"You bought tickets for *The Maybury*," Evan countered. "You knew we would find the treasure and have been planning to steal it for days."

The lady's eyes widened. "You've been spying on me?"

"That's what we do, madam," Mr D'Angelo said. "Hunt wicked devils who seek to harm the innocent."

"I'm afraid you made a fatal mistake trusting Mr Ramsey." Evan kicked Mr Ramsey's shoe to get his attention, for he had consumed far too much wine and struggled to follow the conversation. "He told Bonnie of your plan. Sold information to Charles Sloane. You'll both be arrested for theft and conspiracy to defraud. Half of the treasure is mine, and no doubt you would have taken your share."

Mr Ramsey jumped in shock. He wiped his mouth with the back of his hand. "I—I did nothing other than protect Miss Hart's interests."

"Worry about your own interests," Mr D'Angelo said. "I gathered your creditors and gave them the money to obtain a writ. By now, there'll be a warrant for your arrest and a cosy little room waiting at the sponging-house."

In shock, Mr Ramsey slipped off the bed. He scrambled to his feet. "No! No! I just need time to pay. Wait!" Spittle dribbled down his chin. "I just need ... need—"

"Your share of the treasure," Vivienne said, indebted to Mr D'Angelo for he knew how to hurt this devil. "What was it you promised Bonnie? A ruby for her loyalty?"

"Fool," the countess grumbled. "Elspeth always said you had the sense of a donkey."

"Do not dare speak of my mother like she's kin." Anger bubbled in Vivienne's throat. Anger turned to rage. "Mr Ramsey told you what he'd learned from my father. While you were tending to my mother, you were pestering her for information, pestering Mrs McCready, too. My mother's last moments should have been calm, peaceful, but I shall never forget the fearful look in her eyes."

"Don't be ridiculous. I've done nothing but care for you since she died." The countess gave a mocking snort. "Is this any way to show your gratitude? Elspeth would be ashamed of *you*, gel!"

Vivienne might have slapped the sneer off the lady's face had Evan not caught her wrist. "Though I feel your frustration," he said, "don't lower yourself to her level. Let's hit her with the truth instead."

Evan removed a key from his waistcoat pocket and opened the tea chest. He presented it to the countess who peered inside like a child at a confectioner's window.

"Fur?" She jerked her head back, confused. "Fur?"

Mr Ramsey found his voice. "The gems are in a fur pouch. No wonder we couldn't hear them rattling in the box."

Vivienne reached inside and removed the letters wrapped in rabbit skin. "Our legacy amounts to nothing more than proof Livingston Sloane served the Crown."

When Livingston died, no doubt it suited Cecil Sloane to have everyone believe his brother was a pirate. After all, should the truth about Cecil's betrayal surface, who would believe the offspring of a criminal?

"Letters!" The countess could not contain her rage. "Letters! Ramsey, you imbecile. You said it was a chest full of precious gems."

Mr Ramsey looked equally shocked and confused. "That's what Mr Wicks told Bonnie. She assured me we never need worry about money again."

D'Angelo laughed. "Money will be the only thing on both your minds for the foreseeable future. Ramsey, should you return to London, I'll make sure the writ is enforced."

"And don't worry about Bonnie," Mr Ashwood said. "Cole discovered something interesting. Sir Malcolm Langley, Chief Magistrate at Bow Street, now has evidence she runs a brothel from the back rooms of the Old Red Crow."

Vivienne smiled. Only a fool would cross the gentlemen of the Order.

Evan closed the lid on the tea chest, the sudden *snap* making the countess jump. "And you seem to have come unstuck, Lady Hollinshead. The earl and his highbrow friends will learn of your treachery. It seems a trip to Boston might be just what's needed."

The countess' arrogant bearing faltered. Her bottom lip quivered as she stared at the tea chest. "But I cannot possibly support myself in Boston, not without the ... without the—"

"Treasure," Vivienne spat. "I'm sure a lady with your cunning will devise a plan."

Evan clutched the box and captured Vivienne's hand. "I don't know about you, but there's somewhere else I would rather be. Something else I would rather be doing. I feel lucky tonight, and a game of questions is long overdue."

"In your excitement, you've forgotten I have the devil's luck."

"I've not forgotten. It's time I answered your questions, banished your fears." His gaze drifted to her nightgown and the satin slippers covered in mud. "You'll go with Ashwood in his carriage. It's too cold to ride with me. And we will continue this conversation at Highwood."

"D'Angelo can ride that beast of his, and I'll take your horse," Mr Ashwood said. "Sloane, you accompany Miss Hart in the carriage."

Evan offered no challenge. "If you're sure."

A knowing look passed between the men.

The countess and Mr Ramsey started whining, lamenting the unfairness of it all, blaming each other, hurling accusations.

It was Mr D'Angelo who gripped Mr Ramsey by the throat and warned him not to try the patience of a man who dined with the devil.

They left the villains to their squabbles and gathered amid the chaos in the taproom. Evan kept a firm grip of her hand as the three gentlemen of the Order arranged to meet at Highwood.

"What about Mrs McCready?"

Evan turned to her. "I suggest we send her back to the Highlands, though I suspect she will want to remain with you."

Vivienne had every reason to distrust the woman, to despise her for what she had done. "I don't want to punish her, Evan."

Judging by his rigid stance, he disagreed. "Buchanan and Mrs McCready have ridden ahead. Let's see what she has to say when we speak to her tomorrow. You decide her fate."

Love filled Vivienne's heart. Evan Sloane did not ride roughshod over a woman's liberty. He did not use his power and influence to exert control.

When finally alone with him inside Mr Ashwood's carriage, she could barely contain the emotion. The urge to climb onto his lap and feel full with him, to devour his mouth, to sate the craving, the hunger, proved impossible to ignore. But she didn't want to be consumed with desire when she confessed her true feelings.

"I don't suppose you brought your playing cards," she said, visually feasting on his masculine form.

"No, the fear of losing you was the only thing on my mind."

Her pulse fluttered to her throat. "Then how will we play?"

"We'll play a different game. The first to blink makes a confession."

"Very well." She sat forward, wide-eyed, determined to concentrate, determined to win, determined to know his secrets.

Evan blinked within seconds.

"Your turn to reveal a secret, Mr Sloane, your turn to confess."

A smile tugged at his mouth. "I'm in love with you, Vivienne. Madly in love. It's beyond any feeling I've ever known."

Her soul soared. Her heart raced so fast she could hardly breathe.

"I'm in love with you, too. It burns inside me like the brightest flame."

"Marry me."

"Yes."

"Let's stop en route, find someone willing to perform the ceremony. Ashwood and D'Angelo will bear witness. Or we can marry at Highwood if you'd rather Buchanan were there. Perhaps you want to wear clean shoes when we exchange vows."

"You have the special licence on your person?"

"Indeed."

"May I ask where?" Already hot between the thighs, she scanned the breadth of his chest, glanced at the placket of his breeches. "Should we encounter a problem, I may need to retrieve the important document."

He laughed. "Memory fails me. It pays to forget some things, as now you'll have to frisk me."

Love and lust thrummed in her veins. She could no longer keep to her side of the carriage. "You're rather skilled in the art of flirtation, Mr Sloane." She slid beside him and trailed her fingers over his muscular thigh. "So skilled I suspect you'll soon have me on my knees."

"That's the plan."

He kissed her then, like he did that day in Mr Golding's office. A kiss that stirred every nerve to life. A kiss so profound she felt the tremors deep in her core.

"Your grandfather would be pleased you've kept his vow." She gathered the hem of her nightgown and came to sit astride him. "Proud you solved the clues."

"You solved the clues, my love." He slipped his arms around her waist, crushed her to his chest. "But make no mistake. I'm the one about to claim the treasure."

CHAPTER 21

Highwood, Bedfordshire
Two weeks later

"I QUITE LIKED the idea of us being Sloane and Hart, an intrepid detective duo. It has a certain ring to it that inspires confidence." Vivienne nestled closer to Evan's chest as they sat beneath the beech tree, attempting to read Thomas Gray's poem, but had barely made it past the first stanza.

"We're Sloane and Sloane, double the trouble, and brimming with heart."

She laughed. "Oh, I like that, too."

"Do you miss the thrill of chasing about in the dark, my love?" He was to return to London to take a new case, knew she longed to assist him. "Perhaps we could play a game of hide and seek in the grounds tonight."

She straightened, excitement evident. "If you find me, will I have to do as you command?"

"Undoubtedly. And when you find me, I shall gladly pay a forfeit." He'd wanted to tell her his secret after dinner this evening, but he lived to make her happy and could no longer contain the news. "I received word from Daventry this morning."

"Has Mr Ramsey found the money to pay his creditors?"

With limited options, Ramsey had returned to London and currently had a caged room at the sponging-house. "There's little hope for him as his debts are extensive."

"Mr Howarth was right. Greed is a plague that scourges the hearts of men."

"And the hearts of women. Lady Hollinshead won't find life easy in Boston." The countess had returned to London, too. But after learning of her treachery, the earl took his wife to Liverpool and insisted she board the boat. "No, Daventry wrote to tell me he is assisting his friend Damian Wycliff in a venture—a house for destitute ladies, a means of helping those down on their luck."

"The options are limited for unmarried women without means. So many travel to town seeking a better future. Many fall foul to unscrupulous devils."

"They're looking for a certain type of lady."

Her eyes widened. Clearly, she had misunderstood.

"Intelligent women with an ability to investigate delicate cases," he said. "Strong women who understand the importance of justice."

Vivienne jerked in surprise. "Lady enquiry agents?"

"Indeed. Miss Trimble is to oversee the running of the house, but Daventry asked if you might like to play a role, offer advice in a professional capacity."

Her mouth fell open.

Oh how he longed to draw her close, slip his tongue inside and explore.

"Me? Mr Daventry thinks I have the necessary experience?"

"He's impressed by your deductive skills. There's one lady living in the house at present, Miss Sands, but Daventry is keen to employ more."

Miss Sands had already received her first task, though Evan was sworn to secrecy. D'Angelo's need to avenge his parents' murder was taking its toll. So much so, Daventry had decided to assist from the shadows. To make sure D'Angelo didn't end up a bloated corpse in the Thames.

Vivienne studied him intently. "You would not object to me offering my assistance?"

"No, love. Though I ask you keep me informed, that you consult me, that you do not place yourself at risk."

He would have to offer assistance, too, for her safety was his priority. And when Buchanan returned from escorting Mrs McCready back to the Highlands, Daventry wished to offer him a role.

Evan barely had time to catch his breath before Vivienne climbed onto his lap and kissed him. He felt the depth of her gratitude with every stroke of her tongue. As always, a passionate kiss quickly progressed to the need for deeper satisfaction.

"Make love to me," she breathed against his mouth. "There's no one here but us."

"And a mermaid clutching a seashell."

Vivienne glanced back over her shoulder at the statue in the middle of the lake. "You should erect a statue of my grandfather. Perhaps it's time to stop paying homage to a mermaid and give credit to the man who did save Livingston's life."

"Why would I worship a mermaid when I have a nymph of my own?" He clutched her hips, moved her back and forth over the hard length of his arousal. "Besides, the mermaid is as old as the house. Some other fellow had a love for the mythical creatures. Perhaps that's where my grandfather got the idea for his tale. Can we make love now?"

She claimed his mouth in response—hot, urgent.

He'd be inside her in seconds.

But then she dragged her lips from his and stilled. "Might your grandfather's last message be a clue to finding a real legacy?"

"Can we not discuss this later?"

Mr Golding had struggled to contain his relief when he flicked to the back of the notebook and read the heartfelt messages. Livingston's words brimmed with praise for their tenacity and courage in making it this far. Money corrupted the best of men, and the exercise should have revealed the truth about whom they could trust.

Lucian Hart's parting words were about love and friendship, about investing in relationships rather than the bank. And because Evan had married Vivienne Hart out of love, not duty, they received a final letter containing one simple message.

Look for the truth everywhere.
In the words of a morbid poet.
In the arms of a mythical mermaid.

"We found the treasure, love. We found each other." And they were too busy expressing the depth of their love to concentrate on cryptic messages. "I believe Livingston spoke metaphorically. Meant one might find love in the last place one expects."

"Shells are said to be a symbol of good fortune. The mermaid in the lake is holding one in her arms. There is no greater truth than what we find in the natural world. And shells connect us to the sea."

"I thought we were making love, not delving into symbolism."

She rolled her hips, rubbed against his erection. "Pander to my whims, and I shall pander to yours."

Evan sighed. "Very well." His wife *was* Peitho, a goddess skilled in the art of seductive persuasion. "What are your thoughts on the morbid poet?"

She reached for the book and flicked to Gray's poem. "I recall reading about gems. Yes, he says that many gems lie in dark caves under the ocean. Like the exceptional deeds of unsung heroes, beauty is often hidden from sight."

Evan was so busy gawping in awe at his wife, finding her logical deductions so damnably arousing, he missed her sudden command.

"Well? Will you do it?" She stood and attempted to pull him to his feet. "Will you swim to the mermaid statue and see what lies below?"

"Swim across the lake? Madam, I'm likely to catch my death."

"I'll come with you."

"You can swim?"

"My father insisted I learn. When a family is owed a debt from a marauding pirate, it pays to be prepared." She glanced out at the lake. "It's not far. The last one there must pay a forfeit."

Before he could stop her, she was out of her pelisse, tugging off her boots. He'd been in the lake before, knew she could touch the bed in most places.

She hurried to the water's edge in her shift. He'd known the minx hadn't bothered with stays, had made it easier for him to fondle her breasts.

She laughed. "Just think, we'll have to spend the rest of the day lounging before a roaring fire."

He couldn't love her any more than he did at that moment.

Like his manhood, his heart was ready to burst.

She excited him on every level.

Giving his weakest performance, he let her win the race. There was nothing he wouldn't do if she asked, and the forfeit would be to his benefit.

Despite searching the lake's murky depths, Evan did not find a treasure chest on the bed. But a quick inspection of the mermaid's shell proved fortuitous.

"Good Lord!" He slipped his hand inside the giant conch shell and removed a leather pouch.

"You see!" Vivienne's teeth chattered as she gripped the statue. "Did I not say we'd been left a legacy?"

They swam to the bank and headed back to the house. Mrs Elkin fussed about, had hot baths drawn, had the fire stoked in their bedchamber. Once warm and dry, they sat before the fire and Evan emptied the contents of the pouch onto the rug.

The vibrant assortment of gems glittered against the firelight.

Vivienne giggled as she held up a large blood-red ruby and observed the facets. "Imagine if the gardener had gone to clean the fountain and thrust his hand inside the shell."

"I doubt Livingston cared who found the treasure. Finding each other was the true prize."

She pushed the gems aside as if they were glass beads of little importance, raised her nightgown to her hips and came to sit astride him. "We should stay in bed for the rest of the day. Lord knows we might catch a fever if we don't."

"My skin is already aflame." He thought of the night she reached into her thigh belt and produced the scroll. What if he'd thrown her out without reading the contract? What if he'd been too blind to see the beauty before him? "And I feel the need to prove I'm not a bore in bed."

"You're never a bore in bed."

"You're contractually obliged to love me, regardless."

She arched a coy brow. "And if I fail to abide by the contract?"

"Then I can make a claim against you." He slipped his hand into her damp hair, cupped her nape and drew her mouth to his. "I can settle between your sweet thighs and take up permanent residence."

THANK YOU!

I hope you enjoyed reading ***Valiant.***

What is troubling D'Angelo?
Is he any closer to finding out who murdered his parents?
More so, will he notice the golden-haired beauty employed to
watch his every move?

Find out in ...

Dark Angel
Gentlemen of the Order - Book 4